Fritz Leiber, the son of a noted stage and screen performer, was born in the United States in 1910. A former actor, he has written many fantasy and science fiction stories, and contributed to *Weird Tales* before the Second World War. Leiber is well known and held in high regard by readers of both science fiction and fantasy: he has received several Hugo and Nebula awards for the former, and he is seen as the doyen of fantasy writers, as the man who practically invented the sword and sorcery genre as it is known today. Most of the leading writers in the field acknowledge their debt to him, but, as is often pointed out, what makes Leiber's fantasy adventures superior to those of the many writers who have followed in his footsteps is the strong vein of dry wit that permeates his work.

By the same author

Novels

Gather Darkness
Conjure Wife
The Green Millennium
Two Sought Adventure
Destiny Times Three
The Big Time
The Silver Eggheads
The Wanderer
Tarzan and the Valley of Gold (based on the film)
A Spectre Is Haunting Texas
Our Lady of Darkness
Swords and Deviltry
Swords Against Death
Swords in the Mist
The Swords of Lankhmar
Swords and Ice Magic

Collections of stories

Night's Black Agents
The Mind Spider
Shadows with Eyes
Ships to the Stars
A Pail of Air
The Night of the Wolf
Secret Songs
Night Monsters
You're All Alone
The Best of Fritz Leiber
The Book of Fritz Leiber
The Second Book of Fritz Leiber
The Worlds of Fritz Leiber

FRITZ LEIBER

Swords Against Wizardry

BOOK 4 IN THE SWORDS SERIES

GRAFTON BOOKS
A Division of the Collins Publishing Group

LONDON GLASGOW
TORONTO SYDNEY AUCKLAND

Grafton Books
A Division of the Collins Publishing Group
8 Grafton Street, London W1X 3LA

A Grafton UK Original 1979
Reprinted 1986, 1987

ISBN 0-583-13089-5

Printed and bound in Great Britain by
Collins, Glasgow

Set in Intertype Plantin

Contents

Author's Introduction

Swords Against Wizardry is the fourth book of the Saga of Fafhrd and the Gray Mouser, immediately following *Swords in the Mist* and followed by *The Swords of Lankhmar*. The two heroes have been comrades in adventure for about a decade.

In 1936 my comrade Harry Otto Fischer conceived, began, and abandoned the story 'The Lords of Quarmall.' Twenty five years later I decided I was up to the pleasant task of solving the mysteries of the tale and completing it without changing his words at all, except to add details of plot. Harry, in some ways a very patient person, laconically commented that he was glad to discover at last how his story ended.

The sections Harry wrote are the history of Quarmall and the introduction of its lord and Flindach, beginning with the last paragraph on page 108 and ending at the middle of 118; the chess game between Gwaay and Hasjarl, 130 to 141; the cremation of Quarmal, 150 to 155; parts of the Mouser's spell, 156; and the idea of the Mouser's tunnel journey, 171.

Now Harry's home is in the hilly city of Clarksburg in the Appalachian heartland, while I bivouac in another hilly city on the West Coast, but the comradeship is as always.

Fritz Leiber
San Francisco, Oct. 19, 1973

This book is dedicated to
HARRY OTTO FISCHER,
who first explored Quarmall
and who wrote ten thousand of these words,
here unchanged,
about that subterranean kingdom.

Additionally, Part Two of this novel –
Stardock – is dedicated to
those two hardy cragsmen,
Poul Anderson and Paul Turner.

I: IN THE WITCH'S TENT

The hag bent over the brazier. Its upward-seeking gray fumes interwove with strands of her downward dangling, tangled black hair. Its glow showed her face to be as dark, jagged-featured, and dirty as the new-dug root-clump of a blackapple tree. A half century of brazier heat and smoke had cured it as black, crinkly, and hard as Mingol bacon.

Through her splayed nostrils and slack mouth, which showed a few brown teeth like old tree stumps irregularly fencing the gray field of her tongue, she garglingly inhaled and bubblingly expelled the fumes.

Such of them as escaped her greedy lungs tortuously found their way to the tent's saggy roof, resting on seven ribs down-curving from the central pole, and deposited on the ancient rawhide their tiny dole of resin and soot. It is said that such a tent, boiled out after decades or preferably centuries of use, yields a nauseous liquid which gives a man strange and dangerous visions.

Outside the tent's drooping walls radiated the dark, twisty alleys of Illik-Ving, an overgrown and rudely boisterous town, which is the eighth and smallest metropolis of the Land of the Eight Cities.

While overhead there shivered in the chill wind the strange stars of the world of Nehwon, which is so like and unlike our own world.

Inside the tent, two barbarian-clad men watched the crouching witch across the brazier. The big man, who had red-blond hair, stared somber-eyed and intently. The little man, who was dressed all in gray, dropped his eyelids, stifled a yawn, and wrinkled his nose.

'I don't know which stinks worse, she or the brazier,' he murmured. 'Or maybe it's the whole tent, or this alley muck we must sit in. Or perchance her familiar is a skunk. Look, Fafhrd, if we must consult a sorcerous personage, we should have sought out Sheelba or Ningauble before ever we sailed north from Lankhmar across the Inner Sea.'

'They weren't available,' the big man answered in a clipped whisper. 'Shh, Gray Mouser, I think she's gone into trance.'

'Asleep, you mean,' the little man retorted irreverently.

The hag's gargling breath began to sound more like a death rattle. Her eyelids fluttered, showing two white lines. Wind stirred the tent's dark walls – or it might be unseen presences fumbling and fingering.

The little man was unimpressed. He said, 'I don't see why we have to consult anyone. It isn't as if we were going outside Nehwon altogether, as we did in our last adventure. We've got the papers – the scrap of ramskin parchment, I mean – and we know where we're going. Or at least you say you do.'

'Shh!' the big man commanded, then added hoarsely, 'Before embarking on any great enterprise, it's customary to consult a warlock or witch.'

The little man, now whispering likewise, countered with, 'Then why couldn't we have consulted a civilized one? – any member in good standing of the Lankhmar Sorcerers Guild. He'd at least have had a comely naked girl or two around, to rest your eyes on when they began to water from scanning his crabbed hieroglyphs and horoscopes.'

'A good earthy witch is more honest than some city rogue tricked out in black cone-hat and robe of stars,' the big man argued. 'Besides, this one is nearer our icy goal and its influences. You and your townsman's lust for luxuries! You'd turn a wizard's workroom into a brothel.'

'Why not?' the little man wanted to know. 'Both species of glamour at once!' Then, jerking his thumb at the hag, 'Earthy, you said? Dungy describes her better.'

'Shh, Mouser, you'll break her trance.'

'Trance?' The little man reinspected the hag. Her mouth had shut and she was breathing wheezingly through her beaky nose alone, the fume-sooty tip of which sought to meet her jutting chin. There was a faint high wailing, as of distant wolves, or nearby ghosts, or perhaps just an odd overtone of the hag's wheezes.

The little man sneered his upper lip and shook his head. His hands shook a little too, but he hid that. 'No, she's only stoned out of her skull, I'd say,' he commented judiciously. 'You shouldn't have given her so much poppy gum.'

'But that's the entire intent of trance,' the big man protested. 'To lash, stone, and otherwise drive the spirit out of the skull and whip it up mystic mountains, so that from their peaks it can spy out the lands of past and future, and mayhaps other-world.'

'I wish the mountains ahead of *us* were merely mystic,' the little man muttered. 'Look, Fafhrd, I'm willing to squat here all night – or at any rate for fifty more stinking breaths or two hundred bored heartbeats – to pleasure your whim. But has it occurred to you that we're in danger in this tent? And I don't mean solely from spirits. There are other rogues than ourselves in Illik-Ving, some perhaps on the same quest as ours, who'd dearly love to scupper us. And here in this blind leather hut we're deer on a skyline – or sitting ducks.'

Just then the wind came back with its fumblings and fingerings, and in addition a scrabbling that might be that of wind-swayed branch tips or of dead men's long fingernails a-scratch. There were faint growlings and wailings too, and with them stealthy footfalls. Both men thought of the Mouser's last warning. Fafhrd and he looked toward the tent's night-slitted skin door and loosened their swords in their scabbards.

At that instant the hag's noisy breathing stopped and with it all other sound. Her eyes opened, showing only whites – milky ovals infinitely eerie in the dark root-tangle of her sharp features and stringy hair. The gray tip of her tongue traveled like a large maggot around her lips.

The Mouser made to comment, but the out-thrust palmside of Fafhrd's spread-fingered hand was more compelling than any *shh*.

In a voice low but remarkably clear, almost a girl's voice, the hag intoned:

'For reasons sorcerous and dim
You travel toward the world's frost rim . . .'

'Dim' is the key word there, the Mouser thought. *Typical witchy say-nothing. She clearly knows naught about us except that we're headed north, which she could get from any gossipy mouth.*

'You north, north, north, and north must go
Through dagger-ice and powder-snow . . .'

More of the same, was the Mouser's inward comment. *But must she rub it in, even the snow? Brr!*

'And many a rival, envy-eyed,
Will dog your steps until you've died . . .'

Aha, the inevitable fright-thrust, without which no fortune-tale is complete!

'But after peril's cleansing fire
You'll meet at last your heart's desire . . .'

And now pat the happy ending! Gods, but the stupidest palm-reading prostitute of Ilthmar could –

'And then you'll find—'

Something silvery gray flashed across the Mouser's eyes, so close its form was blurred. Without a thought he ducked back and drew Scalpel.

The razor-sharp spear-blade, driven through the tent's side as if it were paper, stopped inches from Fafhrd's head and was draged back.

A javelin hurtled out of the hide wall. This the Mouser struck aside with his sword.

Now a storm of cries rose outside. The burden of some was, 'Death to the strangers!' Of others, 'Come out, dogs and be killed!'

The Mouser faced the skin door, his gaze darting.

Fafhrd, almost as quick to react as the Mouser, hit on a somewhat irregular solution to their knotty tactical problem: that of men besieged in a fortress whose walls neither protect them nor permit outward viewing. At first step, he leaped to the tent's central pole and with a great heave drew it from the earth.

The witch, likewise reacting with good solid sense, threw herself flat on the dirt.

'We decamp!' Fafhrd cried. 'Mouser, guard our front and guide me!'

And with that he charged toward the door, carrying the whole tent with him. There was a rapid series of little explosions as the somewhat brittle old thongs that tied its rawhide sides to its pegs snapped. The brazier tumbled over, scattering coals. The hag was overpassed. The Mouser, running ahead of Fafhrd, threw wide the door-slit. He had to use Scalpel at once, to parry a sword thrust out of the dark, but with his other hand he kept the door spread.

The opposing swordsman was bowled over, perhaps a bit startled at being attacked by the tent. The Mouser trod on him. He thought he heard ribs snap as Fafhrd did the same, which seemed a nice if brutal touch. Then he was crying out, 'Veer left now, Fafhrd! Now to the right a little! There's an alley coming up on our left. Be ready to turn sharp into it when I give the word. Now!' And grasping the door's hide edges, the Mouser helped swing the tent as Fafhrd pivoted.

From behind came cries of rage and wonder, also a screeching that sounded like the hag, enraged at the theft of her home.

The alley was so narrow that the tent's sides dragged against buildings and fences. At the first sign of a soft spot in the dirt underfoot, Fafhrd drove the tent-pole into it, and they both dashed out of the tent, leaving it blocking the alley.

The cries behind them grew suddenly louder as their pursuers turned into the alley, but Fafhrd and the Mouser did not run off over-swiftly. It seemed certain their attackers would spend considerable time scouting and assaulting the empty tent.

They loped together through the outskirts of the sleeping city toward their own well-hidden camp outside it. Their nostrils sucked in the chill, bracing air funneling down from the best pass through the Trollstep Mountains, a craggy chain which walled off the Land of Eight Cities from the vast plateau of the Cold Waste to the north.

Fafhrd remarked, 'It's unfortunate the old lady was interrupted just when she was about to tell us something important.'

The Mouser snorted. 'She'd already sung her song, the sum of which was zero.'

'I wonder who those rude fellows were and what were their motives?' Fafhrd asked. 'I thought I recognized the voice of that ale-swiller Gnarfi, who has an aversion to bear-meat.'

'Scoundrels behaving as stupidly as we were,' the Mouser answered. 'Motives? – as soon impute 'em to sheep! Ten dolts following an idiot leader.'

'Still, it appears that someone doesn't like us,' Fafhrd opined.

'Was that ever news?' the Gray Mouser retorted.

II: STARDOCK

Early one evening, weeks later, the sky's gray cloud-armor blew away south, smashed and dissolving as if by blows of an acid-dipped mace. The same mighty northeast wind contemptuously puffed down the hitherto impregnable cloud wall to the east, revealing a grimly majestic mountain range running north to south and springing abruptly from the plateau, two leagues high, of the Cold Waste – like a dragon fifty leagues long heaving up its spike-crested spine from icy entombment.

Fafhrd, no stranger to the Cold Waste, born at the foot of these same mountains and childhood climber of their lower slopes, named them off to the Gray Mouser as the two men stood together on the crunchy hoarfrosted eastern rim of the hollow that held their camp. The sun, set for the camp, still shone from behind their backs onto the western faces of the major peaks as he named them – but it shone not with any romanticizing rosy glow, but rather with a clear, cold, detail-pinning light fitting the peaks' dire aloofness.

'Travel your eye to the first great northerly upthrust,' he told the Mouser, 'that phalanx of heaven-menacing ice-spears shafted with dark rock and gleaming green – that's the Ripsaw. Then, dwarfing them, a single ivory-icy tooth, unscalable by any sane appraisal – the Tusk, he's called. Another unscalable then, still higher and with south wall a sheer precipice shooting up a league and curving outward toward the needletop: he is White Fang, where my father died – the canine of the Mountains of the Giants.

'Now begin again with the first snow dome at the south of the chain,' continued the tall fur-cloaked man, copper-bearded and copper-maned, his head otherwise bare to the frigid air, which was as quiet at ground level as sea-deep beneath storm. 'The Hint, she's named, or the Come On. Little enough she looks, yet men have frozen nighting on her slopes and been whirled to death by her whimsical queenly avalanches. Then a far vaster snow dome, true queen to the Hint's princess, a hemisphere of purest white, grand enough to roof the council hall of all the gods that ever were or will be – she is Gran Hanack, whom my father was first of men to mount and master. Our town of tents was pitched *there* near her base. No mark of it now, I'll guess, not even a midden.

'After Gran Hanack and nearest to us of them all, a huge flat-topped pillar, a pedestal for the sky almost, looking to be of green-shot snow but in truth all snow-pale granite scoured by the storms : Obelisk Polaris.

'Lastly,' Fafhrd continued, sinking his voice and gripping his smaller comrade's shoulder, 'let your gaze travel up the snow-tressed, dark-rocked, snowcapped peak between the Obelisk and White Fang, her glittering skirt somewhat masked by the former, but taller than they as they are taller than the Waste. Even now she hides behind her the mounting moon. She is Stardock, our quest's goal.'

'A pretty enough, tall, slender wart on this frostbit patch of Nehwon's face,' the Gray Mouser conceded, writhing his shoulder from Fafhrd's grip. 'And now at last tell me, friend, why you never climbed this Stardock in your youth and seized the treasure there, but must wait until we get a clue to it in a dusty, hot, scorpion-patrolled desert tower a quarter world away – and waste half a year getting here.'

Fafhrd's voice grew a shade unsure as he answered, 'My father never climbed her; how should I? Also, there were no legends of a treasure on Stardock's top in my father's clan . . . though there was a storm of other legends about Stardock, each forbidding her ascent. They called my father the Legend Breaker and shrugged wisely when he died on White Fang . . . Truly, my memory's not so good for those days, Mouser – I got many a mind-shattering knock on my head before I learned to deal all knocks first . . . and then I was hardly a boy when the clan left the Cold Waste – though the rough hard walls of Obelisk Polaris had been my upended playground . . .'

The Mouser nodded doubtfully. In the stillness they heard their tethered ponies munching the ice-crisped grass of the hollow, then a faint unangry growl from Hrissa the ice-cat, curled between the tiny fire and the piled baggage – likely one of the ponies had come cropping too close. On the great icy plain around them, nothing moved – or almost nothing.

The Mouser dipped gray lambskin-gloved fingers into the bottom of his pouch and from the pocket there withdrew a tiny oblong of parchment and read from it, more by memory than sight:

'Who mounts white Stardock, the Moon Tree,
'Past worm and gnome and unseen bars,
'Will win the key to luxury:
'The Heart of Light, a pouch of stars.'

Fafhrd said dreamily, 'They say the gods once dwelt and had their smithies on Stardock and from thence, amid jetting fire and showering sparks, launched all the stars; hence her name. They say diamonds, rubies, smaragds – all great gems – are the tiny pilot models the gods made of the stars . . . and then threw carelessly away across the world when their great work was done.'

'You never told me that before,' the Mouser said, looking at him sharply.

Fafhrd blinked his eyes and frowned puzzledly. 'I am beginning to remember childhood things.'

The Mouser smiled thinly before returning the parchment to its deep pocket. 'The guess that a pouch of stars might be a bag of gems,' he listed, 'the story that Nehwon's biggest diamond is called the Heart of Light, a few words on a ramskin scrap in the topmost room of a desert tower locked and sealed for centuries – small hints, those, to draw two men across this murdering, monotonous Cold Waste. Tell me, Old Horse, were you just homesick for the miserable white meadows of your birth to pretend to believe 'em?'

'Those small hints,' Fafhrd said, gazing now toward White Fang, 'drew other men north across Nehwon. There must have been other ramskin scraps, though why they should be discovered at the same time, I cannot guess.'

'We left all such fellows behind at Illik-Ving, or Lankhmar even, before we ever mounted the Trollsteps,' the Mouser asserted with complete confidence. 'Weak sisters, they were, smelling loot but quailing at hardship.'

Fafhrd gave a small headshake and pointed. Between them and White Fang rose the tiniest thread of black smoke.

'Did Gnarfi and Kranarch seem weak sisters? – to name but two of the other seekers,' he asked when the Mouser finally saw and nodded.

'It could be,' the Mouser agreed gloomily. 'Though aren't there any ordinary travelers of this Waste? Not that we've seen a man-shaped soul since the Mingol.'

Fafhrd said thoughtfully, 'It might be an encampment of the Icy Gnomes . . . though they seldom leave their caves except at High Summer, now a month gone . . .' He broke off, frowning puzzledly. 'Now how did I know that?'

'Another childhood memory bobbing to the top of the black pot?' the Mouser hazarded. Fafhrd shrugged doubtfully.

'So, for choice, Kranach and Gnarfi,' the Mouser concluded. 'Two strong brothers, I'll concede. Perhaps we should have picked a fight with 'em at Illik-Ving,' he suggested. 'Or perhaps even now . . . a swift march by night . . . a sudden swoop—'

Fafhrd shook his head. 'Now we're climbers, not killers,' he said. 'A man must be all climber to dare Stardock.' He directed the Mouser's gaze back toward the tallest mountain. 'Let's rather study her west wall while the light holds.

'Begin first at her feet,' he said. 'That glimmering skirt falling from her snowy hips, which are almost as high as the Obelisk – that's the White Waterfall, where no man may live.

'Now to her head again. From her flat tilted snowcap hang two great swelling braids of snow, streaming almost perpetually with avalanches, as if she combed 'em day and night – the Tresses, those are called. Between them's a wide ladder of dark rock, marked at three points by ledges. The topmost of the three ledge-banks is the Face – d'you note the darker ledges marking eyes and lips? The midmost of the three is called the Roosts; the lowermost – level with Obelisk's wide summit – the Lairs.'

'What lairs and roosts there?' the Mouser wanted to know.

'None may say, for none have climbed the Ladder,' Fafhrd replied. 'Now as to our route up her – it's most simple. We scale Obelisk Polaris – a trustworthy mountain if there ever was one – then cross by a dippling snow-saddle (there's the danger-stretch of our ascent!) to Stardock and climb the Ladder to her top.'

'How do we climb the Ladder in the long blank stretches between the ledges?' the Mouser asked with childlike innocence, almost. 'That is, if the Lairers and Roosters will honor our passports and permit us to try.'

Fafhrd shrugged. 'There'll be a way, rock being rock.'

'Why's there no snow on the Ladder?'

'Too steep.'

'And supposing we climb it to the top,' the Mouser finally asked, 'how do we lift our black-and-blue skeletonized bodies over the brim of Stardock's snowy hat, which seems to outcurve and downcurve most stylishly?'

'There's a triangular hole in it somewhere called the Needle's Eye,' Fafhrd answered negligently. 'Or so I've heard. But never you fret, Mouser, we'll find it.'

'Of course we will,' the Mouser agreed with an airy certainty that almost sounded sincere, 'we who hop-skip across shaking snow bridges and dance the fantastic up vertical walls without ever touching hand to granite. Remind me to bring a longish knife to carve our initials on the sky when we celebrate the end of our little upward sortie.'

His gaze wandered slightly northward. In another voice he continued, 'The dark north wall of Stardock now – that looks steep enough, to be sure, but free of snow to the very top. Why isn't that our route – rock, as you say with such unanswerable profundity, being rock.'

Fafhrd laughed unmockingly. 'Mouser,' he said, 'do you mark against the darkening sky that long white streamer waving south from Stardock's top? Yes, and below it a lesser streamer – can you distinguish that? That second one comes through the Needle's Eye! Well, those streamers from Stardock's hat are called the Grand and Petty Pennons. They're powdered snow blasted off Stardock by the northeast gale, which blows at least seven days out of eight, never predictably. That gale would pluck the stoutest climber off the north wall as easily as you or I might puff dandelion down from its darkening stem. Stardock's self shields the Ladder from the gale.'

'Does the gale never shift around to strike the Ladder?' the Mouser inquired lightly.

'Only occasionally,' Fafhrd reassured him.

'Oh, that's great,' the Mouser responded with quite overpowering sincerity and would have returned to the fire, except just then the darkness began swiftly to climb the Mountains of the Giants, as the sun took his final dive far to the west, and the gray-clad man stayed to watch the grand spectacle.

It was like a black blanket being pulled up. First the glittering skirt of the White Waterfall was hidden, then the Lairs on the Ladder and then the Roosts. Now all the other peaks were gone, even the Tusk's and White Fang's gleaming cruel tips, even the greenish-white roof of Obelisk Polaris. Now only Stardock's snow hat was left and below it the Face between the silvery Tresses. For a moment the ledges called the Eyes gleamed, or seemed to. Then all was night.

Yet there was a pale afterglow about. It was profoundly silent and the air utterly unmoving. Around them, the Cold Waste seemed to stretch north, west, and south to infinity.

And in that space of silence something went whisper-gliding through the still air, with the faint rushy sound of a great sail in a moderate breeze. Fafhrd and the Mouser both stared all around wildly. Nothing. Beyond the little fire, Hrissa the ice-cat sprang up hissing. Still nothing. Then the sound, whatever had made it, died away.

Very softly, Fafhrd began, 'There is a legend . . .' A long pause. Then with a sudden headshake, in a more natural voice: 'The memory slips away, Mouser. All my mind-fingers couldn't clutch it. Let's patrol once around the camp and so to bed.'

From first sleep the Mouser woke so softly that even Hrissa, back pressed against him from his knees to his chest on the side toward the fire, did not rouse.

Emerging from behind Stardock, her light glittering on the

southern Tress, hung the swelling moon, truly a proper fruit of the Moon Tree. Strange, the Mouser thought, how small the moon was and how big Stardock, silhouetted against the moon-pale sky.

Then, just below the flat top of Stardock's hat, he saw a bright, pale blue twinkling. He recalled that Ashsha, pale blue and brightest of Nehwon's stars, was near the moon tonight and he wondered if he were seeing her by rare chance through the Needle's Eye, proving the latter's existence. He wondered too what great sapphire or blue diamond – perhaps the Heart of Light? – had been the gods' pilot model for Ashsha, smiling drowsily the while at himself for entertaining such a silly, lovely myth. And then, embracing the myth entirely, he asked himself whether the gods had left any of their full-scale stars, unlaunched, on Stardock. Then Ashsha, if it were she, winked out.

The Mouser felt cozy in his cloak lined with sheep's-wool and now thong-laced into a bag by the horn hooks around its hem. He stared long and dreamily at Stardock until the moon broke loose from her and a blue jewel twinkled on top of her hat and broke loose too – now Ashsha surely. He wondered unfearfully about the windy rushing he and Fafhrd had heard in the still air – perhaps only a long tongue of a storm licking down briefly. If the storm lasted, they would climb up into it.

Hrissa stretched in her sleep. Fafhrd grumbled low in a dream, wrapped in his own great thong-laced cloak stuffed with eiderdown.

The Mouser dropped his gaze to the ghostly flames of the dying fire, seeking sleep himself. The flames made girl-bodies, then girl-faces. Next a ghostly pale green girl-face – perhaps an afterimage, he thought at first – appeared beyond the fire, staring at him through close-slitted eyes across the flame tops. It grew more distinct as he gazed at it, but there was no trace of hair or body about it – it hung against the dark like a mask.

Yet it was weirdly beautiful: narrow chin, high-arched cheeks, wine-dark short lips slightly pouted, straight nose that went up without a dip into the broad, somewhat low forehead – and then the mystery of those fully lidded eyes seeming to peer at him through wine-dark lashes. And all, save lashes and lips, of palest green, like jade.

The Mouser did not speak or stir a muscle, simply because the face was very beautiful to him – just as any man might hope for the moment never to end when his naked mistress unconsciously or by secret design assumes a particularly charming attitude.

Also, in the dismal Cold Waste, any man treasures illusions, though knowing them almost certainly to be such.

Suddenly the eyes parted wide, showing only the darkness behind, as if the face were a mask indeed. The Mouser did start then, but still not enough to wake Hrissa.

Then the eyes closed, the lips puckered with taunting invitation; then the face began swiftly to dissolve as if were being literally wiped away. First the right side went, then the left, then the center, last of all the dark lips and the eyes. For a moment the Mouser fancied he caught a winy odor; then all was gone.

He contemplated waking Fafhrd and almost laughed at the thought of his comrade's surly reactions. He wondered if the face had been a sign from the gods, or a sending from some black magician castled on Stardock, or Stardock's very soul perhaps – though then where had she left her glittering tresses and hat and her Ashsha eye? – or only a random creation of his own most clever brain, stimulated by sexual privation and tonight by beauteous if devilishly dangerous mountains. Rather quickly he decided on the last explanation and he slumbered.

Two evenings later, at the same hour, Fafhrd and the Gray Mouser stood scarcely a knife cast from the west wall of Obelisk Polaris, building a cairn from pale greenish rock-shards fallen over the millennia. Among this scanty scree were some bones, many broken, of sheep or goats.

As before, the air was still though very cold, the Waste empty, the set sun bright on the mountain faces.

From this closest vantage point the Obelisk was foreshortened into a pyramid that seemed to taper up forever, vertically. Encouragingly, his rock felt diamond-hard while the lowest reaches of the wall at any rate were thick with bumpy handholds and footholds, like pebbled leather.

To the south, Gran Hanack and the Hint were hidden. To the north White Fang towered monstrously, yellowish white in the sunlight, as if ready to rip a hole in the graying sky. Bane of Fafhrd's father, the Mouser recalled.

Of Stardock, there could be seen the dark beginning of the wind-blasted north wall and the north end of the deadly White Waterfall. All else of Stardock the Obelisk hid.

Save for one touch: almost straight overhead, seeming now to come from Obelisk Polaris, the ghostly Grand Pennon streamed southwest.

From behind Fafhrd and the Mouser as they worked came the tantalizing odor of two snow hares roasting by the fire, while before it Hrissa tore flesh slowly and savoringly from the carcass of a third she'd coursed down. The ice-cat was about the size and shape of a cheetah, though with long tufty white hair. The Mouser had bought her from a far-ranging Mingol trapper just north of the Trollsteps.

Beyond the fire the ponies eagerly chomped the last of the grain, strengthening stuff they'd not tasted for a week.

Fafhrd wrapped his sheathed longsword Graywind in oiled silk and laid it in the cairn, then held out a big hand to the Mouser.

'Scalpel?'

'I'm taking my sword with me,' the Mouser stated, then added justifyingly, 'it's but a feather to yours.'

'Tomorrow you'll find what a feather weighs,' Fafhrd foretold. The big man shrugged and placed by Graywand his helmet, a bear's hide, a folded tent, shovel and pickax, gold bracelets from his wrists and arms, quills, ink papyrus, a large copper pot, and some books and scrolls. The Mouser added various empty and near-empty bags, two hunting spears, skis, an unstrung bow with a quiver of arrows, tiny jars of oily paint and squares of parchment, and all the harness of the ponies, many of the items wrapped against damp like Graywand.

Then, their appetites quickening from the roast-fumes, the two comrades swiftly built two top courses, roofing the cairn.

Just as they turned toward supper, facing the raggedly gilt-edged flat western horizon, they heard in the silence the rushy sail-like noise again, fainter this time but twice: once in the air to the north and, almost simultaneously, to the south.

Again they stared around swiftly but searchingly, yet there was nothing anywhere to be seen except – again Fafhrd saw it first – a thread of black smoke very near White Fang, rising from a point on the glacier between that mountain and Stardock.

'Gnarfi and Kranarch, if it be they, have chosen the rocky north wall for their ascent,' the Mouser observed.

'And it will be their bane,' Fafhrd predicted, up-jerking his thumb at the Pennon.

The Mouser nodded with less certainty, then demanded, 'Fafhrd, what *was* that sound? You've lived here.'

Fafhrd's brow crinkled and his eyes almost shut. 'Some legend of great birds . . .' he muttered questioningly, '. . . or of great fish – no, that couldn't be right.'

'Memory pot still seething all black?' the Mouser asked. Fafhrd nodded.

Before he left the cairn, the Northerner laid beside it a slab of salt. 'That,' he said, 'along with the ice-filmed pool and herbage we just passed, should hold the ponies here for a week. If we don't return, well, at least we showed 'em the way between here and Illik-Ving.'

Hrissa smiled up from her bloody tidbit, as if to say, 'No need to worry about me or my rations.'

Again the Mouser woke as soon as sleep had gripped him tight, this time with a surge of pleasure, as one who remembers a rendezvous. And again, this time without any preliminary star-staring or flame-gazing, the living mask faced him across the sinking fire: every same expression-quirk and feature – short lips, nose and forehead one straight line – except that tonight it was ivory pale with greenish lips and lids and lashes.

The Mouser was considerably startled, for last night he had stayed awake, waiting for the phantom girl-face – and even trying to make it come again – until the swelling moon had risen three handbreadths above Stardock . . . without any success whatever. His mind had known that the face had been an hallucination on the first occasion, but his feelings had insisted otherwise – to his considerable disgust and the loss of a quarter night's sleep.

And by day he had secretly consulted the last of the four short stanzas on the parchment scrap in his pouch's deepest pocket:

Who scales the Snow King's citadel
Shall father his two daughter's sons;
Though he must face foes fierce and fell,
His seed shall live while time still runs.

Yesterday that had seemed rather promising – at least the fathering and daughters part – though today, after his lost sleep, the merest mockery.

But now the living mask was there again and going through all the same teasing antics, including the shuddersome yet somehow thrilling trick of opening wide its lids to show not eyes but a dark backing like the rest of the night. The Mouser was enchanted in a shivery way, but unlike the first night he was full-mindedly alert and he tested for illusions by blinking and squinting his own eyes and silently shifting his head about in his hood – with no effect whatever on the living mask. Then he quietly unlaced the thong from the top hooks of his cloak – Hrissa was sleeping against Fafhrd tonight – and slowly reached out his hand and picked up a pebble and flicked it across the pale flames at a point somewhere below the mask.

Although he knew there wasn't anything beyond the fire but scattered scree and ringingly hard earth, there wasn't the faintest sound of the pebble striking anywhere. He might have thrown it off Nehwon.

At almost the same instant, the mask smiled tauntingly.

The Mouser was very swiftly out of his cloak and on his feet.

But even more swiftly the mask dissolved away – this time in one swift stroke from forehead to chin.

He quickly stepped, almost lunged, around the fire to the spot where the mask had seemed to hang, and there he stared around searchingly. Nothing – except a fleeting breath of wine or spirits of wine. He stirred the fire and stared around again. Still nothing. Except that Hrissa woke beside Fafhrd and bristled her moustache and gazed solemnly, perhaps scornfully, at the Mouser, who was beginning to feel rather like a fool. He wondered if his mind and his desires were playing a silly game against each other.

The he trod on something. His pebble, he thought, but when he picked it up, he saw it was a tiny jar. It could have been one of his own pigment jars, but it was too small, hardly bigger than a joint of his thumb, and made not of hollowed stone but some kind of ivory or other tooth.

He knelt by the fire and peered into it, then dipped in his little finger and gingerly rubbed the tip against the rather hard grease inside. It came out ivory-hued. The grease had an oily, not winy odor.

The Mouser pondered by the fire for some time. Then with a glance at Hrissa, who had closed her eyes and laid back her moustache again, and at Fafhrd, who was snoring softly, he returned to his cloak and to sleep.

He had not told Fafhrd a word about his earlier vision of the living mask. His surface reason was that Fafhrd would laugh at such calf-brained nonsense of smoke-faces; his deeper reason the one which keeps any man from mentioning a pretty new girl even to his dearest friend.

So perhaps it was the same reason which next morning kept Fafhrd from telling his dearest friend what happened to him late that same night. Fafhrd dreamed he was feeling out the exact shape of a girl's face in absolute darkness while her slender hands caressed his body. She had a rounded forehead, very long eye-lashed eyes, in-dipping nose bridge, apple cheeks, an impudent snub nose – it *felt* impudent! – and long lips whose grin his big gentle fingers could trace clearly.

He woke to the moon glaring down at him aslant from the south. It shivered the Obelisk's interminable wall, turning rock-knobs to black shadow bars. He also woke to acute disappointment that a dream had been only a dream. Then he would have sworn that he felt fingertips briefly brush his face and that he heard a faint silvery chuckle which receded swiftly. He sat up like a mummy in his laced cloak and stared around.

The fire had sunk to a few red ember-eyes, but the moonlight was bright and by it he could see nothing at all.

Hrissa growled at him reproachfully for a silly sleep-breaker. He damned himself for mistaking the afterimage of a dream for reality. He damned the whole girl-less, girl-vision-breeding Cold Waste. A bit of the night's growing chill spilled down his neck. He told himself he should be fast asleep like the wise Mouser over there, gathering strength for tomorrow's great effort. He lay back and after some time he slumbered.

Next morning the Mouser and Fafhrd woke at the first gray of dawn, the moon still bright as a snowball in the west, and quickly breakfasted and readied themselves and stood facing Obelisk Polaris in the stinging cold, all girls forgotten, their manhood directed solely at the mountain.

Fafhrd stood in high-laced boots with newly-sharpened thick hobnails. He wore a wolfskin tunic, fur turned in but open now from neck to belly. His lower arms and legs were bare. Short-wristed rawhide gloves covered his hands. A rather small pack, wrapped in his cloak, rode high on his back. Clipped to it was a large coil of black hempen rope. On his stout unstudded belt, his sheathed ax on his right side balanced on the other a knife, a small waterskin, and a bag of iron spikes headed by rings.

The Mouser wore his ramskin hood, pulled close around his face now by its drawstring, and on his body a tunic of gray silk, triple layered. His gloves were longer than Fafhrd's and fur-lined. So were his slender boots, which were footed with crinkly behemoth hide. On *his* belt, his dagger Cat's Claw and his waterskin balanced his sword Scalpel, its scabbard thonged loosely to his thigh. While to his cloak-wrapped pack was secured a curiously thick, short, black bamboo rod headed with a spike at one end and at the other a spike and large hook, somewhat like that of a shepherd's crook.

Both men were deeply tanned and leanly muscular, in best trim for climbing, hardened by the Trollsteps and the Cold Waste, their chests a shade larger than ordinary from weeks of subsisting on the latter's thin air.

No need to search out the best-looking ascent – Fafhrd

had done that yesterday as they'd approached the Obelisk.

The ponies were cropping again, and one had found the salt and was licking it with his thick tongue. The Mouser looked around for Hrissa to cuff her cheek in farewell, but the ice-cat was sniffling out a spoor beyond the campsite, her ears a-prick.

'She makes a cat-parting,' Fafhrd said. 'Good.'

A faint shade of rose touched the heavens and the glacier by White Fang. Scanning toward the latter, the Mouser drew in his breath and squinted hard, while Fafhrd gazed narrowly from under the roof of his palm.

'Brownish figures,' the Mouser said at last. 'Kranarch and Gnarfi always dressed in brown leather, I recall. But I make them more than two.'

'I make them four,' Fafhrd said. 'Two strangely shaggy – clad in brown fur suits, I guess. And all four mounting from the glacier up the rock wall.'

'Where the gale will—' the Mouser began, then looked up. So did Fafhrd.

The Grand Pennon was gone.

'You said that sometimes—' the Mouser started.

'Forget the gale and those two and their rough-edged reinforcements,' Fafhrd said curtly. He faced around again at Obelisk Polaris. So did the Mouser.

Squinting up the greenish-white slope, head bent sharply back, the Mouser said, 'This morning he seems somewhat steeper even than that north wall and rather extensive upward.'

'Pah!' Fafhrd retorted. 'As a child I would climb him before breakfast. Often.' He raised his clenched right rawhide glove as if it held a baton, and cried, 'We go!'

With that he strode forward and without a break began to walk up the knobbly face – or so it seemed, for although he used handholds he kept his body far out from the rock, as a good climber should.

The Mouser followed in Fafhrd's steps and holds, stretching his legs farther and keeping somewhat closer to the cliff.

Midmorning and they were still climbing without a break. The Mouser ached or stung in every part. His pack was like a fat man on his back, Scalpel a sizable boy clinging to his belt. And his ears had popped five times.

Just above, Fafhrd's boots clashed rock-knobs and into rock-holes with an unhesitating mechanistic rhythm the Mouser had begun to hate. Yet he kept his eyes resolutely fixed on them. Once he had looked down between his own legs and decided not to do that again.

It is not good to see the blue of distance, or even the gray-blue of middle distance, below one.

So he was taken by surprise when a small white bearded face, bloodily encumbered, came bobbing up alongside and past him.

Hrissa halted on a ledgelet by Fafhrd and took great whistling breaths, her tufted belly-skin pressing up against her spine with each exhalation. She breathed only through her pinkish nostrils because her jaws were full of two snow hares, packed side by side, with dead heads and hind-quarters a-dangle.

Fafhrd took them from her and dropped them in his pouch and laced it shut.

Then he said, just a shade grandiloquently, 'She has proved her endurance and skill, and she has paid her way. She is one of us.'

It had not occurred to the Mouser to doubt any of that. It seemed to him simply that there were three comrades now climbing Obelisk Polaris. Besides, he was most grateful to Hrissa for the halt she had brought. Partly to prolong it, he carefully pressed a handful of water from his bag and stretched it to her to lap. Then he and Fafhrd drank a little too.

All the long summer day they climbed the west wall of the cruel but reliable Obelisk. Fafhrd seemed tireless. The Mouser got his second wind, lost it, and never quite got his third. His whole body was one great leaden ache, beginning deep in his bones and filtering outward, like refined poison, through his flesh. His vision became a bobbing welter of real and remembered rock-knobs, while the necessity of never missing one single grip or foot-placement seemed the ruling of an insane schoolmaster god. He silently cursed the whole maniacal

Stardock project, cackling in his brain at the idea that the luring stanzas on the parchment could be anything but pipe dreams. Yet he would not cry quits or seek again to prolong the brief breathers they took.

He marveled dully at Hrissa's leaping and hunching up beside them. But by mid-afternoon he noted she was limping and once he saw a light blood-print of two pads where she'd set a paw.

They made camp at last almost two hours before sunset, because they'd found a rather wide ledge – and because a very light snowfall had begun, the tiny flakes sifting silently down like meal.

They made a fire of resin-pellets in the tiny claw-footed brazier Fafhrd packed, and they heated over it water for herb tea in their single narrow high pot. The water was a long time getting even lukewarm. With Cat's Claw the Mouser stirred two dollops of honey into it.

The ledge was as long as three men stretched out and as deep as one. On the sheer face of Obelisk Polaris that much space seemed an acre, at least.

Hrissa stretched slackly behind the tiny fire. Fafhrd and the Mouser huddled to either side of it, their cloaks drawn around them, too tired to look around, talk, or even think.

The snowfall grew a little thicker, enough to hide the Cold Waste far below.

After his second swallow of sweetened tea, Fafhrd asserted they'd come at least two-thirds of the way up the Obelisk.

The Mouser couldn't understand how Fafhrd could pretend to know that, any more than a man could tell by looking at the shoreless waters of the Outer Sea how far he'd sailed across it. To the Mouser they were simply in the exact center of a dizzily tip-tilted plain of pale granite, green-tinged and now snow-sprinkled. He was still too weary to outline this concept to Fafhrd, but he managed to make himself say, 'As a child you would climb up and down the Obelisk before breakfast?'

'We had rather late breakfasts then,' Fafhrd explained gruffly.

'Doubtless on the afternoon of the fifth day,' the Mouser concluded.

After the tea was drunk, they heated more water and left the hacked and disjointed bits of one of the snow hares in the fluid until they turned gray, then slowly chewed them and drank the dull soup. At about the same time Hrissa became a little interested in the flayed carcass of the other hare set before her nose – by the brazier to keep it from freezing. Enough interested to begin to haggle it with her fangs and slowly chew and swallow.

The Mouser very gently examined the pads of the ice-cat's paws. They were worn silk-thin, there were two or three cuts in them, and the white fur between them was stained deep pink. Using a feather touch, the Mouser rubbed salve into them, shaking his head the while. Then he nodded once and took from his pouch a large needle, a spool of thin thong, and a small rolled hide of thin, tough leather. From the last he cut with Cat's Claw a shape rather like a very fat pear and stitched from it a boot for Hrissa.

When he tried it on the ice-cat's hind paw, she let it be for a little, then began to bite at it rather gently, looking up queerly at the Mouser. He thought, then very carefully bored holes in it for the ice-cat's non-retracting claws, then drew the boot up the leg snugly until the claws protruded fully and tied it there with the drawstring he'd run through slits at the top.

Hrissa no longer bothered the boot. The Mouser made others, and Fafhrd joined in and cut and stitched one too.

When Hrissa was fully shod in her four clawed paw-mittens, she smelled each, then stood up and paced back and forth the length of the ledge a few times, and finally settled herself by the still-warm brazier and the Mouser, chin on his ankle.

The tiny grains of snow were still falling ruler-straight, frosting the ledge and Fafhrd's coppery hair. He and the Mouser began to pull up their hoods and lace their cloaks about them for the night. The sun still shone through the snowfall, but its light was filtered white and brought not an atom of warmth.

Obelisk Polaris was not a noisy mountain, as many are – a-drip with glacial water, rattling with rock slides, and even with rock strata a-creak from uneven loss or gain of heat. The silence was profound.

The Mouser felt an impulse to tell Fafhrd about the living girl-mask or illusion he'd seen by night, while simultaneously Fafhrd considered recounting to the Mouser his own erotic dream.

At that moment there came again, without prelude, the rushing in the silent air and they saw, clearly outlined by the falling snow, a great flat undulating shape.

It came swooping past them, rather slowly, about two spear-lengths out from the ledge.

There was nothing at all to be seen except the flat, flakeless space the thing made in the airborne snow and the eddies it raised; it in no way obscured the snow beyond. Yet they felt the gust of its passage.

The shape of this invisible thing was most like that of a giant skate or stingray four yards long and three wide; there was even the suggestion of a vertical fin and a long, lashing tail.

'Great invisible fish!' the Mouser hissed, thrusting his hand down in his half-laced cloak and managing to draw Scalpel in a single sweep. 'Your mind was most right, Fafhrd, when you thought it wrong!'

As the snow-sketched apparition glided out of sight around the buttress ending the ledge to the south, there came from it a mocking rippling laughter in two voices, one alto, one soprano.

'A sightless fish that laughs like girls – most monstrous!' Fafhrd commented shakenly, hefting his ax, which he'd got out swiftly too, though it was still attached to his belt by a long thong.

They crouched there then for a while, scrambled out of their cloaks, and with weapons ready, awaited the invisible monster's return, Hrissa standing between them with fur bristling. But after a while they began to shake from the cold and so they perforce got back into their cloaks and laced them, though still gripping their weapons and prepared to throw off the upper lacings in a flash. Then they briefly discussed the weirdness just witnessed, insofar as they could, each now confessing his earlier visions or dreams of girls.

Finally the Mouser said, 'The girls might have been riding the invisible thing, lying along its back – and invisible too! Yet, what *was* the thing?'

This touched a small spot in Fafhrd's memory. Rather unwillingly he said, 'I remember waking once as a child in the night and hearing my father say to my mother, "... like great thick quivering sails, but the ones you can't see are the worst." They stopped speaking then, I think because they heard me stir.'

The Mouser asked, 'Did your father ever speak of seeing girls in the high mountains – flesh, apparition, or witch, which is a mixture of the two; visible or invisible?'

'He wouldn't have mentioned 'em if he had,' Fafhrd replied. 'My mother was a very jealous woman and a devil with a chopper.'

The whiteness they'd been scanning turned swiftly to darkest gray. The sun had set. They could no longer see the falling snow. They pulled up their hoods and laced their cloaks tight and huddled together at the back of the ledge with Hrissa close between them.

Trouble came early the next day. They roused with first light, feeling battered and nightmare-ridden, and uncramped themselves with difficulty while the morning ration of strong herb tea and powdered meat and snow were stewed in the same pot to a barely uncold aromatic gruel. Hrissa gnawed her rewarmed hare's bones and accepted a little bear's fat and water from the Mouser.

The snow had stopped during the night, but the Obelisk was powdered with it on every step and hold, while under the snow was ice – the first-fallen snow melted by yesterday afternoon's meager warmth on the rock and quickly refrozen.

So Fafhrd and the Mouser roped together, and the Mouser swiftly fashioned a harness for Hrissa by cutting two holes in the long side of an oblong of leather. Hrissa protested somewhat when her forelegs were thrust through the holes and the ends of the oblong double-stitched together snugly over her shoulders. But when an end of Fafhrd's black hempen rope was tied around her harness where the stitching was, she simply lay down flat on the ledge, on the warm spot where the brazier had stood, as if to say, 'This debasing tether I will not accept, though humans may.'

But when Fafhrd slowly started up the wall and the Mouser followed and the rope tightened on Hrissa, and when she had looked up and seen them still roped like herself, she followed sulkily after. A little later she slipped off a bulge – her boots, snug as they were, must have been clumsy to her after naked pads – and swung scrabbling back and forth several long moments before she was supporting her own weight again. Fortunately the Mouser had a firm stance at the time.

After that, Hrissa came on more cheerily, sometimes even climbing to the side ahead of the Mouser and smiling back at him – rather sardonically, the Mouser fancied.

The climbing was a shade steeper than yesterday with an even greater insistence that each hand- and foothold be perfect. Gloved fingers must grip stone, not ice; spikes must clash through the brittle stuff to rock. Fafhrd roped his ax to his right wrist and used its hammer to tap away treacherous thin platelets and curves of the glassy frozen water.

And the climbing was more wearing because it was harder to avoid tenseness. Even looking sideways at the steepness of the wall tightened the Mouser's groin with fear. He wondered *what if the wind should blow?* – and fought the impulse to cling flat to the cliff. Yet at the same time sweat began to trickle down his face and chest, so that he had to throw back his hood and loosen his tunic to his belly to keep his clothes from sogging.

But there was worse to come. It had looked as though the slope above were gentling, but now, drawing nearer, they perceived a bulge jutting out a full two yards some seven yards above them. The under-slope was pocked here and there – fine handholds, except that they opened down. The bulge extended as far as they could see to either side, at most points looking worse.

They found themselves the best and highest holds they could, close together, and stared up at their problem. Even Hrissa, a-cling by the Mouser, seemed subdued.

Fafhrd said softly, 'I mind me now they used to say there was an out-jutting around the Obelisk's top. His crown, I think my father called it. I wonder . . .'

'Don't you know?' the Mouser demanded, a shade harshly.

Standing rigid on his holds, his arms and legs were aching worse than ever.

'O Mouser,' Fafhrd confessed, 'in my youth I never climbed Obelisk Polaris farther than halfway to last night's camp. I only boasted to raise our spirits.'

There being nothing to say to that, the Mouser shut his lips, though somewhat thinly. Fafhrd began to whistle a tuneless tune and carefully fished a small grapnel with five dagger-sharp flukes from his pouch and tied it securely to the long end of their black rope still coiled on his back. Then stretching his right arm as far out as he might from the cliff, he whirled the grapnel in a smallish circle, faster and faster, and finally hurled it upward. They heard it clash against rock somewhere above the bulge, but it did not catch on any crack or hump and instantly came sliding and then dropping down, missing the Mouser by hardly a handbreadth, it seemed to him.

Fafhrd drew up the grapnel – with some delays, since it tended to catch on every crack or hump below them – and whirled and hurled it again. And again and again and again, each time without success. Once it stayed up, but Fafhrd's first careful tug on the rope brought it down.

Fafhrd's sixth cast was his first really bad one. The grapnel never went out of sight at all. As it reached the top of the throw, it glinted for an instant.

'Sunlight!' Fafhrd hissed happily. 'We're almost to the summit!'

'That "almost" is a whopper, though,' the Mouser commented, but even he couldn't keep a cheerful note out of his voice.

By the time Fafhrd had failed on seven more casts, all cheerfulness was gone from the Mouser again. His aches were horrible, his hands and feet were numbing in the cold, and his brain was numbing too, so that the next time Fafhrd cast and missed, he was so unwise as to follow the grapnel with his gaze as it fell.

For the first time today he really looked out and down. The Cold Waste was a pale blue expanse almost like the sky – and seeming even more distant – all its copses and mounds and tiny tarns having long since become pinpoints and vanished.

Many leagues to the west, almost at the horizon, a jagged pale gold band showed where the shadows of the mountains ended. Midway in the band was a blue gap – Stardock's shadow continuing over the edge of the world.

Giddily the Mouser snatched his gaze back to Obelisk Polaris . . . and although he could still see the granite, it didn't seem to count any more – only four insecure holds on a kind of pale green nothingness, with Fafhrd and Hrissa somehow suspended beside him. His mind could no longer accept the Obelisk's steepness.

As the urge to hurl himself down swelled in him, he somehow transformed it into a sardonic snort, and he heard himself say with daggerish contempt, 'Leave off your foolish fishing, Fafhrd! I'll show you now how Lankhmarian mountain science deals with a trifling problem such as this which has baffled all your barbarian whirling and casting!'

And with that he unclipped from his pack with reckless speed the thick black bamboo pike or crook and began cursingly with numb fingers to draw out and let snap into place its telescoping sections until it was four times its original length.

This tool of technical climbing, which indeed the Mouser had brought all the way from Lankhmar, had been a matter of dispute between them the whole trip, Fafhrd asserting it was a tricksy toy not worth the packing.

Now, however, Fafhrd made no comment, but merely coiled up his grapnel and thrust his hands into his wolf-skin jerkin against his sides to warm them and, mild-eyed, watched the Mouser's furious activity. Hrissa shifted to a perch closer to Fafhrd and crouched stoically.

But when the Mouser shakily thrust the narrower end of his black tool toward the bulge above, Fafhrd reached out a hand to help him steady it, yet could not refrain from saying, 'If you think to get a good enough hold with the crook on the rim to shinny up that stick—'

'Quiet, you loutish kibitzer!' the Mouser snarled and with Fafhrd's help thrust pike-end into a pock in the rock hardly a finger's length from the rim. Then he seated the spiked foot of the pole in a small, deep hollow just above his head. Next he snapped out two short recessed lever-arms from the base of the pole and began to rotate them. It soon became clear that they controlled a great screw hidden in the pole, for the latter lengthened until it stood firmly between the two pocks in the rock, while the stiff black shaft itself bent a little.

At that instant a sliver of rock, being pressed by the pole, broke off from the rim. The pole thrummed as it straightened and the Mouser, screaming a curse, slipped off his holds and fell.

It was good then that the rope between the two comrades was short and that the spikes of Fafhrd's boots were seated firmly, like so many demon-forged dagger-points, in the rock of his footholds – for as the strain came suddenly on Fafhrd's belt and on his rope-gripping left hand, he took it without plummeting after the Mouser, only bending his knees a little and grunting softly, while his right hand snatched hold of the vibrating pole and saved it.

The Mouser had not even fallen far enough to drag Hrissa from her perch, though the rope almost straightened between them. The ice-cat, her tufted neck bent sharply between foreleg and chest, peered down with great curiosity at the dangling man.

His face was ashen. Fafhrd made no mark of that, but simply handed him the black pole, saying, 'It's a good tool. I've screwed it back short. Seat it in another pock and try again.'

Soon the pole stood firm between the hollow by the Mouser's head and a pock a hand's width from the rim. The bow-like bend in the pole faced downward. Then they put the Mouser first on the rope, and he went climbing up and out along the pole, hanging from it back downward, his boot-edges finding tiny holds on the pole's section-shoulders – out into and over the vast, pale blue-gray space which had so lately dizzied him.

The pole began to bend a little more with the Mouser's weight, the pike end slipping a finger's span in the upper pock with a horrible tiny grating sound, but Fafhrd gave the screw another turn and the pole held firm.

Fafhrd and Hrissa watched the Mouser reach its end, where he paused briefly. Then they saw him reach up his left arm until it was out of sight to the elbow above the rim, meanwhile gripping with his right hand the crook and twining his legs around the shaft. He appeared to feel about with his left hand and find something. Then he moved out and up still further and very slowly his head and after it, in a sudden swift sweep, his right arm went out of sight above the rim.

For several long moments they saw only the bottom half of the bent Mouser, his dark crinkly-soled boots twined securely to the end of the pole. Then, rather slowly, like a gray snail, and with a final push of one boot against the top of the crook, he went entirely out of sight.

Fafhrd slowly paid out rope after him.

After some time the Mouser's voice, quite ghostly yet clear, came down to them: 'Hola! I've got the rope anchored around a boss big as a tree stump. Send up Hrissa.'

So Fafhrd put Hrissa on the rope ahead of him, knotting it to her harness with a sheepshank.

Hrissa fought desperately for a moment against being swung into space, but as soon as it was done hung deathly still. Then as she was drawn slowly up, Fafhrd's knot began to slip. The ice-cat swiftly snatched at the rope with her teeth and gripped it far back between her jaws. The moment she came near the rim, her clawed mittens were ready and she scrabbled and was dragged out of sight.

Soon word came down from the Mouser that Hrissà was safe and Fafhrd might follow. He frowningly tightened the screw another half turn, though the pole creaked ominously, and then very gently climbed out along it. The Mouser now kept the rope taut from above, but for the first stretch it could hardly take more than a few pounds of Fafhrd's weight off the pole.

The upper spike once again grated horribly a bit in its pock, but it still held firm. Helped more by the rope now, Fafhrd got his hands and head over the rim.

What he saw was a smooth, gentle rock slope, which could be climbed by friction, and at the top of it the Mouser and Hrissa standing backgrounded by blue sky and gilded by sunlight.

Soon he stood beside them.

The Mouser said, 'Fafhrd, when we get back to Lankhmar remind me to give Glinthi the Artificer thirteen diamonds from the pouch of them we'll find on Stardock's hat: one for each section and joint of my climbing pole, one each for the spikes at the ends and two for each screw.'

'Are there two screws?' Fafhrd asked respectfully.

'Yes, one at each end,' the Mouser told him and then made Fafhrd brace the rope for him so that he could climb down the slope and, bending all his upper body down over the rim, shorten the pole by rotating its upper screw until he was able to drag it triumphantly back over the top with him.

As the Mouser telescoped its sections together again, Fafhrd said to him seriously, 'You must thong it to your belt as I do my ax. We must not chance losing Glinthi's help on the rest of this journey.'

Throwing back their hoods and opening their tunics wide to the hot sun, Fafhrd and the Mouser looked around, while Hrissa luxuriously stretched and worked her slim limbs and neck and body, the white fur of which hid her bruises.

Both men were somewhat exalted by the thin air and filled brain-high with the ease of mind and spirit that comes with a great danger skilfully conquered.

Rather to their amazement, the southward swinging sun had climbed barely halfway to noon. Perils which had seemed demihours long had lasted minutes only.

The summit of Obelisk Polaris was a great rolling field of pale rock too big to measure by Lankhmar acres. They had arrived near the southwest corner, and the gray-tinted stone meadow seemed to stretch east and north almost indefinitely. Here and there were hummocks and hollows, but they swelled and dipped most gently. There were a few scattered large boulders, not many, while off to the east were darker indistinct shapes which might be bushes and small trees footed in cracks filled with blown dirt.

'What lies east of the mountain chain?' the Mouser asked. 'More Cold Waste?'

'Our clan never journeyed there,' Fafhrd answered. He frowned. 'Some taboo on the whole area, I think. Mist always masked the east on my father's great climbs – or so he told us.'

'We could have a look now,' the Mouser suggested.

Fafhrd shook his head. 'Our course lies there,' he said,

pointing northeast, where Stardock rose like a giantess standing tall but asleep, or feigning sleep, looking seven times as big and high at least as she had before the Obelisk hid her top two days ago.

The Mouser said, a shade dolefully, 'All our brave work scaling the Obelisk has only made Stardock higher. Are you sure there's not another peak, perhaps invisible, on top of her?'

Fafhrd nodded without taking his eyes off her, who was empress without consort of the Mountains of the Giants. Her Tresses had grown to great swelling rivers of snow and now the two adventurers could see faint stirrings in them – avalanches slipping and tumbling.

The Southern Tress came down in a great dipping double curve toward the northwest corner of the mighty rock summit on which they stood.

At the top, Stardock's corniced snow hat, its upper rim glittering with sunlight as if it were edged around with diamonds, seemed to nod toward them a trifle more than it ever had before, and the demurely-eyed Face with it, like a great lady hinting at possible favors.

But the gauzy, long pale veils of the Grand and Petty Pennons no longer streamed from her Hat. The air atop Stardock must be as still at the moment as it was where they stood upon the Obelisk.

'What devil's luck that Kranarch and Gnarfi should tackle the north wall the one day in eight the gale fails!' Fafhrd cursed. 'But 'twill be their destruction yet – yes, and of their two shaggy-clad henchmen too. This calm can't hold.'

'I recall now,' the Mouser remarked, 'that when we caroused with 'em in Illik-Ving, Gnarfi drunken-claimed he could whistle up winds – had learned the trick from his grandmother – and could whistle 'em down too, which is more to the point.'

'The more reason for us to hasten!' Fafhrd cried, upping his pack and slipping his big arms through the wide shoulder straps. 'On, Mouser! Up, Hrissa! We'll have a bite and sup before the snow ridge.'

'You mean we must tackle that freezing, treacherous problem today?' demurred the Mouser, who would dearly have loved to strip and bake in the sun.

'Before noon!' Fafhrd decreed. And with that he set them a stiff walking pace straight north, keeping close to the summit's west edge, as if to countermand from the start any curiosity the Mouser might have about a peek to the east. The latter followed with only minor further protests; Hrissa came on limpingly, lagging at first far behind, but catching up as her limp went and her cat-zest for newness grew.

And so they marched across the great, strange rolling granite plain of Obelisk's top, patched here and there with limestone stretches white as marble. Its sun-drenched silence and uniformity became eerie after a bit. The shallowness of its hollows was deceptive: Fafhrd noted several in which battalions of armed men might have hidden a-crouch, unseen until one came within a spear's cast.

The longer they strode along, the more closely Fafhrd studied the rock his hobnails clashed. Finally he paused to point out a strangely rippled stretch.

'I'd swear that once was seabottom,' he said softly.

The Mouser's eyes narrowed. Thinking of the great invisible fishlike flier they had seen last evening, its raylike form undulating through the snowfall, he felt gooseflesh crawling on him.

Hrissa slunk past them, head a-weave.

Soon they passed the last boulder, a huge one, and saw, scarcely a bowshot ahead, the glitter of snow.

The Mouser said, 'The worst thing about mountain climbing is that the easy parts go so quickly.'

'Hist!' warned Fafhrd, sprawling down suddenly like a great four-legged water beetle and putting his cheek to the rock. 'Do you hear it, Mouser!'

Hrissa snarled, staring about, and her white fur bristled.

The Mouser started to stoop, but realized he wouldn't have to, so fast the sound was coming on: a general high-pitched drumming, as of five hundred fiends rippling their giant thick fingernails on a great stone drumhead.

Then, without pause, there came surging straight toward them over the nearest rock swelling to the southeast, a great wide-fronted stampede of goats, so packed together and their fur so glossy white that they seemed for a flash like an onrushing of living snow. Even the great curving horns of their leaders were ivory-hued. The Mouser noted that a stretch of the sunny air just above their center shimmered and wavered as it will above a fire. Then he and Fafhrd were racing back toward the last boulder with Hrissa bounding ahead.

Behind them the devil's tattoo of the stampede grew louder and louder.

They reached the boulder and vaulted atop it, where Hrissa already crouched, hardly a pounding heartbeat before the white horde. And well it was that Fafhrd had his ax out the instant they won there, for the midmost of the great billies sprang high, forelegs tucked up and head bowed to present his creamy horns – so close Fafhrd could see their splintered tips. But in that same instant Fafhrd got him in his snowy shoulder with a great swashing deep-cleaving blow so heavy that the beast was carried past them to the side and crashed on the short slope leading down to the rim of the west wall.

Then the white stampede was splitting around the great boulder, the animals so near and packed that there was no longer room for leaping, and the din of their hooves and the gasping and now the frightened bleating was horrendous, and the caprid stench was stifling, while the boulder rocked with their passage.

In the worst of the bruit there was a momentary down-rushing of air, briefly dispelling the stench, as something passed close above their heads, rippling the sky like a long flapping blanket of fluid glass, while through the clangor could be heard for a moment a harsh, hateful laughter.

The lesser tongue of the stampede passed between the boulder and the rim, and of these goats many went tumbling over the edge with bleats like screams of the damned, carrying with them the body of the great billy Fafhrd had maimed.

Then as sudden in its departure as a snow squall that dismasts a ship in the Frozen Sea, the stampede was past them and pounding south, swinging east somewhat from the deadly rim, with the last few of the goats, chiefly nannies and kids, bounding madly after.

Pointing his arm toward the sun as if for a sword-thrust,

the Mouser cried furiously, 'See there, where the beams twist all askew above the herd! It's the same flier as just now over-passed us and last night we saw in the snowfall – the flier who raised the stampede and whose riders guided it against us! Oh, damn the two deceitful ghostly bitches, luring us on to a goaty destruction stinking worse than a temple orgy in the City of Ghouls!'

'I thought this laughter was far deeper,' Fafhrd objected. 'It was not the girls.'

'So they have a deep-throated pimp – does that improve them in your eyes? Or your great flapping love-struck ears?' the Mouser demanded angrily.

The drumming of the stampede had died away even swifter than it had come and in the new-fallen silence they heard now a happy half-obstructed growling. Hrissa, springing off the boulder at stampede-end, had struck down a fat kid and was tearing at its bloodied white neck.

'Ah, I can smell it broiling now!' the Mouser cried with a great smile, his preoccupations altering in less than an instant. 'Good Hrissa! Fafhrd, if those be treelets and bushes and grass to the east – and they must be that, for what else feeds these goats? – there's sure to be dead wood – why, there may even be mint! – and we can . . .'

'You'll eat the flesh raw for lunch or not at all!' Fafhrd decreed fiercely. 'Are we to risk the stampede again? Or give the sniggering flier a chance to marshal against us some snow lions? – which are sure to be here too, to prey on the goats. And are we to present Kranarch and Gnarfi the summit of Stardock on a diamond-studded silver platter? – if this devil's lull holds tomorrow too and they be industrious strong climbers, not nice-bellied sluggards like one I could name!'

So, with only a gripe or two more from the Mouser, the kid was swiftly bled, gutted and skinned, and some of its spine-meat and haunches wrapped and packed for supper. Hrissa drank some more blood and ate half the liver and then followed the Mouser and Fafhrd as they set off north toward the snow ridge. The two men were chewing thin-sliced peppered collops of raw kid, but striding swiftly and keeping a wary eye behind for another stampede.

The Mouser expected now at last to get a view of the eastern depths, by peering east along the north wall of Obelisk Polaris, but here again he was foiled by the first great swell of the snow-saddle.

However, the northern view was fearsomely majestic. A full half league below them now and seen almost vertically on, the White Waterfall went showering down mysteriously, twinkling even in the shadow.

The ridge by which they must travel first curved up a score of yards, then dipped smoothly down to a long snow-saddle another score of yards below them, then slowly curved up into the South Tress, down which they could now plainly see avalanches trickling and tumbling.

It was easy to see how the northeast gale, blowing almost continually but missing the Ladder, would greatly pile up snow between the taller mountain and the Obelisk – but whether the rocky connection between the two mountains underlay the snow by only a few yards or by as much as a quarter league was impossible to know.

'We must rope again,' Fafhrd decreed. 'I'll go first and cut steps for us across the west slope.'

'What need we steps in this calm?' the Mouser demanded. 'Or to go by the west slope? You just don't want me to see the east, do you? The top of the ridge is broad enough to drive two carts across abreast.'

'The ridge-top in the wind's path almost certainly overhangs emptiness to the east and would break away,' Fafhrd explained. 'Look you, Mouser; do I know more about snow and ice or do you?'

'I once crossed the Bones of the Old Ones with you,' the Mouser retorted, shrugging. 'There was snow there, I recall.'

'Pooh, the mere spillings of a lady's powderbox compared to this. No, Mouser, on this stretch my word is law.'

'Very well,' the Mouser agreed.

So they roped up rather close – in order, Fafhrd, Mouser, and Hrissa – and without more ado Fafhrd donned his gloves and thonged his ax to his wrist and began cutting steps for them around the shoulders of the snow swell.

It was rather slow work, for under a dusting of powder

snow the stuff was hard and for each step Fafhrd must make at least two cuts – first an in-chopping back hand one to make the step, then a down-chop to clear it. And as the slope grew steeper, he must make the steps somewhat closer together. The steps he made were rather small, at least for his great boots, but they were sure.

Soon the ridge and the Obelisk cut off the sun. It grew very chill. The Mouser closed his tunic and drew his hood around his face, while Hrissa, between her short leaps from step to step, performed a kind of tiny cat-jig on them, to keep her gloved paws from freezing. The Mouser reminded himself to stuff them a bit with lamb's wool when he renewed the salve. He had his pike out now, telescoped short and thonged to his wrist.

They passed the shoulder of the swell and came opposite the beginning of the snow-saddle, but Fafhrd did not cut steps up toward it. Rather, the steps he now was cutting descended at a sharper angle than the saddle dipped, though the slope they were crossing was becoming quite steep.

'Fafhrd,' the Mouser protested quietly, 'we're heading for Stardock's top, not the White Waterfall.'

'You said, "Very well,"' Fafhrd retorted between chops. 'Besides, who does the work?' His ax rang as it bit into ice.

'Look, Fafhrd,' the Mouser said, 'there are two goats crossing to Stardock along the saddletop. No, three.'

'We should trust goats? Ask yourself why they've been sent.' Again Fafhrd's ax rang.

The sun swung into view as it coursed southward, sending their three shadows ranging far ahead of them. The pale gray of the snow turned glittery white. The Mouser unhooded to the yellow rays. For a while the enjoyment of their warmth on the back of his head helped him keep his mouth shut, but then the slope grew steeper yet, as Fafhrd continued remorselessly to cut steps downward.

'I seem to recall that our purpose was to *climb* Stardock, but my memory must be disordered,' the Mouser observed. 'Fafhrd, I'll take your word we must keep away from the top of the ridge, but do we have to keep away so *far*? And the three goats have all skipped across.'

Still, '"Very well," you said,' was all Fafhrd would answer, and this time there was a snarl in his voice.

The Mouser shrugged. Now he was bracing himself with his pike continuously, while Hrissa would pause studyingly before each leap.

Their shadows went less than a spear's cast ahead of them now, while the hot sun had begun to melt the surface snow, sending down trickles of ice water to wet their gloves and make their footing unsure.

Yet still Fafhrd kept cutting steps downward. And now of a sudden he began to cut them downward more steeply still, adding with taps of his ax a tiny handhold above each step – and these handholds were needed!

'Fafhrd,' the Mouser said dreamily, 'perhaps an ice-sprite has whispered to you the secret of levitation, so that from this fine takeoff you can dive, level out, and then go spiring to Stardock's top. In that case I wish you'd teach myself and Hrissa how to grow wings in an instant.'

'Hist!' Fafhrd spoke softly yet sharply at that instant. 'I have a feeling. Something comes. Brace yourself and watch behind us.'

The Mouser drove his pike in deep and rotated his head. As he did, Hrissa leaped from the last step behind to the one on which the Mouser stood, landing half on his boot and clinging to his knee – yet this done so dexterously the Mouser was not dislodged.

'I see nothing,' the Mouser reported, staring almost sunward. Then, words suddenly clipped: 'Again the beams twist like a spinning lantern! The glints on the icy ripple and wave. 'Tis the flier come again! Cling!'

There came the rushing sound, louder than ever before and swiftly mounting, then a great sea-wave of air, as of a great body passing swiftly only spans away; it whipped their clothes and Hrissa's fur and forced them to cling fiercely to their holds, though Fafhrd made a full-armed swipe with his ax. Hrissa snarled. Fafhrd almost louted forward off his holds with the momentum of his blow.

'I'll swear I scored on him, Mouser,' he snarled, recovering. 'My ax touched something besides air.'

'You harebrained fool!' the Mouser cried. 'Your scratches will anger him and bring him back.' He let go of the chopped ice-hold with his hand and, steadying himself by his pike, he searched the sun-bright air ahead and around for ripples.

'More like I've scared him off,' Fafhrd asserted, doing the same. The rushy sound faded and did not return; the air became quiet, and the steep slope grew very still; even the water-drip faded.

Turning back to the wall with a grunt of relief, the Mouser touched emptiness. He grew still as death himself. Turning his eyes only he saw that upward from a point level with his knees the whole snow ridge had vanished – the whole saddle and a section of the swell to either side of it – as if some great god had reached down while the Mouser's back was turned and removed that block of reality.

Giddily he clung to his pike. He was standing atop a newly created snow-saddle now. Beyond and below its raw, fresh-fractured white eastern slope, the silently departed great snow-cornice was falling faster and faster, still in one hill-size chunk.

Behind them the steps Fafhrd had cut mounted to the new snow rim, then vanished.

'See, I chopped us down far enough only in the nick,' Fafhrd grumbled. 'My judgment was faulty.'

The falling cornice was snatched downward out of sight, so that the Mouser and Fafhrd at last could see what lay east of the Mountains of the Giants: a rolling expanse of dark green that might be treetops except that from here even giant trees would be tinier than glass blades – an expanse even farther below them than the Cold Waste at their backs. Beyond the green-carpeted depression, another mountain range loomed like the ghost of one.

'I have heard legends of the Great Rift Valley,' Fafhrd murmured. 'A mountainsided cup for sunlight, its warm floor a league below the Waste.'

Their eyes searched.

'Look,' the Mouser said, 'how trees climb the eastern face of Obelisk almost to his top. Now the goats don't seem so strange.'

They could see nothing, however, of the east face of Stardock.

'Come on!' Fafhrd commanded. 'If we linger, the invisible growl-laughter flier may gather courage to return despite my ax-nick.'

And without further word he began resolutely to cut steps onward . . . and still a little down.

Hrissa continued to peer over the rim, her bearded chin almost resting on it, her nostrils a-twitch as if she faintly scented gossamer threads of meat-odor mounting from the leagues' distant dark green, but when the rope tightened on her harness, she followed.

Perils came thick now. They reached the dark rock of the Ladder only by chopping their way along a nearly vertical ice wall in the twinkly gloom under a close-arching waterfall of snow that shot out from an icy boss above them – perhaps a miniature version of the White Waterfall that was Stardock's skirt.

When they stepped at last, numb with cold and hardly daring to believe they'd made it, onto a wide dark ledge, they saw a jumble of bloody goat tracks in the snow around.

Without more warning than that, a long snowbank between that step and the next above reared up its nearest white end a dozen feet and hissed fearsomely, showing it to be a huge serpent with head as big as an elk's, all covered with shaggy snow-white fur. Its great violet eyes glared like those of a mad horse and its jaws gaped to show slashing-teeth like a shark's and two great fangs jutting a mist of pale ichor.

The furred serpent hesitated for two sways between the nearer, taller man with flashing ax and the farther, smaller one with thick black stick. In that pause Hrissa, with snarling hisses of her own, sprang forward past the Mouser on the downslope side and the furred serpent struck at this newest and most active foe.

Fafhrd got a blast of its hot acrid breath, and the vapor trail from its nearer fang bathed his left elbow.

The Mouser's attention was fixed on a fur-wisped violet eye as big as a girl's fist.

Hrissa looked down the monster's gaping dark red gullet

rimmed by slaver-swimming ivory knives and the two ichor-jetting fangs.

Then the jaws clashed shut, but in the intervening instant Hrissa had leaped back more swiftly even than she'd advanced.

The Mouser plunged the pike-end of his climbing pole into the glaring violet eye.

Swinging his ax two-handed, Fafhrd slashed at the furry neck just back of the horse-like skull, and there gushed out red blood which steamed as it struck the snow.

Then the three climbers were scrambling upward, while the monster writhed in convulsions which shook the rock and spattered with red alike the snow and its snow-white fur.

At what they hoped was a safe distance above it, the climbers watched it dying, though not without frequent glances about for creatures like it or other perilous beasts.

Fafhrd said, 'A hot-blooded serpent, a snake with fur – it goes against experience. My father never spoke of such; I doubt he ever met 'em.'

The Mouser answered, 'I'll wager they find their prey on the east slope of Stardock and come here only to lair or breed. Perhaps the invisible flier drove the three goats over the snow-saddle to lure this one.' His voice grew dreamy. 'Or perhaps there's a secret world inside Stardock.'

Fafhrd shook his head, as if to clear it of such imagination-snaring visions. 'Our way lies upward,' he said. 'We'd best be well above the Lairs before nightfall. Give me a dollop of honey when I drink,' he added, loosening his water bag as he turned and scanned up the Ladder.

From its base the Ladder was a dark narrow triangle climbing to the blue sky between the snowy, ever-tumbling Tresses. First there were the ledges on which they stood, easy at first, but swiftly growing steeper and narrower. Next an almost blank stretch, etched here and there with shadows and ripplings hinting at part-way climbing routes, but none of them connected. Then another band of ledges, the Roosts. Then a stretch still blanker than the first. Finally another ledge-band, narrower and shorter – the Face – and atop all what seemed a tiny pen-stroke of white ink: the brim of Stardock's pennonless snowy hat.

All the Mouser's aches and weariness came back as he squinted up the Ladder while feeling in his pouch for the honey jar. Never, he was sure, had he seen so much distance compressed into so little space by vertical foreshortening. It was as if the gods had built a ladder to reach the sky, and after using it had kicked most of the steps away. But he clenched his teeth and prepared to follow Fafhrd.

All their previous climbing began to seem book-simple compared to what they now struggled through, step by straining step, all the long summer afternoon. Where Obelisk Polaris had been a stern schoolmaster, Stardock was a mad queen, tireless in preparing her shocks and surprises, unpredictable in her wild caprices.

The ledges of the Lairs were built of rock that sometimes broke away at a touch, and they were piled with loose gravel. Also, the climbers made acquaintance with Stardock's rocky avalanches, which brought stones whizzing and spattering down around them without warning, so that they had to press close to the walls and Fafhrd regretted leaving his helmet in the cairn. Hrissa first snarled at each pelting pebble which hit near her, but when at last struck in the side by a small one, showed fear and slunk close to the Mouser, trying until rebuked to push between the wall and his legs.

And once they saw a cousin of the white worm they had slain rear up man-high and glare at them from a distant ledge, but it did not attack.

They had to work their way to the northernmost point of the topmost ledge before they found, at the very edge of the Northern Tress, almost underlying its streaming snow, a scree-choked gulley which narrowed upward to a wide vertical groove – or chimney, as Fafhrd called it.

And when the treacherous scree was at last surmounted, the Mouser discovered that the next stretch of the ascent was indeed very like climbing up the inside of a rectangular chimney of varying width and with one of the four walls missing – that facing outward to the air. Its rock was sounder than that of the Lairs, but that was all that could be said for it.

Here all tricks of climbing were required and the utmost of

main strength into the bargain. Sometimes they hoisted themselves by cracks wide enough for finger- and toeholds; if a crack they needed was too narrow, Fafhrd would tap into it one of his spikes to make a hold, and this spike must, if possible, be unwedged after use and recovered. Sometimes the chimney narrowed so that they could walk up it laboriously with shoulders to one wall and boot soles to the other. Twice it widened and became so smooth-walled that the Mouser's extensible climbing-pike had to be braced between wall and wall to give them a necessary step.

And five times the chimney was blocked by a huge rock or chockstone which in falling had wedged itself fast, and these fearsome obstructions had to be climbed around on the outside, generally with the aid of one of more of Fafhrd's spikes driven between chockstone and wall, or his grapnel tossed over it.

'Stardock has wept millstones in her day,' the Mouser said of these gigantic barriers, jerking his body aside from a whizzing rock for a period to his sentence.

This climbing was generally beyond Hrissa and she often had to be carried on the Mouser's back, or left on a chockstone or one of the rare paw-wide ledges and hoisted up when opportunity offered. They were strongly tempted, especially after they grew death-weary, to abandon her, but could not forget how her brave feint had saved them from the white worm's first stroke.

All this, particularly the passing of the chockstones, must be done under the pelting of Stardock's rocky avalanches – so that each new chockstone above them was welcomed as a roof, until it had to be surmounted. Also, snow sometimes gushed into the chimney, overspilling from one of the snowy avalanches forever whispering down the North Tress – one more danger to guard against. Ice water runneled too from time to time down the chimney, drenching boots and gloves and making all holds unsure.

In addition, there was less nourishment in the air, so that they had more often to halt and gasp deeply until their lungs were satisfied. And Fafhrd's left arm began to swell where the venomous mist from the worm's fang had blown around it, until he could hardly bend its swollen fingers to grip crack or rope. Besides, it itched and stung. He plunged it again and again into snow to no avail.

Their only allies on this most punishing ascent were the hot sun, heartening them by its glow and offsetting the growing frigidity of the thin still air, and the very difficulty and variety of the climb itself, which at least kept their minds off the emptiness around and beneath them – the latter a farther drop than they'd ever stood over on the Obelisk. The Cold Waste seemed like another world, poised separate from Stardock in space.

Once they forced themselves to eat a bite and several times sipped water. And once the Mouser was seized with mountain sickness, ending only when he had retched himself weary.

The only incident of the climb unrelated to Stardock's mad self occurred when they were climbing out around the fifth chockstone, slowly, like two large slugs, the Mouser first this time and bearing Hrissa, with Fafhrd close behind. At this point the North Tress narrowed so that a hump of the North Wall was visible across the snow stream.

There was a whirring unlike that of any rock. Another whirring then, closer and ending in a *thunk*. When Fafhrd scrambled atop the chockstone and into the shelter of the walls, he had a cruelly barbed arrow through his pack.

At cost of a third arrow whirring close by his head, the Mouser peeped out north with Fafhrd clinging to his heels and swiftly dragging him back.

''Twas Kranarch all right; I saw him twang his bow,' the Mouser reported. 'No sight of Gnarfi, but one of their new comrades clad in brown fur crouched behind Kranarch, braced on the same boss. I couldn't see his face, but 'tis a most burly fellow, short of leg.'

'They keep apace of us,' Fafhrd grunted.

'Also, they scruple not to mix climbing with killing,' the Mouser observed as he broke off the tail of the arrow piercing Fafhrd's pack and yanked out the shaft. 'Oh, comrade, I fear your sleeping cloak is sixteen times holed. And that little bladder of pine liniment – it got holed too. Ah, what fragrance!'

'I'm beginning to think those two men of Illik-Ving aren't sportsmen,' Fafhrd asserted. 'So . . . up and on!'

They were all dog-weary, even cat-Hrissa, and the sun was barely ten fingerbreadths (at the end of an outstretched arm) above the flat horizon of the Waste; and something in the air had turned Sol white as silver – he no longer sent warmth to combat the cold. But the ledges of the Roosts were close above now, and it was possible to hope they would offer a better camp site than the chimney.

So although every man and cat muscle protested against it, they obeyed Fafhrd's command.

Halfway to the Roosts it began to snow, powdery grains falling arrow-straight like last night, but thicker.

This silent snowfall gave a sense of serenity and security which was most false, since it masked the rockfalls which still came firing down the chimney like the artillery of the God of Chance.

Five yards from the top a fist-size chunk struck Fafhrd glancingly on the right shoulder, so that his good arm went numb and hung useless, but the little climbing that remained was so easy he could make it with boots and puffed-up, barely-usable left hand.

He peeped cautiously out of the chimney's top, but the Tress here had thickened up again, so that there was no sight of the North Wall. Also the first ledge was blessedly wide and so overhung with rock that not even snow had fallen on its inner half, let alone stones. He scrambled up eagerly, followed by the Mouser and Hrissa.

But even as they cast themselves down to rest at the back of the ledge, the Mouser wriggling out of his heavy pack and unthonging his climbing-pike from his wrist – for even *that* had become a torturesome burden – they heard a now-familiar rushing in the air and there came a great flat shape swooping slowly through the sun-silvered snow which outlined it. Straight at the ledge it came and this time it did not go past, but halted and hung there, like a giant devil fish nuzzling the sea's rim, while ten narrow marks, each of suckers in line, appeared in the snow on the ledge's edge, as of ten short tentacles gripping there.

From the center of this monstrous invisibility rose a smaller snow-outlined invisibility of the height and thickness of a man.

Midway up this shape was one visible thing: a slim sword of dark gray blade and silvery hilt, pointed straight at the Mouser's breast.

Suddenly the sword shot forward, almost as fast as if hurled, but not quite, and after it, as swiftly, the man-size pillar, which now laughed harshly from its top.

The Mouser snatched up one-handed his unthonged climbing pike and thrust at the snow-sketched figure behind the sword.

The gray sword snaked around the pike and with a sudden sharp twist swept it from the Mouser's fatigue-slack fingers.

The black tool, on which Glinthi the Artificer had expended all the evenings of the Month of the Weasel three years past, vanished into the silvery snowfall and space.

Hrissa backed against the wall frothing and snarling, a-tremble in every limb.

Fafhrd fumbled frantically for his ax, but his swollen fingers could not even unsnap the sheath binding its head to his belt.

The Mouser, enraged at the loss of his precious pike to the point where he cared not a whit whether his foe was invisible or not, drew Scalpel from its sheath and fiercely parried the gray sword as it came streaking in again.

A dozen parries he had to make and was pinked twice in the arm and pressed back against the wall almost like Hrissa, before he could take the measure of his foe, now out of the snowfall and wholly invisible, and go himself on the attack.

Then, glaring at a point a foot above the gray sword – a point where he judged his foe's eyes to be (if his foe carried his eyes in his head) – he went stamping forward, beating at the gray blade, slipping Scalpel around it with the tiniest disengages, seeking to bind it with his own sword, and ever thrusting impetuously at invisible arm and trunk.

Three times he felt his blade strike flesh and once it bent briefly against invisible bone.

His foe leaped back onto the invisible flier, making narrow footprints in the slush gathered there. The flier rocked.

In his fighting rage the Mouser almost followed his foe onto that invisible, living, pulsating platform, yet prudently stopped at the brink.

And well it was he did so, for the flier dropped away like a skate in flight from a shark, shaking its slush into the snowfall. There came a last burst of laughter more like a wail, fading off and down in the silvery murk.

The Mouser began to laugh himself, a shade hysterically, and retreated to the wall. There he wiped off his blade and felt the stickiness of invisible blood, and laughed a wild high laugh again.

Hrissa's fur was still on end – and was a long time flattening.

Fafhrd quit trying to fumble out his ax and said seriously. 'The girls couldn't have been with him – we'd have seen their forms or footprints on the slush-backed flier. I think he's jealous of us and works against 'em.'

The Mouser laughed – only foolishly now – for a third time.

The murk turned dark gray. They set about firing the brazier and making ready for night. Despite their hurts and supreme weariness, the shock and fright of the last encounter had excited new energy from them and raised their spirits and given them appetites. They feasted well on thin collops of kid frizzled in the resin-flames or cooked pale gray in water that, strangely, could be sipped without hurt almost while it boiled.

'Must be nearing the realm of the Gods,' Fafhrd muttered. 'It's said they joyously drink boiling wine – and walk hurtlessly through flames.'

'Fire is just as hot here, though,' the Mouser said dully. 'Yet the air seems to have less nourishment. On what do you suppose the Gods subsist?'

'They are ethereal and require neither air nor food,' Fafhrd suggested after a long frown of thinking.

'Yet you just now said they drink wine.'

'Everybody drinks wine,' Fafhrd asserted with a yawn, killing the discussion and also the Mouser's dim, unspoken speculation as to whether the feebler air, pressing less strongly on heating liquid, let its bubbles escape more easily.

Power of movement began to return to Fafhrd's right arm and his left was swelling no more. The Mouser salved and bandaged his own small wounds, then remembered to salve

Hrissa's pads and tuck into her boots a little pine-scented eider-down tweaked from the arrow-holes in Fafhrd's cloak.

When they were half laced up in their cloaks, Hrissa snuggled between them – and a few more precious resin-pellets dropped in the brazier as a bedtime luxury – Fafhrd got out a tiny jar of strong wine of Ilthmar, and they each took a sup of it, imagining those sunny vineyards and that hot, rich soil so far south.

A momentary flare from the brazier showed them the snow falling yet. A few rocks crashed nearby and a snowy avalanche hissed, then Stardock grew still in the frigid grip of night. The climbers' eyrie seemed most strange to them, set above every other peak in the Mountains of the Giants – and likely all Nehwon – yet walled with darkness like a tiny room.

The Mouser said softly, 'Now we know what roosts in the Roosts. Do you suppose there are dozens of those invisible mantas carpeting around us on ledges like this, or a-hung from them? Why don't they freeze? Or does someone stable them? And the invisible folk, what of them? No more can you call 'em mirage – you saw the sword, and I fought the man-thing at the other end of it. Yet invisible! How's that possible?'

Fafhrd shrugged and then winced because it hurt both shoulders cruelly. 'Made of some stuff like water or glass,' he hazarded. 'Yet pliant and twisting the light less – and with no surface shimmer. You've seen sand and ashes made transparent by firing. Perhaps there's some heatless way of firing monsters and men until they are invisible.'

'But how light enough to fly?' the Mouser asked.

'Thin beasts to match thin air,' Fafhrd guessed sleepily.

The Mouser said, 'And then those deadly worms – and the Fiend knows what perils above.' He paused. 'And yet we must still climb Stardock to the top, mustn't we? Why?'

Fafhrd nodded. 'To beat out Kranarch and Gnarfi . . .' he muttered. 'To beat out my father . . . the mystery of it . . . the girls . . . O Mouser, could you stop here any more than you could stop after touching half of a woman?'

'You don't mention diamonds any more,' the Mouser noted. 'Don't you think we'll find them?'

Fafhrd started another shrug and mumbled a curse that turned into a yawn.

The Mouser dug in his pouch to the bottom pocket and brought out the parchment and blowing on the brazier read it all by the resin's last flaming:

> Who mounts white Stardock, the Moon Tree,
> Past worm and gnome and unseen bars,
> Will win the key to luxury:
> The Heart of Light, a pouch of stars.
> The gods who once ruled all the world
> Have made that peak their citadel,
> From whence the stars were one time hurled
> And paths lead on to Heav'n and Hell.
> Comes, heroes, past the Trollstep rocks.
> Come, best of men, across the Waste.
> For you, glory each door unlocks.
> Delay not, up, and come in haste.
> Who scales the Snow King's citadel
> Shall father his two daughters' sons;
> Though he must face foes fierce and fell,
> His seed shall live while time still runs.

The resin burnt out. The Mouser said, 'Well, we've met a worm and one unseen fellow who sought to bar our way – and two sightless witches who might be Snow King's daughters for all I know. Gnomes now – they would be a change, wouldn't they? You said something about Ice Gnomes, Fafhrd. What was it?'

He waited with an unnatural anxiety for Fafhrd's answer. After a bit he began to hear it: soft regular snores.

The Mouser snarled soundlessly, his demon of restlessness now became a fury despite all his aches. He shouldn't have thought of girls – or rather of one girl who was nothing but a taunting mask with pouting lips and eyes of black mystery seen across a fire.

Suddenly he felt stifled. He quickly unhooked his cloak and despite Hrissa's questioning mew felt his way south along the ledge. Soon snow, sifting like ice needles on his flushed face, told him he was beyond the overhang. Then the snow stopped. Another overhang, he thought – but he had not moved. He strained his eyes upward, and there was the black expanse of Stardock's topmost quarter silhouetted against a band of sky pale with the hidden moon and specked by a few faint stars. Behind him to the west, the snowstorm still obscured the sky.

He blinked his eyes and then he swore softly, for now the black cliff they must climb tomorrow was a-glow with soft scattered lights of violet and rose and palest green and amber. The nearest, which were still far above, looked tinily rectangular, like gleam-spilling windows seen from below.

It was as if Stardock were a great hostelry.

Then freezing flakes pinked his face again, and the band of sky narrowed to nothing. The snowfall had moved back against Stardock once more, hiding all stars and other lights.

The Mouser's fury drained from him. Suddenly he felt very small and foolhardy and very, very cold. The mysterious vision of the lights remained in his mind, but muted, as if part of a dream. Most cautiously he crept back the way he had come, feeling the radiant warmth of Fafhrd and Hrissa and the burnt-out brazier just before he touched his cloak. He laced it around him and lay for a long time doubled up like a baby, his mind empty of everything except frigid blackness. At last he slumbered.

Next day started gloomy. The two men chafed and wrestled each other as they lay, to get the stiffness a little out of them and enough warmth in them to rise. Hrissa withdrew from between them limping and sullen.

At any rate, Fafhrd's arms were recovered from their swelling and numbing, while the Mouser was hardly aware of his own arm's little wounds.

They breakfasted on herb tea and honey and began climbing the Roosts in a light snowfall. This last pest stayed with them all morning except when gusty breezes blew it back from Stardock. On these occasions they could see the great smooth cliff separating the Roosts from the ultimate ledges of the Face. By the glimpses they got, the cliff looked to be without any climbing routes whatever, or any marks at all – so that Fafhrd laughed at the Mouser for a dreamer with his tale of windows spilling colored light – but finally as they neared the cliff's base they began to distinguish what seemed to be a narrow crack – a hairline to vision – mounting its center.

They met none of the invisible flat fliers, either a-wing or a-perch, though whenever gusts blew strange gaps into the snowfall, the two adventurers would firm themselves on their perches and grip for their weapons, and Hrissa would snarl.

The wind slowed them little though chilling them much, for the rock of the Roosts was true.

And they still had to watch out for stony peltings, though these were fewer than yesterday, perhaps because so much of Stardock now lay below them.

They reached the base of the great cliff at the point where the crack began, which was a good thing, since the snowfall had grown so heavy that a hunt for it would have been difficult.

To their joy, the crack proved to be another chimney, scarcely a yard across and not much more deep, and as knobbly inside with footholds as the cliff outside was smooth. Unlike yesterday's chimney, it appeared to extend upward indefinitely without change of width and as far as they could see there were no chockstones. In many ways it was like a rock ladder half sheltered from the snow. Even Hrissa could climb here, as on Obelisk Polaris.

They lunched on food warmed against their skins. They were afire with eagerness, yet forced themselves to take time to chew and sip. As they entered the chimney, Fafhrd going first, there came three faint growling booms – thunder perhaps and certainly ominous, yet the Mouser laughed.

With never-failing footholds and opposite wall for back-brace, the climbing was easy, except for the drain on main strength, which required rather frequent halts to gulp down fresh stores of the thin air. Only twice did the chimney narrow so that Fafhrd had to climb for a short stretch with his body outside it; the Mouser, slighter framed, could stay inside.

It was an intoxicating experience, almost. Even as the day grew darker from the thickening snowfall and as the crackling booms returned sharper and stronger – thunder now for sure, since they were heralded by brief palings up and down the chimney – snow-muted lightning flashes – the Mouser and Fafhrd felt as merry as children mounting a mysterious twisty stairway in a haunted castle. They even wasted a little breath in joking calls which went echoing faintly up and down the rugged shaft as it paled and gloomed with the lightning.

But then the shaft grew by degrees almost as smooth as the outer cliff and at the same time it began gradually to widen, first a handbreadth, then another, then a finger more, so that they had to mount more perilously, bracing shoulders against one wall and boots against the other and so 'walking' up with pushes and heaves. The Mouser drew up Hrissa and the ice-cat crouched on his pitching, rocking chest – no inconsiderable burden. Yet both men still felt quite jolly – so that the Mouser began to wonder if there might not be some actual intoxicant in air near Heaven.

Being a head or two taller than the Mouser, Fafhrd was better equipped for this sort of climbing and was still able to go on at that moment when the Mouser realized that his body was stretched almost straight between shoulders and boot soles – with Hrissa a-crouch on him like a traveler on a little bridge. He could mount no farther – and was hazy about how he had managed to come this far.

Fafhrd came down like a great spider at the Mouser's call and seemed not much impressed by the latter's plight – in fact, a lightning flash showed his great bearded face all a-grin.

'Abide you here a bit,' he said. ' 'Tis not so far to the top. I think I glimpsed it the last flash but one. I'll mount and draw you up, putting all the rope between you and me. There's a crack by your head – I'll knock in a spike for safety's sake. Meanwhile, rest.'

Whereupon Fafhrd did all of these things so swiftly and was on his upward way again so soon that the Mouser forebore to utter any of the sardonic remarks churning inside his rigid belly.

Successive lightning flashes showed the Northerner's long-limbed form growing smaller at a gratifyingly rapid rate until he looked hardly bigger than a trap spider at the end of his tube. Another flash and he was gone, but whether because he had reached the top or passed a bend in the chimney the Mouser couldn't be sure.

The rope kept paying upward, however, until there was only a small loop below the Mouser. He was aching abominably now and was also very cold, but gritted his teeth against the pain. Hrissa chose this moment to prowl up and down her small human bridge, restlessly. There was a blinding lightning flash and a crash of thunder that shook Stardock. Hrissa cringed.

The rope grew taut, tugging at the belt of the Mouser, who started to put his weight on it, holding Hrissa to his chest, but then decided to wait for Fafhrd's call. This was a good decision on his part, for just then the rope went slack and began to fall on the Mouser's belly like a stream of black water. Hrissa crouched away from it on his face. It came pelting endlessly, but finally its upper end hit the Mouser under the breastbone with a snap. The only good thing was that Fafhrd didn't come hurtling down with it. Another blinding mountain-shaking crash showed the upper chimney utterly empty.

'Fafhrd!' the Mouser called. '*Fafhrd!*' There came back only the echo.

The Mouser thought for a bit, then reached up and felt by his ear for the spike Fafhrd had struck in with a single offhand slap of his ax-hammer. Whatever had happened to Fafhrd, nothing seemed to remain to do but tie rope to spike and descend by it to where the chimney was easier.

The spike came out at the first touch and went clattering shrilly down the chimney until a new thunderblast drowned the small sound.

The Mouser decided to 'walk' down the chimney. After all, he'd come up that way the last few score of yards.

The first attempt to move a leg told him his muscles were knotted by cramp. He'd never be able to bend his leg and straighten it again without losing his purchase and falling.

The Mouser thought of Glinthi's pike, lost in white space, and he slew that thought.

Hrissa crouched on his chest and gazed down into his face with an expression the next levin-glare showed to be sad yet critical, as if to ask, 'Where is this vaunted human ingenuity?'

Fafhrd had barely eased himself out of the chimney onto the wide, deep rock-roofed ledge at its top, when a door two yards high, a yard wide, and two spans thick had silently opened in the rock at the back of the ledge.

The contrast was most remarkable between the roughness of that rock and the ruler-flat smoothness of the dark stone forming the thick sides of the door and the lintel, jambs, and threshold of the doorway.

Soft pink light spilled out and with it a perfume whose heavy fumes were cargoed with dreams of pleasure barges afloat in a rippling sunset sea.

Those musky narcotic fumes, along with the alcoholic headiness of the thin air, almost made Fafhrd forget his purpose, but touching the black rope was like touching Hrissa and the Mouser at its other end. He unknotted it from his belt and prepared to secure it around a stout rock pillar beside the open door. To get enough rope to make a good knot he had to draw it up quite tight.

But the dream-freighted fumes grew thicker, and he no longer felt the Mouser and Hrissa in the rope. Indeed, he began to forget his two comrades altogether.

And then a silvery voice – a voice he knew well from having heard it laugh once and once chuckle – called, 'Come in, barbarian. Come in to me.'

The end of the black rope slipped from his fingers unnoticed and hissed softly across the rock and down the chimney.

Stooping a little, he went through the doorway which silently closed behind him just in time to shut out the Mouser's desperate call.

He was in a room lit by pink globes hanging at the level of his head. Their soft warm radiance colored the hangings and rugs of the room, but especially the pale spread of the great bed that was its only furniture.

Beside the bed stood a slim woman whose black silk robe concealed all of her except her face, yet did not disguise her body's sleek curves. A black lace mask hid the rest of her.

She looked at Fafhrd for seven thudding heartbeats, then sat down on the bed. A slender arm and hand clothed all in black lace came from under her robe and patted the spread beside her and rested there. Her mask never wavered from Fafhrd's face.

He shouldered out of his pack and unbuckled his ax belt.

The Mouser finished pounding all the thin blade of his dagger into the crack by his ear, using the firestone from his pouch for hammer, so that sparks showered from every cramped stroke of stone against pommel – small lightning flashes to match the greater flares still chasing up and down the chimney, while their thunder crashed an obbligato to the Mouser's taps. Hrissa crouched on his ankles, and from time to time the Mouser glared at her, as if to say, 'Well, cat?'

A gust of snow-freighted wind roaring up the chimney momentarily lifted the lean shaggy beast a span above him and almost blew the Mouser loose, but he tightened his pushing muscles still more and the bridge, arching upward a trifle, held firm.

He had just finished knotting an end of the black rope around the dagger's crossguard and grip – and his fingers and forearms were almost useless with fatigue – when a window two feet high and five wide silently opened in the back of the chimney, its thick rock shutter sliding aside, not a span away from the Mouser's inward shoulder.

A red glow sprang from the window and somewhat illumined four faces with piggy black eyes and with low hairless domes above.

The Mouser considered them. They were all four of extreme ugliness, he decided dispassionately. Only their wide white teeth, showing between their grinning lips which almost joined ear to swinish ear, had any claim to beauty.

Hrissa sprang at once through the red window and disappeared. The two faces between which she jumped did not flicker a black button-eye.

Then eight short brawny arms came out and easily pried the Mouser out and lifted him inside. He screamed faintly from a sudden increase in the agony of his cramps. He was aware of thick dwarfish bodies clad in hairy black jerkins and breeks – and one in a black hairy skirt – but all with thick-nailed splay-feet bare. Then he fainted.

When he came to, it was because he was being punishingly massaged on a hard table, his body naked and slick with warm oil. He was in a low, ill-lit chamber and still closely surrounded by the four dwarves, as he could tell from the eight horny hands squeezing and thumping his muscles before he ever opened his eyes.

The dwarf kneading his right shoulder and banging the top of his spine crinkled his warty eyelids and bared his beautiful white teeth bigger than a giant's in what might be intended for a friendly grin. Then he said in an atrocious Mingol patois, 'I am Bonecracker. This is my wife Gibberfat. Cosseting your body on the larboard side are my brothers Legcruncher and Breakskull. Now drink this wine and follow me.'

The wine stung, yet dispelled the Mouser's dizziness, and it was certainly a blessing to be free of the murderous massage – and also apparently of the cramp-lumps in his muscles.

Bonecracker and Gibberfat helped him off the slab while Legcruncher and Breakskull rubbed him quickly down with rough towels. The warm low-ceiling room rocked dizzily for a moment; then he felt wondrous fine.

Bonecracker waddled off into the dimness beyond the smoky torches. With never a question the Mouser followed the dwarf. Or were these Fafhrd's Ice Gnomes? he wondered.

Bonecracker pulled aside heavy drapes in the dark. Amber light fanned out. The Mouser stepped from rock-roughness onto down-softness. The drapes swished to behind him.

He was alone in a chamber mellowly lit by hanging globes like great topazes – yet he guessed they would bounce aside like puffballs if touched. There was a large wide couch and beyond it a low table against the arras-hung wall with an ivory stool set before it. Above the table was a great silver mirror, while on it were fantastic small bottles and many tiny ivory jars.

No, the room was not altogether empty. Hrissa, sleekly groomed, lay curled in a far corner. She was not watching the Mouser, however, but a point above the stool.

The Mouser felt a shiver creeping on him, yet not altogether one of fear.

A dab of palest green leaped from one of the jars to the point Hrissa was watching and vanished there. But then he saw a streak of reflected green appear in the mirror. The riddlesome maneuver was repeated, and soon in the mirror's silver there hung a green mask, somewhat clouded by the silver's dullness.

Then the mask vanished from the mirror and simultaneously reappeared unblurred hanging in the air above the ivory stool. It was the mask the mouser knew achingly well – narrow chin, high-arched cheeks, straight nose and forehead.

The pouty wine-dark lips opened a little and a soft throaty voice asked, 'Does my visage displease you, man of Lankhmar?'

'You jest cruelly, O Princess,' the Mouser replied, drawing on all his aplomb and sketching a courtier's bow, 'for you are Beauty's self.'

Slim fingers, half outlined now in pale green, dipped into the unguent jar and took up a more generous dab.

The soft throaty voice that so well matched half the laughter he had once heard in a snowfall, now said, 'You shall judge all of me.'

Fafhrd woke in the dark and touched the girl beside him. As soon as he knew she was awake too, he grasped her by the hips. When he felt her body stiffen, he lifted her into the air and held her above him as he lay flat on his back.

She was wondrous light, as if made of pastry or eiderdown, yet when he laid her beside him again, her flesh felt as firm as any, though smoother than most.

'Let us have a light, Hirriwi, I beg you,' he said.

'That were unwise, Faffy,' she answered in a voice like a curtain of tiny silver bells lightly brushed. 'Have you forgotten that now I am wholly invisible? – which might tickle some men, yet you, I think . . .'

'You're right, you're right, I like you real,' he answered, gripping her fiercely by the shoulders to emphasize his feelings, then guiltily jerking away his hands as he thought of how delicate she must be.

The silver bells clashed in full laughter, as if the curtain of them had been struck a great swipe. 'Have no fears,' she told him. 'My airy bones are grown of matter stronger than steel. It is a riddle beyond your philosophers and relates to the invisibility of my race and of the animals from which it sprang. Think how strong tempered glass can be, yet light goes through it. My cursed brother Faroomfar has the strength of a bear for all his slimness while my father Oomforafor is a very lion despite his centuries. Your friend's encounter with Faroomfar was no final test – but oh how it made him howl – Father raged at him – and then there are the cousins. Soon as this night be ended – which is not soon, my dear; the moon still climbs – you must return down Stardock. Promise me that. My heart grows cold at the thought of the dangers you've already faced – and was like ice I know not how many times this last three-day.'

'Yet you never warned us,' he mused. 'You lured me on.'

'Can you doubt why?' she asked. He was feeling her snub nose then and her apple cheeks, and so he felt her smile too. 'Or perhaps you resent it that I let you risk your life a little to win here to this bed?'

He implanted a fervent kiss on her wide lips to show her how little true that was, but she thrust him back after a moment.

'Wait, Faffy dear,' she said. 'No, wait, I say! I know you're greedy and impetuous, but you can at least wait while the moon creeps the width of a star. I asked you to promise me you would descend Stardock at dawn.'

There was a rather long silence in the dark.

'Well?' she prompted. 'What shuts your mouth?' she queried impatiently. 'You've shown no such indecision in certain other matters. Time wastes, the moon sails.'

'Hirriwi,' Fafhrd said softly, 'I must climb Stardock.'

'Why?' she demanded ringingly. 'The poem has been fulfilled. You have your reward. Go on, and only frigid fruitless perils await you. Return, and I'll guard you from the air – yes, and your companion too – to the very Waste.' Her sweet voice faltered a little. 'O Faffy, am I not enough to make you forego the conquest of a cruel mountain? In addition to all else, I love you – if I understand rightly how mortals use that word.'

'No,' he answered her solemnly in the dark. 'You are wondrous, more wondrous than any wench I've known – and I love you, which is not a word I bandy – yet you only make me hotter to conquer Stardock. Can you understand that?'

Now there was silence for a while in the other direction.

'Well,' she said at length, 'you are masterful and will do what you will do. And I have warned you. I could tell you more, show you reasons counter, argue further, but in the end I know I would not break your stubborness – and time gallops. We must mount our own steeds and catch up with the moon. Kiss me again. Slowly. So.'

The Mouser lay across the foot of the bed under the amber globes and contemplated Keyaira, who lay lengthwise with her slender apple green shoulders and tranquil sleeping face propped by many pillows.

He took up the corner of a sheet and moistened it with wine from a cup set against his knee and with it rubbed Keyaira's slim right ankle – so gently that there was no change in her narrow bosom's slow-paced rise and fall. Presently he had cleared away all the greenish unguent from a patch as big as half his palm. He peered down at his handwork. This time he expected surely to see flesh, or at least the green cosmetic on the underside of her ankle, but no, he saw through the irregular little rectangle he'd wiped only the bed's tufted coverlet reflecting the amber light from above. It was a most fascinating and somewhat unnerving mystery.

He glanced questioningly over at Hrissa, who lay on an end of the low table, the thin-glassed, fantastic perfume bottles standing around her, while she contemplated the occupants of the bed, her white tufted chin set on her folded paws. It seemed to the Mouser that she was looking at him with disapproval, so he hastily smoothed back unguent from other parts of Keyaira's leg until the peephole was once more greenly covered.

There was a low laugh. Keyaira propped on her elbows now, was gazing at him through slitted heavy-lashed eyelids.

'We invisibles,' she said in a humorous voice truly or feignedly heavy with sleep, 'show only the outward side of any cosmetic or raiment on us. It is a mystery beyond our seers.'

'You are Mystery's queenly self a-walk through the stars,' the Mouser pronounced, lightly caressing her green toes. 'And I the most fortunate of men. I fear it's a dream and I'll wake on Stardock's frigid ledges. How is it I am here?'

'Our race is dying out,' she said. 'Our men have become sterile. Hirriwi and I are the only princesses left. Our brother Faroomfar hotly wished to be our consort – he still boasts his virility – 'twas he you dueled with – but our father Oomforafor said, "It must be new blood – the blood of heroes." So the cousins and Faroomfar, he much against his will, must fly hither and yon and leave those little rhymed lures written on ramskin in perilous, lonely spots apt to tempt heroes.'

'But how can visibles and invisibles mate?' he asked.

She laughed with delight. 'Is your memory *that* short, Mouse?'

'I mean, have progeny,' he corrected himself, a little irked, but not much, that she had hit on his boyhood nickname. 'Besides, wouldn't such offspring be cloudy, a mix of seen and unseen?'

Keyaira's green mask swung a little from side to side.

'My father thinks such mating will be fertile and that the children will breed true to invisibility – that being dominant over visibility – yet profit greatly in other ways from the admixture of hot, heroic blood.'

'Then your father commanded you to mate with me?' the Mouser asked, a little disappointed.

'By no means, Mouse,' she assured him. 'He would be furious if he dreamt you were here, and Faroomfar would go mad. No, I took a fancy to you, as Hirriwi did to your comrade, when first I spied on you on the Waste – very fortunate that was for you, since my father would have got your seed, if you had won to Stardock's top, in quite a different fashion. Which reminds me, Mouse, you must promise me to descend Stardock at dawn.'

'That is not so easy a promise to give,' the Mouser said. 'Fafhrd will be stubborn, I know. And then there's that other matter of a bag of diamonds, if that's what a pouch of stars means – oh, it's but a trifle, I know, compared to the embraces of a glorious girl . . . still . . .'

'But if I say I love you? – which is only truth . . .'

'Oh Princess,' the Mouser sighed, gliding his hand to her knee. 'How can I leave you at dawn? Only one night . . .'

'Why, Mouse,' Keyaira broke in, smiling roguishly and

twisting her green form a little, 'do you not know that every night is an eternity? Has not any girl taught you that yet, Mouse? I am astonished. Think, we have half an eternity left us yet – which is also an eternity, as your geometer, whether white-bearded or dainty-breasted, should have taught you.'

'But if I am to sire many children—' the Mouser began.

'Hirriwi and I are somewhat like queen bees,' Keyaira explained, 'but think not of that. We have eternity tonight, 'tis true, but only if we make it so. Come closer.'

A little later, plagiarizing himself somewhat, the Mouser said softly, 'The sole fault of mountain climbing is that the best parts go so swiftly.'

'They can last an eternity,' Keyaira breathed in his ear. 'Make them last, Mouse.'

Fafhrd woke shaking with cold. The pink globes were gray and tossing in icy gusts from the open door. Snow had blown in on his clothes and gear scattered across the floor and was piled inches deep on the threshold, across which came also the only illumination – leaden daylight.

A great joy in him fought all these grim gray sights and conquered them.

Nevertheless he was naked and shivering. He sprang up and beat his clothes against the bed and thrust his limbs into their icy stiffness.

As he was buckling his ax belt, he remembered the Mouser down in the chimney, helpless. Somehow all night, even when he'd spoken to Hirriwi of the Mouser, he'd never thought of that.

He snatched up his pack and sprang out on the ledge. From the corner of his eye he caught something moving behind him. It was the massive door closing.

A titan gust of snow-fisted wind struck him. He grabbed the rough rock pillar to which he'd last night planned to tie the rope and hugged it tight. The gods help the Mouser below! Someone came sliding and blowing along the ledge in the wind and snow and hugged the pillar lower down.

The gust passed. Fafhrd looked for the door. There was no sign of it. All the piled snow was redrifted. Keeping close hold of pillar and pack with one hand, he felt over the rough wall with the other. Fingernails no more than eyes could discover the slightest crack.

'So you got tossed out too?' a familiar voice said gayly. '*I* was tossed out by Ice Gnomes, I'll have you know.'

'Mouser!' Fafhrd cried. 'Then you weren't—? I thought—'

'You never thought of me once all night, if I know you,' the Mouser said. 'Keyaira assured me you were safe and somewhat more than that. Hirriwi would have told you the same of me if you'd asked her. But of course you didn't.'

'Then you too—?' Fafhrd demanded, grinning with delight.

'Yes, Prince Brother-in-Law,' the Mouser answered him, grinning back.

They pommeled each other around the pillar a bit – to battle chill, but in sheer high spirits too.

'Hrissa?' Fafhrd asked.

'Warm inside, the wise one. They don't put out the cat here, only the man. I wonder, though . . . Do you suppose Hrissa was Keyaira's to begin with and that she foresaw and planned . . .' His voice trailed off.

No more gusts had come. The snowfall was so light they could see almost a league – up to the Hat above the snow-streaked ledges of the Face and down to where the Ladder faded out.

Once again their minds were filled, almost overpowered by the vastness of Stardock and by their own predicament: two half-frozen mites precariously poised on a frozen vertical world only distantly linked with Nehwon.

To the south there was a pale silver disk in the sky – the sun. They'd been abed till noon.

'Easier to fashion an eternity out of an eighteen-hour night,' the Mouser observed.

'We galloped the moon deep under the sea,' Fafhrd mused.

'Your girl promise to make you go down?' the Mouser asked suddenly.

Fafhrd nodded his head. 'She tried.'

'Mine too. And not a bad idea. The summit smells, by her account. But the chimney looks stuffed with snow. Hold my ankles while I peer over. Yes, packed solid all the way down. So—'

'Mouser,' Fafhrd said, almost gloomily, 'whether there's a way down or no, I must climb Stardock.'

'You know,' the Mouser answered, 'I am beginning to find something in that madness myself. Besides, the east wall of Stardock may hold an easy route to that lush-looking Rift Valley. So let's do what we can with the bare seven hours of light left us. Daytime's no stuff to fashion eternities.'

Mounting the ledges of the Face was both the easiest and hardest climbing they'd had yet to do. The ledges were wide, but some of them sloped outward and were footed with rotten shale that went skidding away into space at a touch, and now and again there were brief traverses which had to be done by narrow cracks and main strength, sometimes swinging by their hands alone.

And weariness and chill and even dizzying faintness came far quicker at this height. They had to halt often to drink air and chafe themselves. While in the back of one deep ledge – Stardock's right eye, they judged – they were forced to spend time firing the brazier with all the remaining resin-pellets, partly to warm food and drink, but chiefly to warm themselves.

Last night's exertions had weakened them too, they sometimes thought, but then the memories of those exertions would return to strengthen them.

And then there were the sudden treacherous wind gusts and the constant yet variable snowfall, which sometimes hid the summit and sometimes let them see it clear against the silvery sky, with great white out-curving brim of the Hat now poised threateningly above them – a cornice like that of the snow-saddle, only now they were on the wrong side.

The illusion grew stronger that Stardock was a separate world from Nehwon in snow-filled space.

Finally the sky turned blue and they felt the sun on their backs – they had climbed above the snowfall at last – and Fafhrd pointed at a tiny nick of blue deep in the brim of the Hat – a nick just visible above the next snow-streaked rock bulge – and he cried, 'The apex of the Needle's Eye!'

At that, something dropped into a snowbank beside them, and there was a muffled clash of metal on rock, while from snow a notched and feathered arrow-end stuck straight up.

They dodged under the protective roof of a bigger bulge as a second arrow and a third clashed against the naked rock on which they'd stood.

'Gnarfi and Kranarch have beaten us, curse 'em,' Fafhrd hissed, 'and set an ambush for us at the Eye, the obvious spot. We must go roundabout and get above 'em.'

'Won't they expect that?

'They were fools to spring their ambush too soon. Besides, we have no other tactic.'

So they began to climb south, though still upward, always keeping rock or snow between them and where they judged the Needle's Eye to be. At last, when the sun was dropping swiftly toward the western horizon, they came swinging back north again and still upward, stamping out steps now in the steepening bank of snow that reversed its curve above them to make the brim of the Hat that now roofed them ominously, covering two-thirds of the sky. They sweated and shook by turns and fought off almost continuous bouts of giddy faintness, yet still strove to move as silently and warily as they might.

At last they rounded one more snow bulge and found themselves looking down a slope at the great bare stretch of rock normally swept by the gale that came through the Needle's Eye to make the Petty Pennon.

On the outward lip of the exposed rock were two men, both clad in suits of brown leather, much scuffed and here and there ripped, showing the inward-turned fur. Lank, black-bearded, elk-faced Kranarch stood whipping his arms against his chest for warmth. Beside him lay his strung bow and some arrows. Stocky boar-faced Gnarfi knelt peeping over the rim. Fafhrd wondered where their two brown-clad bulky servitors were.

The Mouser dug into his pouch. At the same moment Kranarch saw them and snatched up his weapon though rather more slowly than he would have in thicker air. With a similar slowness the Mouser drew out the fist-size rock he had picked up several ledges below for just such a moment as this.

Kranarch's arrow whistled between his and Fafhrd's heads.

A moment later the Mouser's rock struck Kranarch full on his bow-shoulder. The weapon fell from his hand and that arm dangled. Then Fafhrd and the Mouser charged recklessly down the snow slope, the former brandishing his unthonged ax, the latter drawing Scalpel.

Kranarch and Gnarfi received them with their own swords, and Gnarfi with a dagger in his left hand as well. The battle that followed had the same dreamlike slowness as the exchange of missiles. First Fafhrd's and the Mouser's rush gave them the advantage. Then Kranarch's and Gnarfi's great strength – or restedness, rather – told, and they almost drove their enemy off the rim. Fafhrd took a slash in the ribs which bit through his tough wolfskin tunic, slicing flesh and jarring bone.

But then skill told, as it generally will, and the two brown-clad men received wounds and suddenly turned and ran through the great white pointy-topped triangular archway of the Needle's Eye. As he ran Gnarfi screeched, 'Graah! Kruk!'

'Doubtless calling for their shaggy-clad servants or bearers,' the Mouser gasped in surmise, resting sword arm on knee, almost spent. 'Farmerish fat country fellows those looked, hardly trained to weapons. We need not fear 'em greatly. I think, even if they come to Gnarfi's call.' Fafhrd nodded, gasping himself. 'Yet they climbed Stardock,' he added dubiously.

Just then there came galloping through the snowy archway on their hind legs with their nails clashing the wind-swept rock and their fang-edged slavering red mouths open wide and their great-clawed arms widespread – two huge brown bears.

With a speed which their human opponents had been unable to sting from them, the Mouser snatched up Kranarch's bow and sent two arrows speeding, while Fafhrd swung his ax in a gleaming circle and cast it. Then the two comrades sprang swiftly to either side, the Mouser wielding Scalpel and Fafhrd drawing his knife.

But there was no need for further fighting. The Mouser's first arrow took the leading bear in the neck, his second straight in its red mouth-roof and brain, while Fafhrd's ax sank to its helve between two ribs on the trailing bear's left side. The great animals pitched forward in their blood and death throes and rolled twice over and went tumbling ponderously off the rim.

'Doubtless both shes,' the Mouser remarked as he watched them fall. 'O those bestial men of Illik-Ving! Still, to charm or train such beasts to carry packs and climb and even give up their poor lives ...'

'Kranarch and Gnarfi are no sportsmen, that's for certain now,' Fafhrd pronounced. 'Don't praise their tricks.' As he stuffed a rag into his tunic over his wound, he grimaced and swore so angrily that the Mouser didn't speak his quip: *Well, bears are only shortened bearers. I'm always right.*

Then the two comrades trudged slowly under the high tent-like arch of snow to survey the domain, highest on all Nehwon, of which they had made themselves masters – refusing from light-headed weariness to think, in that moment of triumph, of the invisible beings who were Stardock's lords. They went warily, yet not too much so, because Gnarfi and Kranarch had run scared and were wounded not trivially – and the latter had lost his bow.

Stardock's top behind the great toppling snow wave of the Hat was almost as extensive north to south as that of Obelisk Polaris, yet the east rim looked little more than a long bow-shot away. Snow with a thick crust beneath a softer layer covered it all except for the north end and stretches of the east rim, where bare dark rock showed.

The surface, both snow and rock, was flatter even than that of the Obelisk and sloped somewhat from north to south. There were no structures or beings visible, nor signs of hollows where either might hide. Truth to tell, neither the Mouser nor Fafhrd could recall ever having seen a lonelier or barer place.

The only oddity they noticed at first were three holes in the snow a little to the south, each about as big as a hogshead but having the form of an equilateral triangle and apparently going down through the snow to the rock. The three triangular holes were the three corners of a larger equilateral triangle.

The Mouser squinted around closely, then shrugged. 'But a

pouch of stars could be a rather small thing, I suppose,' he said. 'While a heart of light – no guessing its size.'

The whole summit was in bluish shadow except for the northernmost end and for a great pathway of golden light from the setting sun leading from the Needle's Eye all the way across the wind-leveled snow to the east rim.

Down the center of this sunroad went Kranarch's and Gnarfi's running footsteps, the snow flecked here and there with blood. Otherwise the snow ahead was printless. Fafhrd and the Mouser followed those tracks, walking east up their long shadows.

'No sign of 'em ahead,' the Mouser said. 'Looks like there *is* some route down the east wall, and they've taken it – at least far enough to set another ambush.'

As they neared the east rim, Fafhrd said, 'I see other prints making north – a spear's cast that way. Perhaps they turned.'

'But where to?' the Mouser asked.

A few steps more and the mystery was solved horribly. They reached the end of the snow and there on the dark bloodied rock, hidden until now by the wind-piled margin of the snow, sprawled the carcasses of Gnarfi and Kranarch, their middle clothes ripped away, their bodies obscenely mutilated.

Even as the Mouser's gorge rose, he remembered Keyaira's lightly-spoken words: 'If you had won to Stardock's top, my father would have got your seed in quite a different fashion.'

Shaking his head and glaring fiercely, Fafhrd walked around the bodies to the east rim and peered down.

He recoiled a step, then knelt and once more peered.

The Mouser's hopeful theory was prodigiously disproved. Never in his life had Fafhrd looked straight down half such a distance.

A few yards below, the east wall vanished inward. No telling how far the east rim jutted out from Stardock's heartrock.

From this point the fall was straight to the greenish gloom of the Great Rift Valley – five Lankhmar leagues, at least. Perhaps more.

He heard the Mouser say over his shoulder, 'A path for birds or suicides. Naught else.'

Suddenly the green below grew bright, though without showing the slightest feature except for a silvery hair, which might be a great river, running down its center. Looking up again, they saw that the sky had gone all golden with a mighty afterglow. They faced around and gasped in wonder.

The last sunrays coming through the Needle's Eye, swinging southward and a little up, glancingly illuminated a transparent, solid symmetric shape big as the biggest oak tree and resting exactly over the three triangular holes in the snow. It might only be described as a sharp-edged solid star of about eighteen points, resting by three of those on Stardock and built of purest diamond or some like substance.

Both had the same thoughts: that this must be a star the gods had failed to launch. The sunlight had touched the fire in its heart and made it shine, but for a moment only and feebly, not incandescently and forever, as it would have in the sky.

A piercingly shrill, silvery trumpet call broke the silence of the summit.

They swung their gaze north. Outlined by the same deep golden sunlight, ghostlier than the star, yet still clearly to be seen in some of its parts against the yellow sky, a tall slender castle lifted transparent walls and towers from the stony end of the summit. Its topmost spires seemed to go out of sight upward rather than end.

Another sound then – a wailing snarl. A pale animal bounded toward them across the snow from the northwest. Leaping aside with another snarl from the sprawled bodies. Hrissa rushed past them south with a third snarl tossed at them.

Almost too late they saw the peril against which she had tried to warn them.

Advancing toward them from west and north across the unmarked snow were a score of sets of footprints. There were no feet in those prints, nor bodies above them, yet they came on – right print, left print, appearing in succession – and ever more rapidly. And now they saw what they had missed at first because viewed end-on: above each paired set of prints a narrow-shafted, narrow-bladed spear, pointed straight toward them, coming on as swiftly as the prints.

They ran south with Hrissa, Fafhrd in the lead. After a

half dozen sprinting steps the Northerner heard a cry behind him. He stopped and then swiftly spun around.

The Mouser had slipped in the blood of their late foes and fallen. When he got to his feet, the gray spear points were around him on all sides save the rim. He made two wild defensive slashes with Scalpel, but the gray spear points came in relentlessly. Now they were in a close semi-circle around him and hardly a span apart, and he was standing on the rim. They advanced another thrust and the Mouser perforce sprang back from them – and down he fell.

There was a rushing sound and chill air sluiced Fafhrd from behind and something sleekly hairy brushed his calves. As he braced himself to rush forward with his knife and slay an invisible or two for his friend, slender unseen arms clasped him from behind and he heard Hirriwi's silvery voice say in his ear, 'Trust us,' and a coppery-golden sister voice say, 'We'll after him,' and then he found himself pulled down onto a great invisible pulsing shaggy bed three spans above the snow, and they told him 'Cling!' and he clung to the long thick unseen hair, and then suddenly the living bed shot forward across the snow and off the rim and there tilted vertically so his feet pointed at the sky and his face at the Great Rift Valley – and then the bed plunged straight down.

The thin air roared past and his beard and mane were whipped back by the speed of that plunge, but he tightened his grip on the handfuls of invisible hair and a slender arm pressed him down from either side, so that he felt through the fur the throbbing heartbeat of the great invisible carpetlike creature they rode. And he became aware that somehow Hrissa had got under his arm, for there was the small feline face beside his, with slitted eyes and with beard-tuft and ears blown back. And he felt the two invisible girls' bodies alongside his.

He realized that mortal eyes, could such have watched, would have seen only a large man clasping a large white cat and falling headfirst through empty space – but he would be falling much faster than any man should fall, even from such a vast height.

Beside him Hirriwi laughed, as if she had caught his thought, but then the laughter broke off suddenly and the roaring of the wind died almost to utter silence. He guessed it was because the swiftly thickening air had deafened him.

The great dark cliffs flashing upward a dozen yards away were a blur. Yet below him the Great Rift Valley was still featurless green – no, the larger details were beginning to show now: forests and glades and curling hair-thin streams and little lakes like dewdrops.

Between him and the green below he saw a dark speck. It grew in size. It was the Mouser! – rather characteristically falling headfirst, straight as an arrow, with hands locked ahead of him and legs pressed together behind, probably in the faint hope that he might hit deep water.

The creature they rode matched the Mouser's speed and then gradually swung its plunge toward him, flattening out more and more from the vertical, so that the Mouser was pressed against them. Arms visible and invisible clasped him then, pulling him closer, so that all five of the plungers were crowded together on that one great sentient bed.

The creature's dive flattened still more then, halting its fall – there was a long moment while they were all pressed stomach-surgingly tight against the hairy back, while the trees still rushed up at them – and then they were coasting above those same treetops and spiraling down into a large glade.

What happened next to Fafhrd and the Mouser went all in a great tumbling rush, much too swiftly: the feel of springy turf under their feet and balmy air sluicing their bodies, quick kisses exchanged, laughing, shouted congratulations that still sounded all muffled like ghost voices, something hard and irregular yet soft-covered pressed into the Mouser's hands, a last kiss – and then Hirriwi and Keyaira had broken away and a great burst of air flattened the grass and the great invisible flier was gone and the girls with it.

They could watch its upward spiraling flight for a little, however, because Hrissa had gone away on it too. The ice-cat seemed to be peering down at them in farewell. Then she too vanished as the golden afterglow swiftly died in the darkening sky overhead.

They stood leaning together for support in the twilight. Then they straightened themselves, yawning prodigiously, and their hearing came back. They heard the gurgling of a brook and the twittering of birds and a small, faint rustle of dry leaves going away from them and the tiny buzz of a spiraling gnat.

The Mouser opened the invisible pouch in his hands.

'The gems seem to be invisible too,' he said, 'though I can feel 'em well enough. We'll have a hard time selling them – unless we can find a blind jeweler.'

The darkness deepened. Tiny cold fires began to glow in his palms: ruby, emerald, sapphire, amethyst, and pure white.

'No, by Issek!' the Gray Mouser said. 'We'll only need to sell them by night – which is unquestionably the best time for trade in gems.'

The new-risen moon, herself invisible beyond the lesser mountains walling the Rift Valley to the east, painted palely now the upper half of the great slender column of Stardock's east wall.

Gazing up at that queenly sight, Fafhrd said, 'Gallant ladies, all four.'

III: THE TWO BEST THIEVES IN LANKHMAR

Through the mazy avenues and alleys of the great city of Lankhmar, Night was a-slink, though not yet grown tall enough to whirl her black star-studded cloak across the sky, which still showed pale, towering wraiths of sunset.

The hawkers of drugs and strong drinks forbidden by day had not yet taken up their bell-tinklings and thin, enticing cries. The pleasure girls had not lit their red lanterns and sauntered insolently forth. Bravos, desperadoes, procurers, spies, pimps, conmen, and other malfeasors yawned and rubbed drowsy sleep from eyes yet thick-lidded. In fact, most of the Night People were still at breakfast, while most of the Day People were at supper. Which made for an emptiness and hush in the streets, suitable to Night's slippered tread. And which created a large bare stretch of dark thick, unpierced wall at the intersection of Silver Street with the Street of the Gods, a crossing-point where there habitually foregathered the junior executives and star operatives of the Thieves Guild; also meeting there were the few free-lance thieves bold and resourceful enough to defy the Guild and the few thieves of aristocratic birth, sometimes most brilliant amateurs, whom the Guild tolerated and even toadied to, on account of their noble ancestry, which dignified a very old but most disreputable profession.

Midway along the bare stretch of wall, where none might conceivably overhear, a very tall and a somewhat short thief drifted together. After a while they began to converse in prison-yard whispers.

A distance had grown between Fafhrd and the Gray Mouser during their long and uneventful trek south from the Great Rift Valley. It was due simply to too much of each other and to an ever more bickering disagreement as to how the invisible jewels, gift of Hirriwi and Keyaira, might most advantageously be disposed of – a dispute which had finally grown so acrimonious that they had divided the jewels, each carrying his share. When they finally reached Lankhmar, they had lodged apart and each made his own contact with jeweler, fence or private buyer. This separation had made their relationship quite scratchy, but in no way diminished their absolute trust in each other.

'Greetings, Little Man,' Fafhrd prison-growled. 'So you've come to sell your share to Ogo the Blind, or at least give him a viewing? – if such expression may be used of a sightless man.'

'How did you know that?' the Mouser whispered sharply.

'It was the obvious thing to do,' Fafhrd answered somewhat condescendingly. 'Sell the jewels to a dealer who could note neither their night-glow nor daytime invisibility. A dealer who must judge them by weight, feel, and what they can scratch or be scratched by. Besides, we stand just across from the door to Ogo's den. It's very well guarded, by the by – at fewest, ten Mingol swordsmen.'

'At least give me credit for such trifles of common knowledge,' the Mouser answered sardonically. 'Well, you guessed right; it appears that by long association with me you've gained some knowledge of how my wit works, though I doubt that it's sharpened your own a whit. Yes, I've already had one conference with Ogo, and tonight we conclude the deal.'

Fafhrd asked equably, 'Is it true that Ogo conducts all his interviews in pitchy dark?'

'Ho! So there are some few things you admit not knowing! Yes, it's quite true, which makes any interview with Ogo risky work. By insisting on absolute darkness, Ogo the Blind cancels at a stroke the interviewer's advantage – indeed, the advantage passes to Ogo, since he is used by a lifetime of it to utter darkness – a long lifetime, since he's an ancient one, to judge by his speech. Nay, Ogo knows not what darkness is, since it's all he's ever known. However, I've a device to trick him there if need be. In my thick, tightly drawstringed pouch I carry fragments of brightest glow-wood, and can spill them out in a trice.'

Fafhrd nodded admiringly and then asked, 'And what's in

that flat case you carry so tightly under your elbow? An elaborate false history of each of the jewels embossed in ancient parchment for Ogo's fingers to read?'

'There your guess fails! No, it's the jewels themselves, guarded in clever wise so that they cannot be filched. Here, take a peek.' And after glancing quickly to either side and overhead, the Mouser opened the case a handbreadth on its hinges.

Fafhrd saw the rainbow-twinkling jewels firmly affixed in artistic pattern to a bed of black velvet, but all closely covered by an inner top consisting of a mesh of stout iron wire.

The Mouser clapped the case shut. 'On our first meeting, I took two of the smallest of the jewels from their spots in the box and let Ogo feel and otherwise test them. He may dream of filching them all, but my box and the mesh thwart that.'

'Unless he steals from you the box itself,' Fafhrd agreed. 'As for myself, I keep my share of the jewels chained to me.' And after such precautionary glances as the Mouser had made, he thrust back his lose sleeve, showing a stout browned-iron bracelet snapped around his wrist. From the bracelet hung a short chain which both supported and kept tightly shut a small, bulging pouch. The leather of the pouch was everywhere sewed across with fine brown wire. He unclicked the bracelet, which opened on a hinge, then clicked it fast again.

'The browned-iron wire's to foil any cutpurse,' Fafhrd explained offhandedly, pulling down his sleeve.

The Mouser's eyebrows rose. Then his gaze followed them as it went from Fafhrd's wrist to his face, while the small man's expression changed from mild approval to bland inquiry. He asked, 'And you trust such devices to guard your half of the gems from Nemia of the Dusk?'

'How did you know my dealings were with Nemia?' Fafhrd asked in tones just the slightest surprised.

'Because she's Lankhmar's only woman fence, of course. All know you favor women when possible, in business as well as erotic matters. Which is one of your greatest failings, if I may say so. Also, Nemia's door lies next to Ogo's, though that's a trivial clue. You know, I presume, that seven Kleshite stranglers protect her somewhat overripe person? Well, at least then you know the sort of trap you're rushing into. Deal with a woman! – surest route to disaster. By the by, you mentioned "dealings". Does that plural mean this is not your first interview with her?'

Fafhrd nodded. 'As you with Ogo . . . Incidentally, am I to understand that you trust men simply because they're men? That were a greater failing than the one you impute to me. Anyhow, as you with Ogo, I go to Nemia of the Dusk a second time, to complete our deal. The first time I showed her the gems in a twilit chamber, where they appeared to greatest advantage, twinkling just enough to seem utterly real. Did you know, in passing, that she always works in twilight or soft gloom? – which accounts for the second half of her name. At all events, as soon as she glimpsed them, Nemia greatly desired the gems – her breath actually caught in her throat – and she agreed at once to my price, which is not low, as basis for further bargaining. However, it happens that she invariably follows the rule – which I myself consider a sound one – of never completing a transaction of any sort with a member of the opposite sex without first testing them in amorous commerce. Hence this second meeting. If the member be old or otherwise ugly, Nemia deputes the task to one of her maids, but in my case, of course . . .' Fafhrd coughed modestly. 'One more point I'd like to make: "overripe" is the wrong expression. "Full-bloomed" or "the acme of maturity" is what you're looking for.'

'Believe me, I'm sure Nemia is the fullest bloom – a late August flower. Such women always prefer twilight for the display of their "perfectly matured" charms,' the Mouser answered somewhat stifledly. He had for some time been hard put to restrain laughter, and now it appeared in quiet little bursts as he said, 'Oh, you great fool! And you've actually agreed to go to bed with her? And expect not to be parted from your jewels (including family jewels?), let alone not strangled, while at that disadvantage? Oh, this is worse than I thought.'

'I'm not always at such a disadvantage in bed as some people may think,' Fafhrd answered with quiet modesty. 'With me, amorous play sharpens instead of dulls the senses. I trust you have as much luck with a man in ebon darkness as I with a woman in soft gloom. Incidentally, why must you have two conferences with Ogo? Not Nemia's reason, surely?'

The Mouser's grin faded and he lightly bit his lip. With elaborate casualness he said, 'Oh, the jewels must be inspected by the Eyes of Ogo – *his* invariable rule. But whatever test is tried, I'm prepared to out-trick it.'

Fafhrd pondered, then asked, 'And what, or who are, or is, the Eyes of Ogo? Does he keep a pair of them in his pouch?'

'Is,' the Mouser said. Then with even more elaborate casualness, 'Oh, some chit of a girl, I believe. Supposed to have an intuitive faculty where gems are concerned. Interesting, isn't it, that a man as clever as Ogo should believe such superstitious nonsense? Or depend on the soft sex in any fashion. Truly, a mere formality.'

' "Chit of a girl",' Fafhrd mused, nodding his head again and yet again and yet again. 'That describes to a red dot on each of her immature nipples the sort of female you've come to favor in recent years. But of course the amorous is not at all involved in this deal of yours, I'm sure,' he added, rather too solemnly.

'In no way whatever,' the Mouser replied, rather too sharply. Looking around, he remarked, 'We're getting a bit of company, despite the early hour. There's Dickon of the Thieves Guild, that old pen-pusher and drawer of the floor plans of houses to be robbed – I don't believe he's actually worked on a job since the Year of the Snake. And there's fat Grom, their sub-treasurer, another armchair thief. Who comes so dramatically a-slither? – by the Black Bones, it's Snarve, our overlord Glipkerio's nephew! Who's that he speaks to? – oh, only Tork the Cutpurse.'

'And there now appears,' Fafhrd took up, 'Vlek, said to be the Guild's star operative these days. Note his smirk and hear how his shoes creak faintly. And there's that gray-eyed, black-haired amateur, Alyx the Picklock – well, at least her boots don't squeak and I rather admire her courage in adventuring here, where the Guild's animosity toward freelance females is as ill a byword as that of the Pimps Guild. And, just now turning from the Street of the Gods, who have we but Countess Kronia of the Seventy-seven Secret Pockets, who steals by madness, not method. There's one bone-bag I'd never trust, despite her emaciated charms and the weakness you lay to me.'

Nodding, the Mouser pronounced, 'And such as these are called the aristocracy of thiefdom! In all honesty I must say that notwithstanding your weaknesses – which I'm glad you admit – one of the two best thieves in Lankhmar now stands beside me. While the other, needless to say, occupies my rat-skin boots.'

Fafhrd nodded back, though carefully crossing two fingers.

Stifling a yawn, the Mouser said, 'By the by, have you yet any thought about what you'll be doing after those gems are stolen from your wrist, or – though unlikely – sold and paid for? I've been approached about – or at any rate been considering a wander toward – in the general direction of the Eastern Lands.'

'Where it's hotter even than in this sultry Lankhmar? Such a stroll hardly appeals to me,' Fafhrd replied, then casually added, 'In any case, I've been thinking of taking ship – er – northward.'

'Toward that abominable Cold Waste once more? No, thank you!' the Mouser answered. Then, glancing south along Silver Street, where a pale star shone close to the horizon, he went on still more briskly, 'Well, it's time for my interview with Ogo – and his silly girl Eyes. Take your sword to bed with you, I advise, and look to it that neither Graywand nor your more vital blade are filched from you in Nemia's dusk.'

'Oh, so first twinkle of the Whale Star is the time set for your appointment too?' Fafhrd remarked, himself stirring from the wall. 'Tell me, is the true appearance of Ogo known to anyone? Somehow the name makes me think of a fat, old, and overlarge spider.'

'Curb your imagination, if you please,' the Mouser answered sharply. 'Or keep it for your own business, where I'll remind you that the only dangerous spider is the female. No, Ogo's true appearance is unknown. But perhaps tonight I'll discover it!'

'I'd like you to ponder that your besetting fault is over-curiosity,' said Fafhrd, 'and that you can't trust even the stupidest girl to be always silly.'

The Mouser turned impulsively and said, 'However tonight's interviews fall out, let's rendezvous after. The Silver Eel?'

Fafhrd nodded and they gripped hands together. Then each rogue sauntered toward his fateful door.

The Mouser crouched a little, every sense a-quiver, in space utterly dark. On a surface before him – a table, he had felt it out to be – lay his jewel box, closed. His left hand touched the box. His right gripped Cat's Claw and with that weapon nervously threatened the inky darkness all around.

A voice which was at once dry and thick croaked from behind him, 'Open the box!'

The Mouser's skin crawled at the horror of that voice. Nevertheless, he complied with the direction. The rainbow light of the meshed jewels spilled upward, dimly showing the room to be low-ceilinged and rather large. It appeared to be empty except for the table and, indistinct in the far left corner behind him, a dark low shape which the Mouser did not like. It might be a hassock or a fat, round, black pillow. Or it might be . . . The Mouser wished Fafhrd hadn't made his last suggestion.

From ahead of him a rippling, silvery voice quite unlike the first called, 'Your jewels, like no others I have ever seen, gleam in the absence of all light.'

Scanning piercingly across the table and box, the Mouser could see no sign of the second caller. Evening out his own voice, so it was not breathy with apprehension, but bland with confidence, he said, to the emptiness, 'My gems are like no others in the world. In fact, they come not from the world, being of the same substance as the stars. Yet you know by your test that one of them is harder than diamond.'

'They are truly unearthly and most beautiful jewels,' the sourceless silvery voice answered. 'My mind pierces them through and through, and they are what you say they are. I shall advise Ogo to pay your asking price.'

At that instant the Mouser heard behind him a little cough and a dry, rapid scuttling. He whirled around, dirk poised to strike. There was nothing to be seen or sensed, except for the hassock or whatever, which had not moved. The scuttling was no longer to be heard.

He swiftly turned back, and there across the table from him, her front illumined by the twinkling jewels, stood a slim naked girl with pale straight hair, somewhat darker skin, and over-large eyes staring entrancedly from a child's tiny-chinned, pouty-lipped face.

Satisfying himself by a rapid glance that the jewels were in their proper pattern under their mesh and none missing, he swiftly advanced Cat's Claw so that its needle point touched the taut skin between the small yet jutting breasts.

'Do not seek to startle me so again!' he hissed. 'Men – aye, and girls – have died for less.'

The girl did not stir by so much as the breadth of a fine hair; neither did her expresion nor her dreamy yet concentrated gaze change, except that her short lips smiled, then parted to say honey-voiced, 'So you are the Gray Mouser. I had expected a crouchy, sear-faced rogue, and I find . . . a prince.' The very jewels seemed to twinkle more wildly because of her sweet voice and sweeter presence, striking opalescent glimmers from her pale irises.

'Neither seek to flatter me!' the Mouser commanded, catching up his box and holding it open against his side. 'I am inured, I'll have you know, to the ensorcelments of all the world's minxes and nymphs.'

'I speak truth only, as I did of your jewels,' she answered guilelessly. Her lips had stayed parted a little and she spoke without moving them.

'Are you the Eyes of Ogo?' the Mouser demanded harshly, yet drawing Cat's Claw back from her bosom. It bothered him a little, yet only a little, that the tiniest stream of blood, like a black thread, led down for a few inches from the prick his dirk had made.

Utterly unmindful of the tiny wound, the girl nodded. 'And I can see through you, as through your jewels, and I discover naught in you but what is noble and fine, save for certain small subtle impulses of violence and cruelty, which a girl like myself might find delightful.'

'There your all-piercing eyes err wholly, for I am a great villain,' the Mouser answered scornfully, though he felt a pulse of fond satisfaction within him.

The girl's eyes widened as she looked over his shoulder somewhat apprehensively, and from behind the Mouser the dry and thick voice croaked once more, 'Keep to business! Yes, I will pay you in gold your offering price, a sum it will take me some hours to assemble. Return at the same time tomorrow night and we'll close the deal. Now shut the box.'

The Mouser had turned around, still clutching his box, when Ogo began to speak. Again he could not distinguish the source of the voice, though he scanned minutely. It seemed to come from the whole wall.

Now he turned back. Somewhat to his disappointment, the naked girl had vanished. He peered under the table, but there was nothing there. Doubtless some trapdoor or hypnotic device ...

Still suspicious as a snake, he returned the way he had come. On close approach, the black hassock appeared to be only that. Then as the door to the outside slid open noiselessly, he swiftly obeyed Ogo's last injunction, snapping shut the box, and departed.

Fafhrd gazed tenderly at Nemia lying beside him in perfumed twilight, while keeping the edge of his vision on his brawny wrist and the pouch pendant from it, both of which his companion was now idly fondling.

To do Nemia justice, even at the risk of imputing a certain cattiness to the Mouser, her charms were neither overblown, nor even ample, but only ... sufficient.

From just behind Fafhrd's shoulder came a spitting hiss. He quickly turned his head and found himself looking into the crossed blue eyes of a white cat standing on the small bedside table beside a bowl of bronze chrysanthemums.

'Ixy!' Nemia called remonstratingly yet languorously.

Despite her voice, Fafhrd heard behind him, in rapid succession, the click of a bracelet opening and the slightly louder click of one closing.

He turned back instantly, to discover only that Nemia had meanwhile clasped on his wrist, beside the browned-iron bracelet, a golden one around which sapphires and rubies marched alternately in single file.

Gazing at him from betwixt the strands of her long dark hair, she said huskily, 'It is only a small token which I give to those who please me . . . greatly.'

Fafhrd drew his wrist closer to his eyes to admire his prize, but mostly to palpate his pouch with the fingers of his other hand, to assure himself that it bulged as tightly as ever.

It did, and in a burst of generous feeling he said, 'Let me give you one of my gems in precisely the same spirit,' and made to undo his pouch.

Nemia's long-fingered hand glided out to prevent. 'No,' she breathed. 'Let never the gems of business be mixed with the jewels of pleasure. Now if you should choose to bring me some small gift tomorrow night, when at the same hour we exchange your jewels for my gold and my letters of credit on Glipkerio, underwritten by Hisvin the Grain Merchant . . .'

'Right,' Fafhrd said briefly, concealing the relief he felt. He'd been an idiot to think of giving Nemia one of the gems – and with it a day's opportunity to discover its abnormalities.

'Until tomorrow,' Nemia said, opening her arms to him.

'Until tomorrow, then,' Fafhrd agreed, embracing her fervently, yet keeping his pouch clutched in the hand to which it was chained – and already eager to be gone.

The Silver Eel was far less than half filled, its candles few, its cupbearers torpid, as Fafhrd and the Gray Mouser entered simultaneously by different doors and made for one of the many empty booths.

The only eye to watch them at all closely was a gray one above a narrow section of pale cheek bordered by dark hair, peering past the curtain of the backmost booth.

When their thick table-candles had been lit and cups set before them and a jug of fortified wine, and fresh charcoal tumbled into the red-seeded brazier at table's end, the Mouser placed his flat box on the table and, grinning, said, 'All's set. The jewels passed the test of the Eyes – a toothsome wenchlet; more of her later. I get the cash tomorrow night – all my offering price! But you, friend, I hardly thought to see you back alive. Drink we up! I take it you escaped from Nemia's divan whole and sound in organs and limbs – as far as you yet know. But the jewels?'

'They came through too,' Fafhrd answered, swinging the pouch lightly out of his sleeve and then back in again. 'And I get my money tomorrow night . . . the full amount of my asking price, just like you.'

As he named those coincidences, his eyes went thoughtful.

They stayed that way while he took two large swallows of wine. The Mouser watched him curiously.

'At one point,' Fafhrd finally mused, 'I thought she was trying the old trick of substituting for mine an identical but worthlessly filled pouch. Since she'd seen the pouch at our first meeting, she could have had a similar one made up, complete with chain and bracelet.'

'But was she—?' the Mouser asked.

'Oh no, it turned out to be something entirely different,' Fafhrd said lightly, though some thought kept two slight vertical furrows in his forehead.

'That's odd,' the Mouser remarked. 'At one point – just one, mind you – the Eyes of Ogo, if she'd been extremely swift, deft, and silent, might have been able to switch boxes on me.'

Fafhrd lifted his eyebrows.

The Mouser went on rapidly, 'That is, if my box had been closed. But it was open, in darkness, and there'd have been no way to reproduce the varicolored twinkling of the gems. Phosphorus or glow-wood? Too dim. Hot coals? No, I'd have felt the heat. Besides, how get that way a diamond's pure white glow? Quite impossible.'

Fafhrd nodded agreement, but continued to gaze over the Mouser's shoulder.

The Mouser started to reach toward his box, but instead with a small self-contemptuous chuckle picked up the jug and began to pour himself another drink in a careful small stream.

Fafhrd shrugged at last, used the back of his forefingers to push over his own pewter cup for a refill, and yawned mightily, leaning back a little and at the same time pushing his spread-fingered hands to either side across the table, as if pushing away from him all small doubts and wonderings.

The fingers of his left hand touched the Mouser's box.

His face went blank. He looked down his arm at the box.

Then to the great puzzlement of the Mouser, who had just begun to fill Fafhrd's cup, the Northerner leaned forward and placed his head ear-down on the box.

'Mouser,' he said in a small voice, 'your box is buzzing.'

Fafhrd's cup was full, but the Mouser kept on pouring. Heavily fragrant wine puddled and began to run toward the glowing brazier.

'When I touched the box, I felt vibration,' Fafhrd went on bemusedly. 'It's buzzing. It's still buzzing.'

With a low snarl, the Mouser slammed down the jug and snatched the box from under Fafhrd's ear. The wine reached the brazier's hot bottom and hissed.

He tore the box open, opened also its mesh top, and he and Fafhrd peered in.

The candlelight dimmed, but by no means extinguished the yellow, violet, reddish, and white twinkling glows rising from various points on the black velvet bottom.

But the candlelight was quite bright enough also to show, at each such point, matching the colors listed, a firebeetle, glow-wasp, nightbee, or diamondfly, each insect alive but delicately affixed to the floor of the box with silver wire. From time to time the wings or wingcases of some buzzed.

Without hesitation, Fafhrd unclasped the brown-iron bracelet from his wrist, unchained the pouch, and dumped it on the table.

Jewels of various sizes, all beautifully cut, made a fair heap.

But they were all dead black.

Fafhrd picked up a big one, tried it with his fingernail, then whipped out his hunting knife and with its edge easily scored the gem.

He carefully drooped it in the brazier's glowing center. After a bit it flamed up yellow and blue.

'Coal,' Fafhrd said.

The Mouser clawed his hands over his faintly twinkling box, as if about to pick it up and hurl it through the wall and across the Inner Sea.

Instead he unclawed his hands and hung them decorously at his sides.

'I am going away,' he announced quietly, but very clearly, and did so.

Fafhrd did not look up. He was dropping a second black gem in the brazier.

He did take off the bracelet Nemia had given him; he brought it close to his eyes, said, 'Brass . . . glass,' and spread his fingers to let it drop in the spilled wine. After the Mouser was gone, Fafhrd drained his brimming cup, drained the Mouser's and filled it again, then went on supping from it as he continued to drop the black jewels one by one in the brazier.

Nemia and the Eyes of Ogo sat cozily side by side on a luxurious divan. They had put on negligees. A few candles made a yellowish dusk.

On a low, gleaming table were set delicate flagons of wines and liqueurs, slim-stemmed crystal goblets, golden plates of sweetmeats and savories, and in the center two equal heaps of rainbow-glowing gems.

'What a quaint bore barbarians are,' Nemia remarked, delicately stifling a yawn, 'though good for one's sensuous self, once in a great while. This one had a little more brains than most. I think he might have caught on, except that I made the two clicks come so exactly together when I snapped back on his wrist the bracelet with the false pouch and at the same time my brass keepsake. It's amazing how barbarians are hypnotized by brass along with any odd bits of glass colored like rubies and sapphires – I think the three primary colors paralyze their primitive brains.'

'Clever, *clever* Nemia,' the Eyes of Ogo cooed with a tender caress. 'My little fellow almost caught on too when I made the switch, but he got interested in threatening me with his knife. Actually jabbed me between the breasts. I think he has a dirty mind.'

'Let me kiss the blood away, darling Eyes,' Nemia suggested. 'Oh, dreadful . . . dreadful.'

While shivering under her treatment – Nemia had a slightly bristly tongue – Eyes said, 'For some reason he was quite nervous about Ogo.' She made her face blank, her pouty mouth hanging slightly open.

The richly draped wall opposite her made a scuttling sound and then croaked in a dry, thick voice, 'Open your box, Gray Mouser. Now close it. Girls, girls! Cease your lascivious play!'

Nemia and Eyes clung to each other laughing. Eyes said in her natural voice, if she had one, 'And he went away still thinking there was a real Ogo. I'm quite certain of that. My, they both must be in a froth by now.'

Sitting back, Nemia said, 'I suppose we'll have to take some special precautions against their raiding us to get their jewels back.'

Eyes shrugged, 'I have my five Mingol swordsmen.'

Nemia said. 'And I have my three and a half Kleshite stranglers.'

'Half?' Eyes asked.

'I was counting Ixy. No, but seriously.'

Eyes frowned for half a heartbeat, then shook her head decisively. 'I don't think we need worry about Fafhrd and the Gray Mouser raiding us back. Because we're girls, their pride will be hurt, and they'll sulk a while and then run away to the ends of the earth on one of those adventures of theirs.'

'Adventures!' said Nemia, as one who says, 'Cesspools and privies!'

'You see, they're really weaklings,' Eyes went on, warming to her topic. 'They have no drive whatever, no ambition, no true passion for money. For instance, if they did – and if they didn't spend so much time in dismal spots away from Lankhmar – they'd have known that the King of Ilthmar has developed a mania for gems that are invisible by day, but glow by night, and has offered half his kingdom for a sack of star-jewels. And then they'd never have had even to consider such an idiotic thing as coming to us.'

'What do you suppose he'll do with them? The King, I mean.'

Eyes shrugged. 'I don't know. Build a planetarium. Or eat them.' She thought a moment. 'All things considered, it might be as well if we got away from here for a few weeks. We deserve a vacation.'

Nemia nodded, closing her eyes. 'It should be absolutely

the opposite sort of place to the one in which the Mouser and Fafhrd will have their next – ugh! – adventure.'

Eyes nodded too and said dreamily, 'Blue skies and rippling water, spotless beach, a tepid wind, flowers and slim slavegirls everywhere . . .'

Nemia said, 'I've always wished for a place that has no weather, only perfection. Do you know which half of Ilthmar's kingdom has the least weather?'

'Precious Nemia,' Eyes murmured, 'you're so civilized. And so very, very clever. Next to one other, you're certainly the best thief in Lankhmar.'

'Who's the other?' Nemia was eager to know.

'Myself, of course,' Eyes answered modestly.

Nemia reached up and tweaked her companion's ear – not too painfully, but enough.

'If there were the least money depending on that,' she said quietly but firmly, 'I'd teach you differently. But since it's only conversation . . .'

'Dearest Nemia.'

'Sweetest Eyes.'

The two girls gently embraced and kissed eath other fondly.

The Mouser glared thin-lipped across a table in a curtained booth in the Golden Lamprey, a tavern not unlike the Silver Eel.

He rapped the teak before him with his fingertip, and the perfumed stale air with his voice, saying, 'Double those twenty gold pieces and I'll make the trip and hear Prince Gwaay's proposal.'

The very pale man opposite him, who squinted as if even the candlelight were a glare, answered softly, 'Twenty-five – and you serve him for one day after arrival.'

'What sort of ass do you take me for?' the Mouser demanded dangerously. 'I might be able to settle all his troubles in one day – I usually can – and what then? No, no preagreed service; I hear his proposal only. And . . . thirty-five gold pieces in advance.'

'Very well, thirty gold pieces – twenty to be refunded if you refuse to serve my master, which would be a risky step, I warn you.'

'Risk is my bed-mate,' the Mouser snapped. 'Ten only to be refunded.'

The other nodded and began slowly to count rilks onto the teak. 'Ten *now*,' he said. 'Ten when you join our caravan tomorrow morning at the Grain Gate. And ten when we reach Quarmall.'

'When we first glimpse the spires of Quarmall,' the Mouser insisted.

The other nodded.

The Mouser moodily snatched the golden coins and stood up. They felt very few in his fist. For a moment he thought of returning to Fafhrd and with him devising plans against Ogo and Nemia.

No, never! He realized he couldn't in his misery and self-rage bear the thought of even looking at Fafhrd.

Besides, the Northerner would certainly be drunk.

And two, or at most three, rilks would buy him certain tolerable and even interesting pleasures to fill the hours before dawn brought him release from this hateful city.

Fafhrd was indeed drunk, being on this third jug. He had burnt up all the black jewels and was now with the greatest delicacy and most careful use of the needle point of his knife, releasing unharmed each of the silver-wired firebeetles, glow-wasps, nightbees, and diamondflies. They buzzed about erratically.

Two cupbearers and the chucker-out had come to protest and now Slevyas himself joined them, rubbing the back of his thick neck. He had been stung and a customer too. Fafhrd had himself been stung twice, but hadn't seemed to notice. Nor did he now pay the slightest attention to the four haranguing him.

The last nightbee was released. It careened off noisily past Slevyas' neck, who dodged his head with a curse. Fafhrd sat back, suddenly looking very wretched. With varying shrugs the master of the Silver Eel and his three servitors made off, one cupbearer making swipes at the air.

Fafhrd tossed up his knife. It came down almost point first, but didn't quite stick in the teak. He laboriously scabbarded it, then forced himself to take a small sip of wine.

As if someone were about to emerge from the backmost booth, there was a stirring of its heavy curtains, which like all the others had stitched to them heavy chain and squares of metal, so that one guest couldn't stab another through them, except with luck and the slimmest stilettos.

But at that moment a very pale man, who held up his cloak to shield his eyes from the candlelight, entered by the side door and made to Fafhrd's table.

'I've come for my answer, Northerner,' he said in a voice soft yet sinister. He glanced at the toppled jugs and spilled wine. 'That is, if you remember my proposition.'

'Sit down,' Fafhrd said. 'Have a drink. Watch out for the glowwasps – they're vicious.' Then, scornfully, 'Remember! Prince Hasjarl of Marquall – Quarmall. Passage by ship. A mountain of gold rilks. Remember!'

Keeping on his feet, the other amended, 'Twenty-five rilks. Provided you take ship with me at once and promise to render a day's service to my prince. Thereafter by what further agreement you and he arrive at.'

He placed on the table a small golden tower of precounted coins.

'Munificent!' Fafhrd said, grabbing it up and reeling to his feet. He placed five of the coins on the table and shoved the rest in his pouch, except for three more, which scattered dulcetly across the floor. He corked and pouched the third wine jug. Coming out from behind the table, he said, 'Lead the way, comrade,' gave the squinty-eyed man a mighty shove toward the side door, and went weaving after him.

In the backmost booth, Alyx the Picklock pursed her lips and shook her head disapprovingly.

IV: THE LORDS OF QUARMALL

The room was dim, almost maddeningly dim to one who loved sharp detail and the burning sun. The few wall-set torches that provided the sole illumination flamed palely and thinly, more like will-o'-the-wisps than true fire, although they released a pleasant incense. One got the feeling that the dwellers of this region resented light and only tolerated a thin mist of it for the benefit of strangers.

Despite its vast size, the room was carved all in somber solid rock – smooth floor, polished curving walls, and domed ceiling – either a natural cave finished by man or else chipped out and burnished entirely by human effort, although the thought of that latter amount of work was nearly intolerable. From numerous deep niches between the torches, metal statuettes and masks and jeweled objects gleamed darkly.

Through the room, bending the feeble bluish flames, came a perpetual cool draft bringing acid odors of damp ground and moist rock which the sweet spicy scent of the torches never quite masked.

The only sounds were the occasional rutch of rock on wood from the other end of the long table, where a game was being played with black and white stone counters – that and, from beyond the room, the ponderous sighing of the great fans that sucked down the fresh air on its last stage of passage from the distant world above and drove it through this region . . . and the perpetual soft thudding of the naked feet of the slaves on the heavy leather tread-belts that drove those great wooden fans . . . and the very faint mechanic gasping of those slaves.

After one had been in this region for a few days, or only a few hours, the sighing of the fans and the soft thudding of the feet and the faint gaspings of the tortured lungs seemed to drone out only the name of this region, over and over.

'Quarmall . . .' they seemed to chant. 'Quarmall . . . Quarmall is all . . .'

The Gray Mouser, upon whose senses and through whose mind these sensations and fancies had been flooding and flitting, was a small man strongly muscled. Clad in gray silks irregularly woven, with tiny thread-tufts here and there, he looked restless as a lynx and as dangerous.

From a great tray of strangely hued and shaped mushrooms set before him like sweetmeats, the Mouser disdainfully selected and nibbled cautiously at the most normal looking, a gray one. Its perfumy savor masking bitterness offended him and he spat it surreptitiously into his palm and dropped that hand under the table and flicked the wet chewed fragments to the floor. Then, while he sucked his cheeks sourly, the fingers of both his hands began to play as slowly and nervously with the hilts of his sword Scalpel and his dagger Cat's Claw as his mind played with his boredoms and murky wonderings.

Along each side of the long narrow table, in great highbacked chairs widely spaced, sat six scrawny old men, bald or shaven of dome and chin, and chicken fluted of jowl, and each clad only in a neat white loincloth. Eleven of these stared intently at nothing and perpetually tensed their meager muscles until even their ears seemed to stiffen, as though concentrating mightily in realms unseen. The twelfth had his chair half turned and was playing across a far corner of the table the board-game that made the occasional tiny rutching noises. He was playing it with the Mouser's employer Gwaay, ruler of the Lower Levels of Quarmall and younger son to Quarmal, Lord of Quarmall.

Although the Mouser had been three days in Quarmall's depths he had come no closer to Gwaay than he was now, so that he knew him only as a pallid, handsome, soft-spoken youth, no realer to the Mouser, because of the eternal dimness and the invariable distance between them, than a ghost.

The game was one the Mouser had never seen before and quite tricky in several respects.

The board looked green, though it was impossible to be certain of colors in the unending twilight of the torches, and it had no perceptible squares or tracks on it, except for a phosphorescent line midway between the opponents, dividing the board into two equal fields.

Each contestant started the game with twelve flat circular counters set along his edge of the board. Gwaay's counters were obsidian-black, his ancient opponent's marble-white, so the Mouser was able to distinguish them despite the dimness.

The object of the game seemed to be to move the pieces randomly forward over uneven distances and get at least seven of them into your opponent's field first.

Here the trickiness was that one moved the pieces not with the fingers but only by looking at them intently. Apparently, if one gazed only at a single piece, one could move it quite swiftly. If one gazed at several, one could move them all together in a line or cluster, but more sluggishly.

The Mouser was not yet wholly convinced that he was witnessing a display of thought-power. He still suspected threads, soundless air-puffings, surreptitious joggings of the board from below, powerful beetles under the counters, and hidden magnets! – for Gwaay's pieces at least could by their color be some sort of loadstone.

At the present moment Gwaay's black counters and the ancient's white ones were massed at the central line, shifting only a little now and then as the push-of-war went first a nail's breadth one way, then the other. Suddenly Gwaay's rearmost counter circled swiftly back and darted toward an open space at the board's edge. Two of the ancient's counters moved to block it. Six of Gwaay's other counters formed a wedge and thrust across the midline through the weak point thus created. As the ancient's two detached counters returned to oppose them, Gwaay's end-running counter sped across. The game was over – Gwaay gave no sign of this, but the ancient began fumblingly to return the pieces to their starting positions with his fingers.

'Ho, Gwaay, that was easily won!' the Mouser called out cockily. 'Why not take on two of them together? The oldster must be a sorcerer of the Second Rank to play so weakly – or even a doddering apprentice of the Third.'

The ancient shot the Mouser a venomous gaze. 'We are, all

twelve of us, sorcerers of the First Rank and have been from our youth,' he proclaimed portentously. 'As you should swiftly learn were one of us to point but a little finger against you.'

'You have heard what he says,' Gwaay called softly to the Mouser without looking at him.

The Mouser, daunted no whit, at least outwardly, called back, 'I still think you could beat two of them together, or seven – or the whole decrepit dozen! If they are of First Rank, you must be of Zero or Negative Magnitude.'

The ancient's lips worked speechlessly and bubbled with froth at the affront, but Gwaay only called pleasantly. 'Were but three of my faithful magi to cease their sorcerous concentrations, my brother Hasjarl's sendings would burst through from the Upper Levels and I would be stricken with all the diseases in the evil compendium, and a few others that exist in Hasjarl's putrescent imagination alone – or perchance I should be erased entirely from this life.'

'If nine out of twelve must be forever a-guarding you, they can't get much sleep,' the Mouser observed, calling back.

'Times are not always so troublous,' Gwaay replied tranquilly. 'Sometimes custom or my father enjoins a truce. Sometimes the dark inward sea quiets. But today I know by certain signs that a major assault is being made on the liver and lights and blood and bones and rest of me. Dear Hasjarl has a double coven of sorcerers hardly inferior to my own – Second Rank, but High Second – and he whips them on. And I am as distasteful to Hasjarl, oh Gray Mouser, as the simple fruits of our manure beds are to your lips. Tonight, furthermore, my father Quarmal casts his horoscope in the tower of the Keep, high above Hasjarl's Upper Levels, so it befits I keep all rat-holes closely watched.'

'If it's magical helpings you lack,' the Mouser retorted boldly, 'I have a spell or two that would frizzle your elder brother's witches and warlocks!' And truth to tell the Mouser had parchment-crackling in his pouch one spell – though one spell only – which he dearly wanted to test. It had been given him by his own wizardly mentor and master Sheelba of the Eyeless Face.

Gwaay replied, more softly than ever, so that the Mouser

felt that if there had been a yard more between them he would not have heard, 'It is your work to ward from my physical body Hasjarl's sword-sendings, in particular those of this great champion he is reputed to have hired. My sorcerers of the First Rank will shield off Hasjarl's sorcerous *billets-doux*. Each to his proper occupation.' He lightly clapped his hands together. A slim slavegirl appeared noiselessly in the dark archway beyond him. Without looking once at her, Gwaay softly commanded, 'Strong wine for our warrior.' She vanished.

The ancient had at last laboriously shuffled the black and white counters into their starting positions and Gwaay regarded his thoughtfully. But before making a move, he called to the Mouser, 'If time still hangs heavy on your hands, devote some of it to selecting the reward you will take when your work is done. And in your search overlook not the maiden who brings you the wine. Her name is Ivivis.'

At that the Mouser shut up. He had already chosen more than a dozen expensive be-charming objects from Gwaay's drawers and niches and locked them in a disused closet he had discovered two levels down. If this should be discovered, he would explain that he was merely making an innocent pre-selection pending final choice, but Gwaay might not view it that way and Gwaay was sharp, judging from the way he'd noted the rejected mushroom and other things.

It had not occurred to the Mouser to preempt a girl or two by locking her in the closet also, though it was admittedly an attractive idea.

The ancient cleared his throat and said chucklingly across the board, 'Lord Gwaay, let this ambitious sworder try his sorcerous tricks. Let him try them on me!'

The Mouser's spirits rose, but Gwaay only raised palm and shook his head slightly and pointed a finger at the board; the ancient began obediently to think a piece forward.

The Mouser's spirits fell. He was beginning to feel very much alone in this dim underworld where all spoke and moved in whispers. True, when Gwaay's emissary had approached him in Lankhmar, the Mouser had been happy to take on this solo job. It would teach his loud-voiced sword-mate Fafhrd a lesson if his small gray comrade (and brain!) should disappear one night without a word . . . and then return perchance a year later with a brimful treasure chest and a mocking smile.

The Mouser had even been happy all the long caravan trip from Lankhmar south to Quarmall, along the Hlal River and past the Lakes of Pleea and through the Mountains of Hunger. It had been a positive pleasure to loll on a swaying camel beyond reach of Fafhrd's hugeness and disputatious talk and boisterous ways, while the nights grew ever bluer and warmer and strange jewel-fiery stars came peering over the southern horizon.

But now he had been three nights in Quarmall since his secret coming to the Lower Levels – three nights and days, or rather one hundred and forty-four interminable demi-hours of buried twilight – and he was already beginning in his secretest mind to wish that Fafhrd were here, instead of half a continent away in Lankhmar – or even farther than that if he'd carried out his misty plans to revisit his northern homeland. Someone to drink with, at any rate – and even a roaring quarrel would be positively refreshing after seventy-two hours of nothing but silent servitors, tranced sorcerers, stewed mushrooms, and Gwaay's unbreakable soft-tongued equanimity.

Besides, it appeared that all Gwaay wanted was a mighty sworder to nullify the threat of this champion Hasjarl was supposed to have hired as secretly as Gwaay had smuggled in the Mouser. If Fafhrd were here, he could be Gwaay's sworder, while Mouser would have better opportunity to peddle Gwaay his magical talents. The one spell he had in his pouch – he had got it from Sheelba in return for the tale of the Perversions of Clutho – would forever establish his reputation as an archimage of deadly might, he was sure.

The Mouser came out of his musings to realize that the slave-girl Ivivis was kneeling before him – for how long she had been there he could not say – and proffering an ebony tray on which stood a squat stone jug and a copper cup.

She knelt with one leg doubled, the other thrust behind her as in a fencing lunge, stretching the short skirt of her green tunic, while her arms reached the tray forward.

Her slim body was most supple – she held the difficult pose effortlessly. Her fine straight hair was pale as her skin – both a sort of ghost color. It occurred to the Mouser that she would look very well in his closet, perhaps cherishing against her bosom the necklace of large black pearls he had discovered piled behind a pewter statuette in one of Gwaay's niches.

However, she was kneeling as far away from him as she could and still stretch him the tray, and her eyes were most modestly downcast, nor would she even flicker up their lids to his gracious murmurings – which were all the approach he thought suitable at this moment.

He seized the jug and cup. Ivivis drooped her head still lower in acknowledgment, then flitted silently away.

The Mouser poured a finger of blood-red, blood-thick wine and sipped. Its flavor was darkly sweet, but with a bitter under-taste. He wondered if it were fermented from scarlet toadstools.

The black and white counters skittered rutchingly in obedience to Gwaay's and the ancient's peerings. The pale torch flames bent to the unceasing cool breeze, while the fan-slaves and their splayed bare feet on the leather belts and the great unseen fans themselves on their ponderous axles muttered unendingly, 'Quarmall . . . Quarmall is downward tall . . . Quarmall . . . Quarmall is all . . .'

In an equally vast room many levels higher yet still underground – a windowless room where torches flared redder and brighter, but their brightness nullified by an acrid haze of incense smoke, so that here too the final effect was exasperating dimness – Fafhrd sat at the table's foot.

Fafhrd was ordinarily a monstrously calm man, but now he was restlessly drumming fist on thumb-root, on the verge of admitting to himself that he wished the Gray Mouser were here, instead of back in Lankhmar or perchance off on some ramble in the desert-patched Eastern Lands.

The Mouser, Fafhrd thought, might have more patience to unriddle the mystification and crooked behavior-ways of these burrowing Quarmallians. The Mouser might find it easier to endure Hasjarl's loathsome taste for torture, and at least the little gray fool would be someone human to drink with!

Fafhrd had been very glad to be parted from the Mouser and from his vanities and tricksiness and chatter when Hasjarl's agent had contacted him in Lankhmar, promising large pay in return for Fafhrd's instant, secret, and solitary coming. Fafhrd had even dropped a hint to the small fellow that he might take ship with some of his Northerner countrymen who had sailed down across the Inner Sea.

What he had not explained to the Mouser was that, as soon as Fafhrd was aboard her, the longship had sailed not north but south, coasting through the vast Outer Sea along Lankhmar's western seaboard.

It had been an idyllic journey, that – pirating a little now and then, despite the sour objections of Hasjarl's agent, battling great storms and also the giant cuttlefish, rays, and serpents which swarmed ever thicker in the Outer Sea as one sailed south. At the recollection Fafhrd's fist slowed its drumming and his lips almost formed a long smile.

But now this Quarmall! This endless stinking sorcery! This torture-besotted Hasjarl! Fafhrd's fist drummed fiercely again.

Rules! – he mustn't explore downward, for that led to the Lower Levels and the enemy. Nor must he explore upward – that way was to Father Quarmal's apartments, sacrosanct. None must know of Fafhrd's presence. He must satisfy himself with such drink and inferior wenches as were available in Hasjarl's limited Upper Levels. (They called these dim labyrinths and crypts *upper!*)

Delays! – they mustn't muster their forces and march down and smash brother-enemy Gwaay; that was unthinkable rashness. They mustn't even shut off the huge treadmill-driven fans whose perpetual creaking troubled Fafhrd's ears and which sent the life-giving air on the first stages of its journey to Gwaay's underworld, and through other rock-driven wells sucked out the stale – no, those fans must never be stopped, for Father Quarmal would frown on any battle-tactic which suffocated valuable slaves; and from anything Father Quarmal frowned on, his sons shrank shuddering.

Instead, Hasjarl's war-council must plot years-long campaigns weaponed chiefly with sorcery and envisioning the conquest of Gwaay's Lower Levels a quarter tunnel – or a quarter mushroom field – at a time.

Mystifications! – mushrooms must be served at all meals

but never eaten or so much as tasted. Roast rat, on the other hand, was a delicacy to be crowed over. Tonight Father Quarmal would cast his own horoscope and for some reason that superstitious starsighting and scribbling would be of incalculable cryptic consequence. All maids must scream loudly twice when familiarities were suggested to them, no matter what their subsequent behavior. Fafhrd must never get closer to Hasjarl than a long dagger's cast – a rule which gave Fafhrd no chance to discover how Hasjarl managed never to miss a detail of what went on around him while keeping his eyes fully closed almost all the time.

Perhaps Hasjarl had a sort of short-range second sight, or perhaps the slave nearest him ceaselessly whispered an account of all that transpired, or perhaps – well, Fafhrd had no way of knowing.

But somehow Hasjarl could see things with his eyes shut.

This paltry trick of Hasjarl's evidently saved his eyes from the irritation of the incense smoke, which kept those of Hasjarl's sorcerers and of Fafhrd himself red and watering. However, since Hasjarl was otherwise a most energetic and restless prince – his bandy-legged misshapen body and mismated arms forever a-twitch, his ugly face always grimacing – the detail of eyes tranquilly shut was peculiarly jarring and shiversome.

All in all, Fafhrd was heartily sick of the Upper Levels of Quarmall though scarcely a week in them. He had even toyed with the notion of double-crossing Hasjarl and hiring out to his brother or turning informer for his father – although they might, as employers, be no improvement whatever.

But mostly he simply wanted to meet in combat this champion of Gwaay's he kept hearing so much of – meet him and slay him and then shoulder his reward (preferably a shapely maiden with a bag of gold in her either hand) and turn his back forever on the accursed dim-tunneled whisper-haunted hill of Quarmall!

In an excess of exasperation he clapped his hand to the hilt of his longsword Graywand.

Hasjarl saw that, although Hasjarl's eyes were closed, for he quickly pointed his gnarly face down the long table at

Fafhrd, between the ranks of the twenty-four heavily-robed, thickly-bearded sorcerers crowded shoulder to shoulder. Then, his eyelids still shut, Hasjarl commenced to twitch his mouth as a preamble to speech and with a twitter-tremble as overture called, 'Ha, hot for battle, eh, Fafhrd boy? Keep him in the sheath! Yet tell me, what manner of man do you think this warrior – the one you protect me against – Gwaay's grim man-slayer? He is said to be mightier than an elephant in strength, and more guileful than the very Zobolds.' With a final spasm Hasjarl managed, still without opening his eyes, to look expectantly at Fafhrd.

Fafhrd had heard all this sort of worrying time and time again during the past week, so he merely answered with a snort:

'Zutt! They all say that about anybody. I know. But unless you get me some action and keep these old flea-bitten beards out of my sight—'

Catching himself up short, Fafhrd tossed off his wine and beat with his pewter mug on the table for more. For although Hasjarl might have the demeanor of an idiot and the disposition of a ocelot, he served excellent ferment of grape ripened on the hot brown southern slopes of Quarmall hill . . . and there was no profit in goading him.

Nor did Hasjarl appear to take offense – or if he did, he took it out on his bearded sorcerers, for he instantly began to instruct one to enuciate his runes more clearly, questioned another as to whether his herbs were sufficiently pounded, reminded a third that it was time to tinkle a certain silver bell thrice, and in general treated the whole two dozen as if they were a roomful of schoolboys and he their eagle-eyed pedagogue – though Fafhrd had been given to understand that they were all magi of the First Rank.

The double coven of sorcerers in turn began to bustle more nervously, each with his particular spell – touching off more stinks, jiggling black drops out of more dirty vials, waving more wands, pin-stabbing more figurines, finger-tracing eldritch symbols more swiftly in the air, mounding up each in front of him from his bag more noisesome fetishes, and so on.

From his hours of sitting at the foot of the table, Fafhrd had learned that most of the spells were designed to inflict a noisome disease upon Gwaay; the Black Plague, the Red Plague, the Boneless Death, the Hairless Decline, the Slow Rot, the Fast Rot, the Green Rot, the Bloody Cough, the Belly Melts, the Ague, the Runs, and even the footling Nose Drip. Gwaay's own sorcerers, he gathered, kept warding off these malefic spells with counter-charms, but the idea was to keep on sending them in hopes that the opposition would some day drop their guard, if only for a few moments.

Fafhrd rather wished Gwaay's gang were able to reflect back the disease-spells on their dark-robed senders. He had become weary even of the abstruse astrologic signs stitched in gold and silver on those robes, and of the ribbons and precious wires knotted cabalistically in their heavy beards.

Hasjarl, his magicians disciplined into a state of furious busyness, opened wide his eyes for a change and with only a preliminary lip-writhe called to Fafhrd, 'So you want action, eh, Fafhrd boy?'

Fafhrd, mightily irked at the last epithet, planted an elbow on the table and wagged that hand at Hasjarl and called back, 'I do. My muscles cry to bulge. You've strong-looking arms, Lord Hasjarl. What say you we play the wrist game?'

Hasjarl tittered evilly and cried, 'I go but now to play another sort of wrist game with a maid suspected of commerce with one of Gwaay's pages. She never screamed even once . . . then. Wouldst accompany me and watch the action, Fafhrd?' And he suddenly shut his eyes again with the effect of putting on two tiny masks of skin – yet shut them so firmly there could be no question of his peering through the lashes.

Fafhrd shrank back in his chair, flushing a little. Hasjarl had divined Fafhrd's distaste for torture on the Northerner's first night in Quarmall's Upper Levels and since then had never missed an opportunity to play on what Hasjarl must view as Fafhrd's weakness.

To cover his embarrassment, Fafhrd drew from under his tunic a tiny book of stitched parchment pages. The Northerner would have sworn that Hasjarl's eyelids had not flickered once since closing, yet now the villain cried, 'The sigil on the cover of that packet tells me it is something of Ningauble of the Seven Eyes. What is it, Fafhrd?'

'Private matters,' the latter retorted firmly. Truth to tell, he was somewhat alarmed. The contents of the packet were such as he dared not permit Hasjarl see. And just as the villain somehow knew, there was indeed on the top parchment the bold black figure of a seven-fingered hand, each finger bearing an eye for a nail – one of the many signs of Fafhrd's wizardly patron.

Hasjarl coughed hackingly. 'No servant of Hasjarl has private matters,' he pronounced. 'However, we will speak of that at another time. Duty calls me.' He bounded up from his chair and fiercely eyeing his sorcerers cried at them barkingly, 'If I find one of you dozing over his spells when I return, it were better for him – aye, and for his mother too – had he been born with slave's chains on his ankles!'

He paused, turning to go, and pointing his face at Fafhrd again, called rapidly yet cajolingly, 'The girl is named Friska. She's but seventeen. I doubt not she will play the wrist game most adroitly and with many a charming exclamation. I will converse with her, at length. I will question her, as I twist the crank, very slowly. And she will answer, she will comment, she will describe her feelings, in sounds if not in words. Sure you won't come?' And trailing an evil titter behind him, Hasjarl strode rapidly from the room, red torches in the archway outlining his monstrous bandy-legged form in blood.

Fafhrd ground his teeth. There was nothing he could do at the moment. Hasjarl's torture chamber was also his guard barrack. Yet the Northerner chalked up in his mind an intention, or perhaps an obligation.

To keep his mind from nasty unmanning imaginings, he began carefully to reread the tiny parchment book which Ningauble had given him as a sort of reward for past services, or an assurance for future ones, on the night of the Northerner's departure from Lankhmar.

Fafhrd did not worry about Hasjarl's sorcerers overlooking what he read. After their master's last threat they were all as furiously and elbow-jostlingly busy with their spells as so many bearded black ants.

Quarmall was first brought to my attention (*Fafhrd read in Ningauble's little handwritten, or tentacle-writ book*) by the report that certain passageways beneath it ran deep under the Sea and extended to certain caverns wherein might dwell some remnant of the Elder Ones. Naturally I dispatched agents to probe the truth of the report: two well-trained and valuable spies were sent (also two others to watch them) to find the facts and accumulate gossip. Neither pair returned nor did they send messages or tokens in explanation, or indeed word of any sort. I was interested; but being unable at that time, to spare valuable material on so uncertain and dangerous a quest, I bided my time until information should be placed at my disposal (as it usually is).

After twenty years my discretion was rewarded. (*So went the crabbed script as Fafhrd continued to read.*) An old man, horribly scarred and peculiarly pallid, was fetched to me. His name was Tamorg, and his tale interesting in spite of the teller's incoherence. He claimed to have been captured from a passing caravan when yet a small lad and carried into captivity within Quarmall. There he served as a slave on the Lower Levels, far below the ground. Here there was no natural light, and the only air was sucked down into the mazy caverns by means of large fans, treadmill-driven; hence his pallor and otherwise unusual appearance.

Tamorg was quite bitter about these fans, for he had been chained at one of those endless belts for a longer time than he cared to think about. (He really did not know exactly how long, since there was, by his own statement, no measure of time in the Lower Levels.) Finally he was released from his onerous walking, as nearly as I could glean from his garbled tale, by the invention or breeding of a specialized type of slave who better served the purpose.

From this I postulate that the Masters of Quarmall are sufficiently interested in the economics of their holdings to improve them: a rarity among overlords. Moreover, if these specialized slaves were bred, the life-span of these overlords must perforce be longer than ordinary; or else the cooperation between father and son is more perfect than any filial relationship I have yet noted.

Tamorg further related that he was put to more work digging, along with eight other slaves likewise taken from the treadmills. They were forced to enlarge and extend certain passages and chambers; so for another space of time he mined and buttressed. This time must have been long, for by close cross-questioning I found that Tamorg digged and walled, single-handed, a passage a thousand and twenty paces long. These slaves were not chained, unless maniacal, nor was it necessary to bind them so; for these Lower Levels seem to be a maze within a maze, and an unlucky slave once strayed from familiar paths stood small chance of retracing his steps. However, rumor has it, Tamorg said, that the Lords of Quarmall keep certain slaves who have memorized each a portion of the ever-extending labyrinth. By this means they are able to traverse with safety and communicate one level to the other.

Tamorg finally escaped by the simple expedient of accidentally breaking through the wall whereat he dug. He enlarged the opening with his mattock and stooped to peer. At that moment a fellow workman pushed against him and Tamorg was thrust head-foremost into the opening he had made. Fortunately it led into a chasm at the botom of which ran a swift but deep underground stream, into which Tamorg fell. As swimming is an art not easily forgotten, he managed to keep afloat until he reached the outer world. For several days he was blinded by the sun's rays and felt comfortable only by dim torchlight.

I questioned him in detail about the many interesting phenomena which must have been before him constantly but he was very unsatisfactory, being ignorant of all observational methods. However I placed him as gatekeeper in the palace of D – whose coming and going I desired to check upon. So much for that source of information.

My interest in Quarmall was aroused (*Ningauble's book went on*) and my appetite whetted by this scanty meal of facts, so I applied myself toward getting more information. Through my connection with Sheelba I made contact with Eeack, the Overlord of Rats; by holding out the lure of secret passages to the granaries of Lankhmar, he was persuaded to visit me. His visit proved both barren and embarrassing. Barren because it turned out that rats are eaten as a delicacy in Quarmall and hunted for culinary purposes by well-trained weasels. Naturally, under such circumstances, any rat within the walls of Quarmall stood little chance of doing liaison work except from the uncertain vantage of a pot. Eeack's personal cohort of countless rats, evil-smelling and famished, consumed all edibles within reach of their sharp teeth; and out of pity for the plight in which I was left Eeack favored me by cajoling Scraa to wake and speak with me.

Scraa (*Ningauble's notes continued*) is one of those eon-old roaches who existed contemporaneously with those monstrous reptiles which once ruled the world, and whose racial memories go back into the mistiness of time before the Elder Ones retreated from the surface. Scraa presented me the following short history of Quarmall neatly inscribed on a peculiar parchment composed of cleverly welded wingcases flattened and smoothed most subtly. I append his document and apologize for his somewhat dry and prosy style.

'The city-state of Quarmall houses a civilization almost unheard of in the sphere of anthropoid organization. Perhaps the closest analogy which might be made is to that of the slave-making ants. The domain of Quarmall is at the present day limited to the small mountain, or large hill, on which it stands; but like a radish the main portion of it lies buried beneath the surface. This was not always so.

'Once the Lords of Quarmall ruled over broad meadows and vast seas; their ships swam between all known ports and their caravans marched the routes from sea to sea. Slowly from the fertile valleys and barren cliffs, from the desert spots and the open sea the grip of Quarmall loosened; not willingly but ever forced did the Lords of Quarmall retreat. Inexorably they were driven, year by year, generation by generation, from all their possessions and rights; until finally they were confined to that last and staunchest stronghold, the impregnable castle of Quarmall. The cause of this driving is lost in the dimness of fable; but it was probably due to those most gruesome practices which even to this day persuade the surrounding countryside that Quarmall is unclean and cursed.

'As the Lords of Quarmall were pushed back, driven in spite of their sorceries and valor, they burrowed under that last, vast stronghold ever deeper and ever broader. Each succeeding Lord dug more deeply into the bowels of the small mount on which sat the Keep of Quarmall. Eventually the memory of past glories faded and was forgotten and the Lords of Quarmall concentrated on their mazy tunneling to the exclusion of the outer world. They would have forgotten the outer world entirely but for their constant and ever increasing need of slaves and of sustenance for those slaves.

'The Lords of Quarmall are magicians of great repute and adepts in the practice of the Art. It is said that by their skill they can charm men into bondage both of body and of soul.'

So much did Scraa write. All in all it is a very unsatisfactory bit of gossip: hardly a word about those intriguing passageways which first aroused my interest; nothing about the conformation of the Land or its inhabitants; not even a map! But then poor ancient Scraa lives almost entirely in the past – the present will not become important to him for another eon or so.

However I believe I know two fellows who might be persuaded to undertake a mission there . . . (*Here Ningauble's notes ended, much to Fafhrd's irritation and suspicious puzzlement – and carking shamed discomfort too, for now he must think again of the unknown girl Hasjarl was torturing.*

Outside the mount of Quarmall the sun was past meridian and shadows had begun to grow. The great white oxen threw their weight against the yoke. It was not the first time nor would it be the last, they knew. Each month as they approached this mucky stretch of road the master whipped and slashed them frantically, attempting to goad them into a speed which they, by nature, were unable to attain. Straining until the harness creaked, they obliged as best they could: for they knew that when this spot was pulled the master would reward them with a bit of salt, a rough caress, and a brief respite from work. It was unfortunate that this particular piece of road stayed mucky long after the rains had ceased; almost from one season to the next. Unfortunate that it took a longer time to pass.

Their master had reason to lash them so. This spot was accounted accursed among his people. From this curved eminence the towers of Quarmall could be spied on; and more important these towers looked down upon the road, even as one looking up could see them. It was not healthy to look on the towers of Quarmall, or to be looked upon by them. There was sufficient reason for this feeling. The master of the oxen spat surreptitiously, made an obvious gesture with his fingers, and glanced fearfully over his shoulder at the sky-thrusting lacy-topped towers as the last mudhole was traversed. Even in this fleeting glance he caught the glimpse of a flash, a brilliant scintillation, from the tallest keep. Shuddering, he leaped into the welcome covert of the trees and thanked the gods he worshiped for his escape.

Tonight he would have much to speak of in the tavern. Men would buy him bowls of wine to swill, and bitter beer of herbs. He could lord it for an evening. Ah! but for his quickness he might even now be plodding soulless to the mighty gates of Quarmall; there to serve until his body was no more and even after. For tales were told of such charmings, and of other things, among the elders of the village: tales that bore no moral but which all men did heed. Was it not only last Serpent Eve that young Twelm went from the ken of men? Had he not jeered at these very tales and, drunken, braved the terraces of Quarmall? Sure, and this was so! And it was also true that his less brave companion had seen him swagger with bravado to the last, the highest terrace, almost to the moat; then when Twelm, alarmed at some unknown cause, turned to run, his twisted-arched body was pulled willy-nilly back into the darkness. Not even a scream was heard to mark the passing of Twelm from this earth and the ken of his fellowmen. Juln, that less brave or less foolhardy companion of Twelm, had spent his time thenceforth in a continual drunken stupor. Nor would he stir from under roofs at night.

All the way to the village the master of the oxen pondered. He tried to formulate in his dim peasant intellect a method by which he might present himself as a hero. But even as he painfully constructed a simple, self-aggrandizing tale, he bethought himself of the fate of that one who had dared to brag of robbing Quarmall's vineyards; the one whose name was spoken only in a hushed whisper, secretly. So the driver decided to confine himself to facts, simple as they were, and trust to the atmosphere of horror that he knew any manifestation of activity in Quarmall would arouse.

While the driver was still whipping his oxen, and the Mouser watching two shadow-men play a thought-game, and Fafhrd swilling wine to drown the thought of an unknown girl in pain – at the same time Quarmal, Lord of Quarmall, was casting his own horoscope for the coming year. In the highest tower of the Keep he labored, putting in order the huge astrolabe and the other massive instruments necessary for his accurate observations.

Through curtains of broidery the afternoon sun beat hotly into the small chamber; beams glanced from the polished surfaces and scintillated into rainbow hues as they reflected askew. It was warm, even for an old man lightly gowned, and Quarmal stepped to the windows opposite the sun and drew the broidery aside, letting the cool moor-breeze blow through his observatory.

He glanced idly out the deep-cut embrasures. In the distance down past the terraced slopes he could see the little, curved brown thread of road which led eventually to the village.

Like ants the small figures on it appeared: ants struggling through some sticky trap; and like ants, even as Quarmal watched, they persisted and finally disappeared. Quarmal sighed as he turned away from the windows. Sighed in a slight disappointment because he regretted not having looked a moment sooner. Slaves were always needed. Besides, it would have been an opportunity for trying out a recently invented instrument or two.

Yet it was never Quarmal's way to regret the past, so with a shrug he turned away.

For an old man Quarmal was not particularly hideous until his eyes were noticed. They were peculiar in their shape and the ball was rich ruby-red. The dead-white iris had that nauseous sheen of pearly iridescence found only in the sea dwellers among living creatures; this character he inherited from his mother, a mer-woman. The pupils, like specks of black crystal, sparkled with incredible malevolent intelligence.

His baldness was accentuated by the long tufts of coarse black hair which grew symmetrically over each ear. Pale, pitted skin hung loosely on his jowls, but was tightly drawn over the high cheekbones. Thin as a sharpened blade, his long jutting nose gave him the appearance of an old hawk or kestrel.

If Quarmal's eyes were the most arresting feature in his countenance, his mouth was the most beautiful. The lips were full and ruddy, remarkable in so aged a man, and they had that peculiar mobility found in some elocutionists and orators and actors. Had it been possible for Quarmal to have known vanity, he might have been vain about the beauty of his mouth; as it was this perfectly molded mouth served only to accentuate the horror of his eyes.

He looked up veiledly now through the iron rondures of the astrolobe at the twin of his own face pushing forth from a windowless square of the opposite wall: it was his own waxen life-mask, taken within the year and most realistically tinted and blackly hair-tufted by his finest artist, save that the white-irised eyes were of necessity closed – though the mask still gave a feeling of peering. The mask was the last in several rows of such, each a little more age-darkened than the succeeding one. Though some were ugly and many were elderly-handsome, there was a strong family resemblance between the shut-eyed faces, for there had been few if any intrusions into the male lineage of Quarmall.

There were perhaps fewer masks than might have been expected, for most Lords of Quarmall lived very long and had sons late. Yet there were also a considerable many, since Quarmall was such an ancient rulership. The oldest masks were of a brown almost black and not wax at all but the cured and mummified face skins of those primeval autocrats. The arts of flaying and tanning had early been brought to an exquisite degree of perfection in Quarmall and were still practiced with jealously prideful skill.

Quarmal dropped his gaze from the mask to his lightly-robed body. He was a lean man, and his hips and shoulders still gave evidence that once he had hawked, hunted, and fenced with the best. His feet were high-arched and his step was still light. Long and spatulate were his knob-knuckled fingers, while fleshy muscular palms gave witness to their dexterity and nimbleness, a necessary advantage to one of his calling. For Quarmal was a sorcerer, as were all the Lords of Quarmall from the eon-mighty past. From childhood up through manhood each male was trained into his calling, like some vines are coaxed to twist and thread a difficult terrace.

As Quarmal returned from the window to attend his duties he pondered on his training. It was unfortunate for the House of Quarmall that he possessed two instead of the usual single heir. Each of his sons was a creditable necromancer and well skilled in other sciences pertaining to the Art; both were exceedingly ambitious and filled with hatred. Hatred not only for one another but for Quarmal their father.

Quarmal pictured in his mind Hasjarl in his Upper Levels below the Keep and Gwaay below Hasjarl in his Lower Levels . . . Hasjarl cultivating his passions as if in some fiery circle of Hell, making energy and movement and logic carried to the ultimate the greatest goods, constantly threatening with whips and tortures and carrying through those threats, and now hiring a great brawling beast of a man to be his sworder . . . Gwaay nourishing restraint as if in Hell's frigidest circle, trying to reduce all life to art and intuitive thought, seeking by meditation to compel lifeless rock to do his bidding and constrain Death by the power of his will, and now hiring a small gray man like Death's younger brother to be his knifer . . . Quarmal thought of Hasjarl and Gwaay and for a moment a strange smile of fatherly pride bent his lips and then he shook his head and his smile became stranger still and he shuddered very faintly.

It was well, thought Quarmal, that he was an old man, far past his prime, even as magicians counted years, for it would be unpleasant to cease living in the prime of life, or even in the twilight of life's day. And he knew that sooner or later, in spite of all protecting charms and precautions, Death would creep silently on him or spring suddenly from some unguarded moment. This very night his horoscope might signal Death's instant escapeless approach; and though men lived by lies, treating truth's very self as lie to be exploited, the stars remained the stars.

Each day Quarmal's sons, he knew, grew more clever and more subtle in their usage of the Art which he had taught them. Nor could Quarmal protect himself by slaying them. Brother might murder brother, or the son his sire, but it was forbidden from ancient times for the father to slay his son. There were no very good reasons for this custom, nor were any needed. Custom in the House of Quarmall stood unchallenged, and it was not lightly defied.

Quarmal bethought him of the babe sprouting in the womb of Kewissa, the childlike favorite concubine of his age. So far as his precautions and watchfulness might have enforced that babe was surely his own – and Quarmal was the most watchful and cynically realistic of men. If that babe lived and proved a boy – as omens foretold it would be – and if Quarmal were given but twelve more years to train him, and if Hasjarl and Gwaay should be taken by the fates or each other . . .

Quarmal clipped off in his mind this line of speculation. To expect to live a dozen more years with Hasjarl and Gwaay growing daily more clever-subtle in their sorceries – or to hope for the dual extinguishment of two such cautious sprigs of his own flesh – were vanity and irrealism indeed!

He looked around him. The preliminaries for the casting were completed, the instruments prepared and aligned; now only the final observations and their interpretation were required. Lifting a small leaden hammer Quarmal lightly struck a brazen gong. Hardly had the resonance faded when the tall, richly appareled figure of a man appeared in the arched doorway.

Flindach was Master of the Magicians. His duties were many but not easily apparent. His power carefully concealed was second only to that of Quarmal. A wearied cruelty sat upon his dark visage, giving him an air of boredom which ill matched the consuming interest he took in the affairs of others. Flindach was not a comely man: a purple wine mark covered his left cheek, three large warts made an isosceles triangle on his right, while his nose and chin jutted like those of an old witch. Startlingly, with an effect of mocking irreverence, his eyes were ruby-whited and pearly-irised like those of his lord; he was a younger offspring of the same mer-woman who had birthed

Quarmal – after Quarmal's father had done with her and following one of Quarmal's bizzare customs, had given her to *his* Master of Magicians.

Now those eyes of Flindach, large and hypnotically staring, shifted uneasily as Quarmal spoke: 'Gwaay and Hasjarl, my sons, work today on their respective Levels. It would be well if they were called into the council room this night. For it is the night on which my doom is to be foretold. And I sense premonitorily that this casting will bear no good. Bid them dine together and permit them to amuse one another by plotting at my death – or by attempting each other's.'

He shut his lips precisely as he finished, and looked more evil than a man expecting Death should look. Flindach, used to terrors in the line of business, could scarcely repress a shudder at the glance bestowed on him; but remembering his position he made the sign of obeisance, and without a word or backward look departed.

The Gray Mouser did not once remove his gaze from Flindach as the latter strode across the domed dim sorcery chamber of the Lower Level until he reached Gwaay's side. The Mouser was mightily intrigued by the warts and wine mark on the cheeks of the richly-robed witch-faced man, and by his eerie red-whited eyes, and he instantly gave this charming visage a place of honor in the large catalog of freak-faces he stored in his memory vaults.

Although he strained his ears, he could not hear what Flindach said to Gwaay or what Gwaay answered.

Gwaay finished the telekinetic game he was playing by sending all his black counters across the midline in a great rutching surge that knocked half his opponent's white counters tumbling into his loinclothed lap. Then he rose smoothly from his tool.

'I sup tonight with my beloved brother in my all-revered father's apartments,' he pronounced mellowly to all. 'While I am there and in the escort of great Flindach here, no sorcerous spells may harm me. So you may rest for a space from your protective concentrations, oh my gracious magi of the First Rank.' He turned to go.

The Mouser, inwardly leaping at the chance to glimpse the

sky again, if only by chilly night, rose springily too from his chair and called out, 'Ho, Prince Gwaay! Though safe from spells, will you not want the warding of my blades at this dinner party? There's many a great prince never made king 'cause he was served cold iron 'twixt the ribs between the soup and the fish. I also juggle most prettily and do conjuring tricks.'

Gwaay half turned back. 'Nor may steel harm me while my sire's hand is stretched above,' he called so softly that the Mouser felt the words were being lobbed like feather balls barely as far as his ear. 'Stay here, Gray Mouser.'

His tone was unmistakably rebuffing, nevertheless the Mouser, dreading a dull evening, persisted, 'There is also the matter of that serious spell of mine of which I told you, Prince – a spell most effective against magi of the *Second* Rank and lower, such as a certain noxious brother employs. Now were a good time—'

'Let there be no sorcery tonight!' Gwaay cut him off sternly, though speaking hardly louder than before. ' 'Twere an insult to my sire and to his great servant Flindach here, a Master of Magicians, even to think of such! Bide quietly, swordsman, keep peace, and speak no more.' His voice took on a pious note. 'There will be time enough for sorcery and swords, if slaying there must be.'

Flindach nodded solemnly at that and they silently departed. The Mouser sat down. Rather to his surprise, he noted that the twelve aged sorcerers were already curled up like pillbugs on their sides on their great chairs and snoring away. He could not even while away time by challenging one of them to the thought-game, hoping to learn by playing, or to a bout at conventional chess. This promised to be a most glum evening indeed.

Then a thought brightened the Mouser's swarthy visage. He lifted his hands, cupping the palms, and clapped them lightly together as he had seen Gwaay do.

The slim slavegirl Ivivis instantly appeared in the far archway. When she saw that Gwaay was gone and his sorcerers slumbering, her eyes became bright as a kitten's. She scampered to the Mouser, her slender legs flashing, seated herself with a last bound on his lap, and clapped her lissome arms around him.

Fafhrd silently faded back into a dark side passage as Hasjarl came hurrying along the torchlit corridor beside a richly robed official with hideously warted and mottled face and red eyeballs, on whose other side strode a pallid comely youth with strangely ancient eyes. Fafhrd had never before met Flindach or, of course, Gwaay.

Hasjarl was clearly in a pet, for he was grimacing insanely and twisting his hands together furiously as though pitting one in murderous battle against the other. His eyes, however, were tightly shut. As he stamped swiftly past, Fafhrd thought he glimpsed a bit of tattooing on the nearest upper eyelid.

Fafhrd heard the red-eyeballed one say, 'No need to run to your sire's banquet-board, Lord Hasjarl. We're in good time.' Hasjarl answered only a snarl, but the pale youth said sweetly, 'My brother is ever a baroque pearl of dutifulness.'

Fafhrd moved forward, watched the three out of sight, then turned the other way and followed the scent of hot iron straight to Hasjarl's torture chamber.

It was a wide, low-vaulted room and the brightest Fafhrd had yet encountered in these murky, misnamed Upper Levels.

To the right was a low table around which crouched five squat brawny men more bandy-legged than Hasjarl and masked each to the upper lip. They were noisily gnawing bones snatched from a huge platter of them, and swilling ale from leather jacks. Four of the masks were black, one red.

Beyond them was a fire of coals in a circular brick tower half as high as a man. The iron grill above it glowed redly. The coals brightened almost to white, then grew more deeply red again, as a twisted half-bald hag in tatters slowly worked a bellows.

Along the walls to either side, there thickly stood or hung various metal and leather instruments which showed their foul purpose by their ghostly hand-and-glove resemblance to various outer surfaces and inward orifices of the human body: boots, collars, masks, iron maidens, funnels, and the like.

To the left a fair-haired pleasingly plump girl in white

under tunic lay bound to a rack. Her right hand in an iron half-glove stretched out tautly toward a machine with a crank. Although her face was tear-streaked, she did not seem to be in present pain.

Fafhrd strode toward her, hurriedly slipping out of his pouch and onto the middle finger of his right hand the massy ring Hasjarl's emissary had given him in Lankhmar as token from his master. It was of silver, holding a large black seal on which was Hasjarl's sign: a clenched fist.

The girl's eyes widened with new fears as she saw Fafhrd coming.

Hardly looking at her as he paused by the rack, Fafhrd turned toward the table of masked messy feasters, who were staring at him gape-mouthed by now. Stretching out toward them the back of his right hand, he called harshly yet carelessly, 'By authority of this sigil, release to me the girl Friska!' From mouth-corner he muttered to the girl, 'Courage!'

The black-masked creature who came hurrying toward him like a terrier appeared either not to recognize at once Hasjarl's sign or else not to reason out its import, for he said only, wagging a greasy finger, 'Begone, barbarian. This dainty morsel is not for you. Think not to quench your rough lusts here. Our Master—'

Fafhrd cried out, 'If you will not accept the authority of the Clenched Fist one way, then you must take it the other.' Doubling up the hand with the ring on it, he smashed it against the torturer's suet-shining jaw so that he stretched himself out on the dark flags, skidded a foot, and lay quietly.

Fafhrd turned at once toward the half-risen feasters and slapping Graywand's hilt but not drawing it, he planted his knuckles on his hips and, addressing himself to the red mask, he barked out rather like Hasjarl, 'Our Master of the Fist had an afterthought and ordered me to fetch the girl Friska so that he might continue her entertainment at dinner for the amusement of those he goes to dine with. Would you have a new servant like myself report to Hasjarl your derelictions and delays? Loose her quickly and I'll say nothing.' He stabbed a finger at the hag by the bellows, 'You! – fetch her outer dress.'

The masked ones sprang to obey quickly enough at that, their tucked-up masks falling over their mouths and chins. There were mumblings of apology, which he ignored. Even the one he had slugged got groggily to his feet and tried to help.

The girl had been released from her wrist-twisting device, Fafhrd supervising, and she was sitting up on the side of the rack when the hag came with a dress and two slippers, the toe of one stuffed with oddments of ornament and such. The girl reached for them, but Fafhrd grabbed them instead and, seizing her by the left arm, dragged her roughly to her feet.

'No time for that now,' he commanded. 'We will let Hasjarl decide how he wants you trigged out for the sport,' and without more ado he strode from the torture chamber, dragging her beside him, though again muttering from mouth-side, 'Courage.'

When they were around the first bend in the corridor and had reached a dark branching, he stopped and looked at her frowningly. Her eyes grew wide with fright; she shrank from him, but then firming her features she said fearful-boldly, 'If you rape me by the way, I'll tell Hasjarl.'

'I don't mean to rape but rescue you, Friska,' Fafhrd assured her rapidly. 'That talk of Hasjarl sending to fetch you was but my trick. Where's a secret place I can hide you for a few days? – until we flee these musty crypts forever! I'll bring you food and drink.'

At that Friska looked far more frightened. 'You mean Hasjarl didn't order this? And that you dream of escaping from Quarmall? Oh stranger, Hasjarl would only have twisted my wrist a little longer, perhaps not maimed me much, only heaped a few more indignities, certainly spared my life. But if he so much as suspected that I had sought to escape from Quarmall . . . Take me back to the torture chamber!'

'That I will not,' Fafhrd said irkedly, his gaze darting up and down the empty corridor. 'Take heart, girl. Quarmall's not the wide world. Quarmall's not the stars and the sea. Where's a secret room?'

'Oh, it's hopeless,' she faltered. 'We could never escape. The stars are a myth. Take me back.'

'And make myself out a fool? No.' Fafhrd retorted harshly. 'We're rescuing you from Hasjarl and from Quarmall too. Make up your mind to it, Friska, for I won't be budged. If you try to scream I'll stop your mouth. *Where's a secret room?*' In his exasperation he almost twisted her wrist, but remembered in time and only brought his face close to hers and rasped, '*Think!*' She had a scent like heather underlying the odor of sweat and tears.

Her eyes went distant then and she said in a small voice, almost dreamlike, 'Between the Upper and the Lower Levels there is a great hall with many small rooms adjoining. Once it was a busy and teeming part of Quarmall, they say, but now debated ground between Hasjarl and Gwaay. Both claim it, neither will maintain it, not even sweep its dust. It is called the Ghost Hall.' Her voice went smaller still. 'Gwaay's page once begged me meet him a little this side of there, but I did not dare.'

'Ha, that's the very place,' Fafhrd said with a grin. 'Lead us to it.'

'But I don't remember the way,' Friska protested. 'Gwaay's page told me, but I tried to forget . . .'

Fafhrd had spotted a spiral stair in the dark branchway. Now he strode instantly toward it, drawing Friska along beside him.

'We know we have to start by going down,' he said with rough cheer. 'Your memory will improve with motion, Friska.'

The Gray Mouser and Ivivis had solaced themselves with such kisses and caresses as seemed prudent in Gwaay's Hall of Sorcery, or rather now of Sleeping Sorcerers. Then, at first coaxed chiefly by Ivivis, it is true, they had visited a nearby kitchen, where the Mouser had readily wheedled from the lumpish cook three large thin slices of medium-rare unmistakable rib-beef, which he had devoured with great satisfaction.

At least one of his appetites mollified, the Mouser had consented that they continue their little ramble and even pause to view a mushroom field. Most strange it had been to see, betwixt the rough-finished pillars of rock, the rows of white button-fungi grow dim, narrow, and converge toward infinity in the ammonia-scented darkness.

At this point they had become teasing in the talks, he taxing

Ivivis with having many lovers drawn by her pert beauty, she stoutly denying it, but finally admitting that there was a certain Klevis, page to Gwaay, for whom her heart had once or twice beat faster.

'And best, Gray Guest, you keep an eye open for him,' she had warned, wagging a slim finger, 'for certain he is the fiercest and most skillful of Gwaay's swordsmen.'

Then to change this topic and to reward the Mouser for his patience in viewing the mushroom field, she had drawn him, they going hand in hand now, to a wine cellar. There she had prettily begged the aged and cranky butler for a great tankard of amber fluid for her companion. It had proved to the Mouser's delight to be purest and most potent essence of grape with no bitter admixture whatever.

Two of his appetites now satisfied, the third returned to the Mouser more hotly. Hand-holding became suddenly merely tantalizing and Ivivis' pale green tunic no more an object for admiration and for compliments to her, but only a barrier to be got rid of as swiftly as possible and with the smallest necessary modicum of decorousness.

Himself taking the lead, he drew her as directly as he could recall the route, and with little speech, toward the closet he had preempted for his loot, two levels below Gwaay's Hall of Sorcery. At last he found the corridor he sought, one hung to either side with thick purple arras and lit by infrequent copper chandeliers which hung each from the rock ceiling on three copper chains and held three thick black candles.

This far Ivivis followed him with only the fewest flirtatious balkings and a minimum of wondering, innocent-eyed questions as to what he intended and why such haste was needful. But now her hesitations became convincing, her eyes began to show a genuine uneasiness, or even fearfulness, and when he stopped by the arras-slit before the door to his closet and with the courtliest of lecherous smirks he could manage indicated to her that they had reached their destination, she drew sharply back, stifling an exclamation with the flat of her hand.

'Gray Mouser,' she whispered rapidly, her eyes at once frightened and beseeching, 'there is a confession I should have made earlier and now must make at once. By one of those malign and mocking coincidences which haunt all Quarmall, you have chosen for your hidey-hole the very chamber where—'

Well it was for the Gray Mouser then that he took seriously Ivivis' look and tone, that he was by nature sense-aware and distrustful, and in particular that his ankles now took note of a slight yet unaccustomed draft from under the arras. For without other warning a fist pointed with a dark dagger punched through the arras-slit at his throat.

With the edge of his left hand, which had been raised to indicate to Ivivis their bedding-place, the Mouser struck aside the black-sleeved arm.

The girl exclaimed, not loudly, 'Klevis!'

With his right hand the Mouser caught hold of the wrist going by him and twisted it. With his spread left hand he simultaneously rammed his attacker in the armpit.

But the Mouser's grip, made by hurried snatch, was imperfect. Moreover, Klevis was not minded to resist and have his arm dislocated or broken in that fashion. Spinning with the Mouser's twist, he also went into a deliberate forward somersault.

The net result was that Klevis lost his cross-gripped dagger, which clattered dully on the thick-carpeted floor, but tore loose unhurt from the Mouser and after two more somersaults came lightly to his feet, at once turning and drawing rapier.

By then the Mouser had drawn Scalpel and his dirk Cat's Claw too, but held the latter behind him. He attacked cautiously, with probing feints. When Klevis counterattacked strongly, he retreated, parrying each fierce thrust at the last moment, so that again and again the enemy blade went whickering close by him.

Klevis lunged with especial fierceness. The Mouser parried, high this time and not retreating. In an instant they were pressed body to body, their rapiers strongly engaged near their hilts and above their heads.

By turning a little, the Mouser blocked Klevis' knee driven at his groin. While with the dirk Klevis had overlooked, he stabbed the other from below, Cat's Claw entering just under Klevis' breastbone to pierce his liver, gizzard, and heart.

Letting go his dirk, the Mouser nudged the body away from him and turned.

Ivivis was facing them, with Klevis' punching-dagger gripped ready for a thrust.

The body thudded to the floor.

'Which of us did you propose to skewer?' the Mouser asked.

'I don't know,' the girl answered in a flat voice. 'You, I suppose.'

The Mouser nodded. 'Just before this interruption, you were saying, "The very chamber where—' What?'

'—where I often met Klevis, to be with him,' she replied.

Again the Mouser nodded. 'So you loved him and—'

'Shut up, you fool!' she interrupted. '*Is he dead?*' There were both deep concern and exasperation in her voice.

The Mouser backed along the body until he stood at the head of it. Looking down, he said, 'As mutton. He was a handsome youth.'

For a long moment they eyed each other like leopards across the corpse. Then, averting her face a little, Ivivis said, 'Hide the body, you imbecile. It tears my heartstrings to see it.'

Nodding, the Mouser stooped and rolled the corpse under the arras opposite the closet door. He tucked in Klevis' rapier beside him. Then he withdrew Cat's Claw from the body. Only a little dark blood followed. He cleaned his dirk on the arras, then let the hanging drop.

Standing up, he snatched the punching-dagger from the brooding girl and flipped it so that it too vanished under the arras.

With one hand he spread wide the slit in the arras. With the other he took hold of Ivivis' shoulder and pressed her toward the doorway which Klevis had left open to his undoing.

She instantly shook loose from his grip, but walked through the doorway. The Mouser followed. The leopard look was still in both their eyes.

A single torch lit the closet. The Mouser shut the door and barred it.

Ivivis snarled at him, summing it up: 'You owe me much, Gray Stranger.'

The Mouser showed his teeth in an unhumorous grin. He

did not stop to see whether his stolen trinkets had been disturbed. It did not even occur to him, then, to do so.

Fafhrd felt relief when Friska told him that the darker slit at the very end of the dark, long, straight corridor they'd just entered was the door to the Ghost Hall. It had been a hurrying, nervous trip, with many peerings around corners and dartings back into dark alcoves while someone passed, and a longer trip vertically downward than Fafhrd had anticipated. If they had now only reached the top of the Lower Levels, this Quarmall must be bottomless! Yet Friska's spirits had improved considerably. Now at times she almost skipped along in her white chemise cut low behind. Fafhrd strode purposefully, her dress and slippers in his left hand, his ax in his right.

The Northerner's relief in no wise diminished his wariness, so that when someone rushed from an inky tunnel-mouth they were passing, he stroked out almost negligently and he felt and heard his ax crunch halfway through a head.

He saw a comely blond youth, now most sadly dead and his comeliness rather spoiled by Fafhrd's ax, which still stood in the great wound it had made. A fair hand opened and the sword it had held fell from it.

'Hovis!' he heard Friska cry. 'O gods! O gods that are not here. Hovis!'

Lifting a booted foot, Fafhrd stamped it sideways at the youth's chest, at once freeing his ax and sending the corpse back into the tunneled dark from which the live man had so rashly hurtled.

After a swift look and listen all about, he turned toward Friska where she stood white-faced and staring.

'Who's this Hovis?' he demanded, shaking her lightly by the shoulder when she did not reply.

Twice her mouth opened and shut again, while her face remained as expressionless as that of a silly fish. Then with a little gasp she said, 'I lied to you, barbarian. I have met Gwaay's page Hovis here. More than once.'

'Then why didn't you warn me, wench?' Fafhrd demanded. 'Did you think I would scold you for your morals, like some city graybeard? Or have you no regard at all for your men, Friska?'

'Oh, do not chide me,' Friska begged miserably. 'Please do not chide me.'

Fafhrd patted her shoulder. 'There, there,' he said. 'I forget you were shortly tortured and hardly of a mind to remember everything. Come on.'

They had taken a dozen steps when Friska began to shudder and sob together in a swiftly mounting crescendo. She turned and ran back, crying, 'Hovis! Hovis, forgive me!'

Fafhrd caught her before three steps. He shook her again and when that did not stop her sobbing, he used his other hand to slap her twice, rocking her head a little.

She stared at him dumbly.

He said not fiercely but somberly, 'Friska, I must tell you that Hovis is where your words and tears can never again reach him. He's dead. Beyond recall. Also, I killed him. That's beyond recall too. But you are still alive. You can hide from Hasjarl. Ultimately, whether you believe it or not, you can escape with me from Quarmall. Now come on with me, and no looking back.'

She blindly obeyed, with only the faintest of moanings.

The Gray Mouser stretched luxuriously on the silver-tipped bearskin he'd thrown on the floor of his closet. Then he lifted on an elbow and, finding the black pearls he'd pilfered, tried them against Ivivis' bosom in the pale cool light of the single torch above. Just as he'd imagined, the pearls looked very well there. He started to fasten them around her neck.

'No, Mouser,' she objected lazily. 'It awakens an unpleasant memory.'

He did not persist, but lying back again, said unguardedly, 'Ah, but I'm a lucky man, Ivivis. I have you and I have an employer who, though somewhat boresome with his sorceries and his endless mild speaking, seems a harmless enough chap and certainly more endurable than his brother Hasjarl, if but half of what I hear of that one is true.'

The voice of Ivivis briskened. 'You think Gwaay harmless? – and kinder than Hasjarl? La, that's a quaint conceit. Why, but a week ago he summoned my late dearest friend, Divis, then his favorite concubine, and telling her it was a necklace of the same stones, hung around her neck an emerald adder, the sting of which is infallibly deadly.'

The Mouser turned his head and stared at Ivivis. 'Why did Gwaay do that?' he asked.

She stared back at him blankly. 'Why, for nothing at all, to be sure,' she said wonderingly. 'As everyone knows, that is Gwaay's way.'

The Mouser said, 'You mean that, rather than say, "I am wearied of you," he killed her?'

Ivivis nodded. 'I believe Gwaay can no more bear to hurt people's feelings by rejecting them than he can bear to shout.'

'It is better to be slain than rejected?' the Mouser questioned ingenuously.

'No, but for Gwaay it is easier on his feelings to slay than to reject. Death is everywhere here in Quarmall.'

The Mouser had a fleeting vision of Klevis' corpse stiffening behind the arras.

Ivivis continued, 'Here in the Lower Levels we are buried before we are born. We live, love, and die buried. Even when we strip, we yet wear a garment of invisible mold.'

The Mouser said, 'I begin to understand why it is necessary to cultivate a certain callousness in Quarmall, to be able to enjoy at all any moments of pleasure snatched from life, or perhaps I mean from death.'

'That is most true, Gray Mouser,' Ivivis said very soberly, pressing herself against him.

Fafhrd started to brush aside the cobwebs joining the two dust-filmed sides of the half open, high, nail-studded door, then checked himself and bending very low ducked under them.

'Do you stoop too,' he told Friska. 'It were best we leave no signs of our entry. Later I'll attend to our footprints in the dust, if that be needful.'

They advanced a few paces, then stood hand in hand, waiting for their eyes to grow accustomed to the darkness. Fafhrd still clutched in his other hand Friska's dress and slippers.

'This is the Ghost Hall?' Fafhrd asked.

'Aye,' Friska whispered close to his ear, sounding fearful. 'Some say that Gwaay and Hasjarl send their dead to battle here. Some say that demons owing allegiance to neither—'

'No more of that girl,' Fafhrd ordered gruffly. 'If I must battle devils or liches, leave me my hearing and my courage.'

They were silent a space then while the flame of the last torch twenty paces beyond the half shut door slowly revealed to them a vast chamber low-domed with huge, rough black blocks pale-mortared for a ceiling. It was set out with a few tatter-shrouded furnishings and showed many small closed doorways. To either side were wide rostra set a few feet above floor level, and toward the center there was, surprisingly, what looked like a dried-up fountain pool.

Friska whispered, 'Some say the Ghost Hall was once the harem of the father lords of Quarmall during some centuries when they dwelt underground between Levels, ere this Quarmal's father coaxed by his sea-wife returned to the Keep. See, they left so suddenly that the new ceiling was neither finish-polished, nor final cemented, nor embellished with drawings, if such were purposed.'

Fafhrd nodded. He distrusted that unpillared ceiling and thought the whole place looked rather more primitive than Hasjarl's polished and leather-hung chambers. That gave him a thought.

'Tell me, Friska,' he said. 'How is it that Hasjarl can see with his eyes closed? Is it that—'

'Why, do you not know that?' she interrupted in surprise. 'Do you not know even the secret of his horrible peeping? He simply—'

A dim velvet shape that chittered almost inaudibly shrill swooped past their faces and with a little shriek Friska hid her face in Fafhrd's chest and clung to him tightly.

In combing his fingers through her heather-scented hair to show her no flying mouse had found lodgment there and in smoothing his palms over her bare shoulders and back to demonstrate that no bat had landed there either, Fafhrd began to forget all about Hasjarl and the puzzle of his second sight – and his worries about the ceiling falling in on them too.

Following custom, Friska shrieked twice, very softly.

Gwaay languidly clapped his white, perfectly groomed hands

and with a slight nod motioned for the waiting slaves to remove the platters from the low table. He leaned lazily into the deep-cushioned chair and through half-closed lids looked momentarily at his companion before he spoke. His brother across the table was not in a good humor. But then it was rare for Hasjarl to be other than in a pet, a temper, or more often merely sullen and vicious. This may have been due to the fact that Hasjarl was a very ugly man, and his nature had grown to confirm to his body; or perhaps it was the other way around. Gwaay was indifferent to both theories; he merely knew that in one glance all his memory had told him of Hasjarl was verified; and he again realized the bitter magnitude of his hatred for his brother. However, Gwaay spoke gently in a low, pleasant voice:

'Well, how now, Brother, shall we play at chess, that demon game they say exists in every world? 'Twill give you a chance to lord it over me again. You always win at chess, you know, except when you resign. Shall I have the board set before us?' and then cajolingly, 'I'll give you a pawn!' and he raised one hand slightly as if to clap again in order that his suggestion might be carried out.

With the lash he carried slung to his wrist Hasjarl slashed the face of the slave nearest him, and silently pointed at the massive and ornate chessboard across the room. This was quite characteristic of Hasjarl. He was a man of action and given to few words, at least away from his home territory.

Besides, Hasjarl was in a nasty humor. Flindach had torn him from his most interesting and exciting amusement: torture! And for what? thought Hasjarl: to play at chess with his prigish brother; to sit and look at his pretty brother's face; to eat food that would surely disagree with him; to wait the answer to the casting, which he already knew – had known for years; and finally to be forced to smile into the horrible blood-whited eyes of his father, unique in Quarmall save for those of Flindach, and toast the House of Quarmall for the ensuing year. All this was most distasteful to Hasjarl and he showed it plainly.

The slave, a bloody welt swift-swelling across his face, carefully slid the chessboard between the two. Gwaay smiled as another slave arranged the chessmen precisely on their squares; he had thought of a scheme to annoy his brother. He had chosen the black as usual and he planned a gambit which he knew his avaricious opponent couldn't refuse; one Hasjarl would accept to his own undoing.

Hasjarl sat grimly back in his chair, arms folded. 'I should have made you take white,' he complained. 'I know the paltry tricks you can do with black pebbles – I've seen you as a girl-pale child darting them through the air to startle the slaves' brats. How am I to know you will not cheat by fingerless shifting your pieces while I deep ponder?'

Gwaay answered gently, 'My paltry powers, as you most justly appraise them, Brother, extend only to bits of basalt, trifles of obsidian and other volcanic rocks conformable to my nether level. While these chess pieces are jet, Brother, which in your great scholarship you surely know is only a kind of coal, vegetable stuff pressed black, not even in the same realm as the very few materials subject to my small magickings. Moreover, for you to miss the slightest trick with those quaint slave-surgeried eyes of yours, Brother, were matter for mighty wonder.'

Hasjarl growled. Not until all was ready did he stir; then, like an adder's strike, he plucked a black rook's pawn from the board and with a sputtering giggle, snarled: 'Remember, Brother? It was a pawn you promised! Move!'

Gwaay motioned the waiting slave to advance his king's pawn. In like manner Hasjarl replied. A moment's pause and Gwaay offered his gambit: pawn to king-bishop's fourth! Eagerly Hasjarl snatched the apparent advantage and the game began in earnest. Gwaay, his face easy-smiling in repose, seeming to be less interested in the game than in the shadow play of the flickering lamps on the figured leather upholsterings of calfskin, lambskin, snakeskin, and even slaveskin and nobler human hide; seeming to move offhand, without plan, yet confidently. Hasjarl, his lips compressed in concentration, was intent on the board, each move a planned action both mental and physical. His concentration made him for the moment oblivious of his brother, oblivious of all but the problem before him; for Hasjarl loved to win beyond all computation.

It had always been this way; even as children the contrast

was apparent. Hasjarl was the elder; older by only a few months which his appearance and demeanor lengthened to years. His long, misshapen torso was ill-borne on short bandy legs. His left arm was perceptibly longer than the right; and his fingers, peculiarly webbed to the first knuckle, were gnarled and stubby with brittle striated nails. It was as if Hasjarl were a poorly reconstructed puzzle put together in such fashion that all the pieces were mismated and awry.

This was particularly true of his features. He possessed his sire's nose, though thickened and coarse-pored; but this was contradicted by the thin-lipped, tightly compressed mouth continually pursed until it had assumed a perpetual sphincter-like appearance. Hair, lank and lusterless, grew low on his forehead; and low, flattened cheekbones added yet another contradiction.

As a lad, led by some perverse whim, Hasjarl had bribed, coaxed, or more probably browbeaten one of the slaves versed in surgery to perform a slight operation on his upper eyelids. It was a small enough thing in itself, yet its implications and results had affected the lives of many men unpleasantly, and never ceased to delight Hasjarl.

That merely the piercing of two small holes, centered over the pupil when the eyes were closed, could produce such qualms in other people was incredible; but it was so. Featherweight grommets of sleekest gold, jade or – as now – ivory – kept the holes from growing shut.

When Hasjarl peered through these tiny apertures it gave the effect of an ambush and made the object of his gaze feel spied upon; but this was the least annoying of his many irritating habits.

Hasjarl did nothing easily but he did all things well. Even in swordplay his constant practice and overly long left arm made him the equal of the athletic Gwaay. His administration of the Upper Levels over which he ruled was above all things economical and smooth; for woe betide the slave who failed in the slightest detail of his duties. Hasjarl saw and punished.

Hasjarl was well nigh the equal of his teacher in the practice of the Art; and he had gathered about him a band of magicians almost the caliber of Flindach himself. But he was not happy in his prowess so hardly won, for between the absolute power which he desired and the realization of that desire stood two obstacles: the Lord of Quarmall whom he feared above all things; and his brother Gwaay whom he hated with a hatred nourished on envy and fed by his own thwarted desires.

Gwaay, antithetically, was supple of limb, well-formed and good to look upon. His eyes, wide-set and pale, were deceptively gentle and kindly; for they masked a will as strong and capable of action as coiled spring-steel. His continual residence in the Lower Levels over which he ruled gave to his pallid smooth skin a peculiar waxy luster.

Gwaay possessed that enviable ability to do all things well, with little exertion and less practice. In a way he was much worse than his brother: for while Hasjarl slew with tortures and slow pain and an obvious personal satisfaction, he at least attached some importance to life because he was so meticulous in its taking; whereas Gwaay smiling gently would slay, without reason, as if jesting. Even the group of sorcerers which he had gathered about him for protection and amusement was not safe from his fatal and swift humors.

Some thought that Gwaay was a stranger to fear, but this was not so. He feared the Lord of Quarmall and he feared his brother; or rather he feared that he would be slain by his brother before he could slay him. Yet so well were his fear and hatred concealed that he could sit relaxed, not two yards from Hasjarl, and smile amusedly, enjoying every moment of the evening. Gwaay flattered himself on his perfect control over all emotion.

The chess game had developed beyond the opening stage, the moves coming slower, and now Hasjarl rapped down a rook on the seventh rank.

Gwaay observed gently, 'Your turreted warrior rushes deep into my territory, Brother. Rumor has it you've hired a brawny champion out of the north. With what purpose, I wonder, in our peace-wrapped cavern world? Could he be a sort of living rook?' He poised, hand unmoving over one of his knights.

Hasjarl giggled. 'And if his purpose is to slash pretty throats, what's that to you? I know naught of this rook-warrior, but 'tis said – slaves' chat, no doubt – that you yourself have had fetched a skilled sworder from Lankhmar. Should I call him a knight?'

'Aye, two can play at a game,' Gwaay remarked with prosy philosophy and lifting his knight, softly but firmly planted it at his king's sixth.

'I'll not be drawn,' Hasjarl snarled. 'You shall not win by making my mind wander.' And arching his head over the board, he cloaked himself again with his all-consuming calculations.

In the background slaves moved silently, tending the lamps and replenishing the founts with oil. Many lamps were needed to light the council room, for it was low-ceiled and massively beamed, and the arras-hung walls reflected little of the yellow rays and the mosaic floor was worn to a dull richness by countless footsteps in the past. From the living rock this room had been carved; long forgotten hands had set the huge cypress beams and inlaid the floor so cunningly. Those gay, time-faded tapestries had been hung by the slaves of some ancient Lord of Quarmall, who had pilfered them from a passing caravan, and so with all the rich adornments. The chessmen and the chairs, the chased lamp sconces and the oil which fed the wicks, and the slaves which tended them: all was loot. Loot from generations back when the Lords of Quarmall plundered far and wide and took their toll from every passing caravan.

High above that warm, luxuriously furnished chamber where Gwaay and Hasjarl played at chess, the Lord of Quarmall finished the final calculations which would complete his horoscope. Heavy leather hangings shut out the stars that had but now twinkled down their benisons and dooms. The only light in that instrument-filled room was the tiny flare of a single taper. By such scant illumination did custom bid the final casting be read, and Quarmal strained even his keen vision to see the Signs and Houses rightly.

As he rechecked the final results his supple lips writhed in a sneer, a grimace of displeasure. *Tonight or tomorrow,* he thought with an inward chill. *At most, late on the morrow.* Truly, he had little time.

Then, as if pleased by some subtle jest, he smiled and nodded, making his skinny shadow perform monstrous gyrations on the curtains and brasured wall.

Finally Quarmal laid aside his crayon, and taking the single candle lighted by its flame seven larger tapers. With the aid of this better light he read once more the horoscope. This time he made no sign of pleasure or any other emotion. Slowly he rolled the intricate diagramed and inscribed parchment into a slender tube, which he thrust in his belt; then rubbing together his lean hands he smiled again. At a nearby table were the ingredients which he needed for his scheme's success: powders, oils, tiny knives, and other materials and instruments.

The time was short. Swiftly he worked, his spatulate fingers performing miracles of dexterity. Once he went on an errand to the wall. The Lord of Quarmall made no mistakes, nor could he afford them.

It was not long before the task was completed to his satisfaction. After extinguishing the last-lit candles, Quarmal, Lord of Quarmall, relaxed into his chair and by the dim light of a single taper summoned Flindach, in order that his horoscope might be announced to those below.

As was his wont, Flindach appeared almost at once. He presented himself confronting his master with arms folded across his chest, and head bowed submissively. Flindach never presumed. His figure was illuminated only to the waist, above that shadow concealed whatever expression of interest or boredom his warted and wine-marked face might show. In like manner the pitted yet sleeker countenance of Quarmal was obscured, only his pale irises gleamed phosphorescent from the shadows like two minute moons in a dark bloody sky.

As if he were measuring Flindach, or as if he saw him for the first time, Quarmal slowly raised his glance from foot to forehead of the figure before him, and looking direct into the shaded eyes of Flindach so like his own, he spoke. 'O Master of Magicians, it is within your power to grant me a boon this night.'

He raised a hand as Flindach would have spoken and swiftly

continued: 'I have watched you grow from boy to youth and from youth to man; I have nurtured your knowledge of the Art until it is only second to my own. The same mother carried us, though I her firstborn and you the child of her last fertile year – that kinship helped. Your influence within Quarmall is almost equal to mine. So I feel that some reward is due your diligence and faithfulness.'

Again Flindach would have spoken, but was dissuaded by a gesture. Quarmal spoke more slowly now, and accompanied his words with staccato taps on the parchment roll. 'We both well know, from hearsay and direct knowledge, that my sons plot my death. And it is also true that in some manner they must be thwarted, for neither of the twain is fit to become the Lord of Quarmall; nor does it seem probable that either will ever reach such wisdom. Under their warring, Quarmall would die of inanition and neglect, as has died the Ghost Hall. Furthermore, each of them, to buttress his sorceries, has secretly hired a sworded champion from afar – you've seen Gwaay's – and this is the beginning of the bringing of free mercenaries into Quarmall and the sure doom of our power.' He stretched a hand toward the dark close-crowded rows of mummied and waxen masks and he asked rhetorically, 'Did the Lords of Quarmall guard and preserve our hidden realm that its councils might be entered, crowded, and at last be captured by foreign captains?

'Now a far more secret matter,' he continued, his voice sinking. 'The concubine Kewissa carries my seed: male-growing, by all omens and oracles – though this is known only to Kewissa and myself, and now to you, Flindach. Should this unborn sprout reach but boyhood brotherless, I might die content, leaving to you his tutelage in all confidence and trust.'

Quarmal paused and sat impassive as an effigy. 'Yet to forestall Hasjarl and Gwaay becomes more difficult each day, for they increase in power and in scope. Their own innate wickedness gives them access to regions and demons heretofore but imagined by their predecessors. Even I, well versed in necromancy, am often appalled.' He paused and quizzically looked at Flindach.

For the first time since he had entered Flindach spoke. His

voice was that of one trained in the recitation of incantations, deep and resonant. 'Master, what you speak is true. Yet how will you encompass their plots? You know, as well as I, the custom that forbids what is perhaps the only means of thwarting them.'

Flindach paused as if he would say more, but Quarmal quickly intervened. 'I have concocted a scheme, which may or may not succeed. The success of it depends almost entirely upon your cooperation.' He lowered his voice almost to a whisper, beckoning for Flindach to step closer. 'The very stones may carry tales, O Flindach, and I would that this plan were kept entirely secret.' Quarmal beckoned again, and Flindach stepped still nearer until he was within arm's reach of his master. Half stooping, he placed himself in such a position that his ear was close to Quarmal's mouth. This was closer than ever he remembered approaching Quarmal, and strange qualms filled his mind, recrudescences of childish old wives' tales. This ancient ageless man with eyes pearl-irised as his own seemed to Flindach not like half brother at all, but like some strange, merciless half father. His burgeoning terror was intensified when he felt the sinewy fingers of Quarmal close on his wrist and gently urge him closer, almost to his knees, beside the chair.

Quarmal's lips moved swiftly, and Flindach controlled his urge to rise and flee as the plan was unfolded to him. With a sibilant phrase, the final phrase, Quarmal finished and Flindach realized the full enormity of that plan. Even as he comprehended it, the single taper guttered and was extinguished. There was darkness absolute.

The chess game progressed swiftly; the only sounds, except the ceaseless shuffle of naked feet and the hiss of lamp wicks, were the dull click of the chessmen and the staccato cough of Hasjarl. The low table off which the twain had eaten was placed opposite the broad arched door which was the only apparent entrance to the council chamber.

There was another entrance. It led to the Keep of Quarmall; and it was toward this arras-concealed door that Gwaay glanced most often. He was positive that the news of the casting would be as usual, but a certain curiosity whelmed him this evening; he felt a faint foreshadowing of some untoward event, even as wind blows gusty before a storm.

An omen had been vouchsafed Gwaay by the gods today; an omen that neither his necromancers nor his own skill could interpret to his complete satisfaction. So he felt that it would be wise to await the development of events prepared and expectant.

Even as he watched the tapestry behind which he knew was the door whence would step Flindach to announce the consequences of the casting, that hanging bellied and trembled as if some breeze blew on it, or some hand pushed against it lightly.

Hasjarl abruptly threw himself back in his chair and cried in his high-pitched voice, 'Check with my rook to your king, and mate in three!' He dropped one eyelid evilly and peered triumphantly at Gwaay.

Gwaay, without removing his eyes from the still swaying tapestry, said in precise, mellow words. 'The knight interposes, Brother, discovering check. I mate in two. You are wrong again, my comrade.'

But even as Hasjarl swept the men with a crash to the floor, the arras was more violently disturbed. It was parted by two slaves and the harsh gong-note, announcing the entrance of some high official, sounded.

Silently from betwixt the hanging stepped the tall lean form of Flindach. His shadowed face, despite the disfiguring wine mark and the treble mole, had a great and solemn dignity. And in its somber expressionlessness – an expressionlessness curiously mocked by a knowing glitter deep in the black pupils of the pearl-irised crimson-balled eyes – it seemed to forebode some evil tiding.

All motion ceased in that long low hall as Flindach, standing in the archway framed in rich tapestries, raised one arm in a gesticulation demanding silence. The attendant well-trained slaves stood at their posts, heads bowed submissively; Gwaay remained as he was, looking directly at Flindach; and Hasjarl, who had half-turned at the gong note, likewise awaited the announcement. In a moment, they knew, Quarmal their father would step from behind Flindach and smiling evilly would announce his horoscope. Always this had been the procedure; and always, since each could remember, Gwaay and Hasjarl had at this moment wished for Quarmal's death.

Flindach, arm lifted in dramatic gesture, began to speak.

'The casting of the horoscope has been completed and the finding has been made. Even as the Heavens foretell is the fate of man fulfilled. I bring this news to Hasjarl and Gwaay, the sons of Quarmal.'

With a swift motion Flindach plucked a slender parchment tube from his belt and, breaking it with his hands, dropped it crumpled at his feet. In almost the same gesture he reached behind his left shoulder and stepping from the shadow of the arch drew a peaked cowl over his head.

Throwing wide both arms, Flindach spoke, his voice seeming to come from afar:

'Quarmal, Lord of Quarmall, rules no more. The casting is fulfilled. Let all within the walls of Quarmall mourn. For three days the place of the Lord of Quarmall will be vacant. So custom demands and so shall it be. On the morrow, when the sun enters his courtyard, that which remains of what was once a great and puissant lord will be given to the flames. Now I go to mourn my master and oversee the obsequies and prepare myself with fasting and with prayer for his passing. Do you likewise.'

Flindach slowly turned and disappeared into the darkness from which he had come.

For the space of ten full heartbeats Gwaay and Hasjarl sat motionless. The announcement came as a thunderclap to both. Gwaay for a second felt an impulse to giggle and smirk like a child who has unexpectedly escaped punishment and is instead rewarded; but in the back of his mind he was half-convinced that he had known all along the outcome of the casting. However, he controlled his childish glee and sat silent, staring.

On the other hand Hasjarl reacted as might be expected of him. He went through a series of outlandish grimaces and ended with an obscene half smothered titter. Then he frowned, and turning said to Gwaay, 'Heard you not what said Flindach? I must go and prepare myself!' and he lurched to his feet and paced silently across the room, out the broad-arched door.

Gwaay remained sitting for another few moments, frowning eyes narrowed in concentration, as if he were puzzling over some abtruse problem which required all his powers to solve. Suddenly he snapped his fingers and, motioning for his slaves to precede him, made ready for his return to the Lower Levels, whence he had come.

Fafhrd had barely left the Ghost Hall when he heard the faint rattle and clink of armed men moving cautiously. His bemusement with Friska's charms vanished as if he had been soused with ice water. He shrank into the deeper darkness and eavesdropped long enough to learn that these were pickets of Hasjarl, guarding against an invasion from Gwaay's Lower Levels – and not tracking down Friska and himself as he'd first feared. Then he made off swiftly for Hasjarl's Hall of Sorcery, grimly pleased that his memory for landmarks and turnings seemed to work as well for mazy tunnels as for forest trails and steep zigzag mountain escalades.

The bizarre sight that greeted him when he reached his goal stopped him on the stony threshold. Standing shin-deep and stark naked in a steaming marble tub shaped like a ridgy sea-shell, Hasjarl was berating and haranguing the great roomful around him. And every man jack of them – sorcerers, officers, overseers, pages bearing great fringy towels and dark red robes and other apparel – was standing quakingly still with cringing eyes, except for the three slaves soaping and laving their Lord with tremulous dexterity.

Fafhrd had to admit that Hasjarl naked was somehow more consistent – ugly everywhere – a kobold birthed from a hot-spring. And although his grotesque child-pink torso and mismated arms were a-writhe and a-twitch in a frenzy of apprehension, he had dignity of a sort.

He was snarling, 'Speak, all of you, is there a precaution I have forgotten, a rite omitted, a rat-hole overlooked that Gwaay might creep through? Oh, that on this night when demons lurk and I must mind a thousand things and dress me for my father's obsequies, I should be served by wittols! Are you all deaf and dumb? Where's my great champion, who should ward me now? Where are my scarlet grommets? Less soap there, you – take that! You, Essem, are we guarded well above? – I don't trust Flindach. And Yissim, have we guards enough below? – Gwaay is a snake who'll strike through any gap. Dark Gods, defend me! Go to the barracks, Yissim, get more men, and reinforce our downward guards – and while you're there, I mind me now, bid them continue Friska's torture. Wring the truth from her! She's in Gwaay's plots – this night has made me certain. Gwaay knew my father's death was imminent and laid invasion plans long weeks agone. Any of you may be his purchased spies! Oh where's my champion? *Where are my scarlet grommets?*'

Fafhrd, who'd been striding forward, quickened his pace at mention of Friska. A simple inquiry at the torture chamber would reveal her escape and his part in it. He must create diversions. So he halted close in front of pink wet steaming Hasjarl and said boldly, 'Here is your champion, Lord. And he counsels not sluggy defense, but some swift stroke at Gwaay! Surely your mighty mind has fashioned many a shrewd attacking stratagem. Launch you a thunderbolt!'

It was all Fafhrd could do to keep speaking forcefully to the end and not let his voice trail off as his attention became engrossed in the strange operation now going on. While Hasjarl crouched stock-still with head a-twist, an ashen-faced bath-slave had drawn out Hasjarl's left upper eyelid by its lashes and was inserting into the hole in it a tiny flanged scarlet ring or grommet no bigger than a lentil. The grommet was carried on the tip of an ivory wand as thin as a straw and the whole deed was being done by the slave with the anxiety of a man refilling the poison pouches of an untethered rattlesnake – if such an action might be imagined for purposes of comparison.

However, the operation was quickly completed, and then on the right eye too – and evidently with perfect satisfaction, since Hasjarl did not slash the slave with the soapy wet lash still dangling from his wrist – and when Hasjarl straightened up he was grinning broadly at Fafhrd.

'You counsel me well, champion,' he cried. 'These other fools could do nothing but shake. There *is* a stroke long-planned that I'll try now, one that won't violate the obsequies.

Essem, take slaves and fetch the dust – you know the stuff I mean – and meet me at the vents! Girls, sluice these suds off with tepid water. Boy, give me my slippers and my toweling robe! – those other clothes can wait. Follow me, Fafhrd!'

But just then his red-grommeted gaze lit on his four-and-twenty bearded and hooded sorcerers standing apprehensive by their chairs.

'Back to your charms at once, you ignoramuses!' he roared at them. 'I did not tell you to stop because I bathed! Back to your charms and send your plagues at Gwaay – red, black and green, nose drip and bloody rot – or I will burn your beards off to the eyelashes as prelude to more dire torturings! Haste, Essem! Come, Fafhrd!'

The Gray Mouser at that same moment was returning from his closet with Ivivis when Gwaay, velvet-shod and followed by barefoot slaves, came around a turn in the dim corridor so swiftly there was no evading him.

The young Lord of the Lower Levels seemed preternaturally calm and controlled, yet with the impression that under the calm was naught but quivering excitement and darting thought – so much so that it would hardly have surprised the Mouser if there had shone forth from Gwaay an aura of Blue Essence of Thunderbolt. Indeed, the Mouser felt his skin begin to prickle and sting as if just such an influence were invisibly streaming from his employer.

Gwaay scanned the Mouser and the pretty slavegirl in a flicker and spoke, his voice dancing rapid and gaysome.

'Well, Mouser, I can see you've sampled your reward ahead of time. Ah, youth and dim retreats and pillowed dreams and amorous hostessings – what else gilds life or makes it worth the guttering sooty candle? Was the girl skillful? Good! Ivivis, dear, I must reward your zeal. I gave Divis a necklace – would you one? Or I've a brooch shaped like a scorpion, ruby-eyed—'

The Mouser felt the girl's hand quiver and chill in his and he cut in quickly with, 'My demon speaks to me, Lord Gwaay, and tells me it's a night when the Fates walk.'

Gwaay laughed. 'Your demon has been listening behind the arras. He's heard tales of my father's swift departure.' As he spoke a drop formed at the end of his nose, between his nostrils. Fascinated, the Mouser watched it grow. Gwaay started to lift the back of his hand to it, then shook it off instead. For an instant he frowned, then laughed again.

'Aye, the Fates trod on Quarmall Keep tonight,' Gwaay said, only now his gay rapid voice was a shade hoarse.

'My demon whispers me further that there are dangerous powers abroad this night,' the Mouser continued.

'Aye, brother love and such,' Gwaay quipped in reply, but now his voice was a croak. A look of great startlement widened his eyes. He shivered as with a chill and drops pattered from his nose. Three hairs came loose from his scalp and fell across his eyes. His slaves shrank back from him.

'My demon warns me we'd best use my Great Spell quickly against those powers,' the Mouser went on, his mind returning as always to Sheelba's untested rune. 'It destroys only sorcerers of the Second Rank and lower. Yours, being of the First Rank, will be untouched. But Hasjarl's will perish.'

Gwaay opened his mouth to reply, but no words came forth, only a moaning nightmarish groan like that of a mute. Hectic spots shone forth high on his cheeks, and now it seemed to the Mouser that a reddish blotch was crawling up the right side of his chin, while on the left black spots were forming. A hideous stench became apparent. Gwaay staggered and his eyes brimmed with a greenish ichor. He lifted his hand to them and its back was yellowish crusted and red-cracked. His slaves ran.

'Hasjarl's sendings!' the Mouser hissed. 'Gwaay's sorcerers still sleep! I'll rouse 'em! Support him, Ivivis!' And turning he sped like the wind down corridor and up ramp until he reached Gwaay's Hall of Sorcery. He entered it, clapping and whistling harshly between his teeth, for true enough the twelve scrawny loinclothed magi were still curled snoring on their wide high-backed chairs. The Mouser darted to each in turn, righting and shaking him with no gentle hands and shouting in his ear, 'To your work! Anti-venom! Guard Gwaay!'

Eleven of the sorcerers roused quickly enough and were soon staring wide-eyed at nothingness, though with their bodies rocking and their heads bobbing for a while from the Mouser's shaking – like eleven small ships just overpassed by a squall.

He was having a little more trouble with the twelfth, though this one was coming awake, soon would be doing his share, when Gwaay appeared of a sudden in the archway with Ivivis at his side, though not supporting him. The young Lord's face gleamed as silvery clear in the dimness as the massy silver mask of him that hung in the niche above the arch.

'Stand aside, Gray Mouser, I'll jog the sluggard,' he cried in a rippingly bright voice and snatching up a small obsidian jar tossed it toward the drowsy sorcerer.

It should have fallen no more than halfway between them. Did he mean to wake the ancient by its shattering? the Mouser wondered. But then Gwaay stared at it in the air and it quickened its speed fearfully. It was as if he had tossed up a ball, then batted it. Shooting forward like a bolt fired point-blank from a sinewy catapult it shattered the ancient's skull and spattered the chair and the Mouser with his brains.

Gwaay laughed, a shade high-pitched, and cried lightly, 'I must curb my excitement! I must! I must! Sudden recovery from two dozen deaths – or twenty-three and the Nose Drip – is no reason for a philosopher to lose control. Oh, I'm a giddy fellow!'

Ivivis cried suddenly, 'The room swims! I see silver fish!'

The Mouser felt dizzy himself then and saw a phosphorescent green hand reach through the archway toward Gwaay – reach out on a thin arm that lengthened to yards. He blinked hard and the hand was gone – but now there were swimmings of purple vapor.

He looked at Gwaay and that one, frowny-eyed now, was sniffling hard then sniffling again, though no new drop could be seen to have formed on his nose-end.

Fafhrd stood three paces behind Hasjarl, who looked in his bunched and high-collared robe of earth-brown toweling rather like an ape.

Beyond Hasjarl on the right there trotted on a thick wide roller-riding leather belt three slaves of monstrous aspect: great splayed feet, legs like an elephant's, huge furnace-bellows chests, dwarfy arms, pinheads with wide toothy mouths and with nostrils bigger than their eyes or ears – creatures bred to run ponderously and nothing else. The moving belt disappeared with a half twist into a vertical cylinder of masonry five yards across and reemerged just below itself, but moving in the opposite direction, to pass under the rollers and complete its loop. From within the cylinder came the groaning of the great wooden fan which the belt whirled and which drove life-sustaining air downward to the Lower Levels.

Beyond Hasjarl on the left was a small door as high as Fafhrd's head in the cylinder. To it there mounted one by one, up four narrow masonry steps, a line of dusky, great-headed dwarves. Each bore on his shoulder a dark bag which when he reached the window he untied and emptied into the clamorous shaft, shaking it out most thoroughly while he held it inside, then folding it and leaping down to give place to the next bag-bearer.

Hasjarl leered over his shoulder at Fafhrd. 'A nosegay for Gwaay!' he cried. ''Tis a king's ransom I strew on the downward gale: powder of poppy, dust of lotus and mandragora, crumble of hemp. A million lewdly pleasant dreams, and all for Gwaay! Three ways this conquers him: he'll sleep a day and miss my father's funeral, then Quarmall's mine by right of sole appearance yet with no bloodshed, which would mar the rites; his sorcerers will sleep and my infectious spells burst through and strike him down in stinking jellied death; his realm will sleep, each slave and cursed page, so we'll conquer all merely by marching down after the business of the funeral. Ho, swifter there!' And seizing a long whip from an overseer, he began to crack it over the squat cones of the tread-slaves' heads and sting their broad backs with it. Their trot changed to a ponderous gallop, the moan of the fan rose in pitch, and Fafhrd waited to hear it shatter crackingly, or see the belt snap, or the rollers break on their axles.

The dwarf at the shaft-window took advantage of Hasjarl's attention being elsewhere to snatch a pinch of powder from his bag and bring it to his nostrils and sniff it down, leering ecstatically. But Hasjarl saw and whipped him about the legs most cruelly. The dwarf dutifully emptied his bag and shook it out while making little hops of agony. However he did not seem much chastened or troubled by his whipping, for as he left the chamber Fafhrd saw him pull his empty bag over his head and waddle off breathing deeply through it.

Hasjarl went on whip-cracking and calling, 'Swifter, I say! For Gwaay a drugged hurricane!'

The officer Yissim raced into the room and darted to his master.

'The girl Friska's escaped!' he cried. 'Your torturers say your champion came with your seal, telling them you had ordered her release – and snatched her off! All this occurred a quarter day ago.'

'Guards!' Hasjarl squealed. 'Seize the Northerner! Disarm and blind the traitor!'

But Fafhrd was gone.

The Mouser, in company with Ivivis, Gwaay and a colorful rabble of drug-induced hallucinations, reeled into a chamber similar to the one from which Fafhrd had just disappeared. Here the great cylindrical shaft ended in a half turn. The fan that sucked down the air and blew it out to refresh the Lower Levels was set vertically in the mouth of the shaft and was visible as it whirled.

By the shaft-mouth hung a large cage of white birds, all lying on its floor with their feet in the air. Besides these telltales, there was stretched on the floor of the chamber its overseer, also overcome by the drugs whirlwinding from Hasjarl.

By contrast, the three pillar-legged slaves ponderously trotting their belt seemed not affected at all. Presumably their tiny brains and monstrous bodies were beyond the reach of any drug, short of its lethal dose.

Gwaay staggered up to them, slapped each in turn, and commanded, 'Stop!' Then he himself dropped to the floor.

The groaning of the fan died away, its seven wooden vanes became clearly visible as it stopped (though for the Mouser they were interwoven with scaly hallucinations), and the only real sound was the slow gasping of the tread-slaves.

Gwaay smiled weirdly at them from where he sprawled and he raised an arm drunkenly and cried, 'Reverse! About face!' Slowly the tread-slaves turned, taking a dozen tiny steps to do it, until they all three faced the opposite direction on the belt.

'Trot!' Gwaay commanded them quickly. Slowly they obeyed and slowly the fan took up again its groaning, but now it was blowing air up the shaft against Hasjarl's downward fanning.

Gwaay and Ivivis rested on the floor for a space, until their brains began to clear and the last hallucinations were chased from view. To the Mouser they seemed to be sucked up the shaft through the fan blades: a filmy horde of blue and purple wraiths armed with transparent saw-toothed spears and cutlasses.

Then Gwaay, smiling in highest excitement with his eyes, said softly and still a bit breathlessly, 'My sorcerers . . . were not overcome . . . I think. Else I'd be dying . . . Hasjarl's two dozen deaths. Another moment . . . and I'll send across the level . . . to reverse the exhaust fan. We'll get fresh air through it. And put more slaves on this belt here – perchance I'll blow my brother's nightmares back to him. Then lave and robe me for my father's fiery funeral and mount to give Hasjarl a nasty shock. Ivivis, as soon as you can walk, rouse my bath girls. Bid them make all ready.'

He reached across the floor and grasped the Mouser strongly at the elbow. 'You, Gray One,' he whispered, 'prepare to work this mighty rune of yours which will smite down Hasjarl's warlocks. Gather your simples, pray your demonic prayers – consulting first with my twelve arch-magi . . . if you can rouse the twelfth from his dark hell. As soon as Quarmal's lich is in the flames, I'll send you word to speak your deadly spell.' He paused and his eyes gleamed with a witchy glare in the dimness. 'The time has come for sorcery and swords!'

There was a tiny scrabbling as one of the white birds staggered to its feet on the cage-bottom. It gave a chirrup that was rather like a hiccup, yet still had a note of challenge in it.

All that night through, all Quarmall was awake. Into the Ordering Room of the Keep, a magician came crying, 'Lord Flindach! The mind-casters have incontrovertible advertisements that the two brothers war against each other. Hasjarl sends sleepy resins down the shafts, while Gwaay blows them back.'

The warty and purple-blotched face of the Master of Magicians looked up from where he sat busy at a table surrounded by a small host awaiting orders.

'Have they shed blood?' he asked.

'Not yet.'

'It is well. Keep enchanted eyes on them.'

Then, gazing sternly in turn from under his hood at those whom he addressed, the Master of Magicians gave his other orders:

To two magicians robed as his deputies: 'Go on the instant to Hasjarl and Gwaay. Remind them of the obsequies and stay with them until they and their companies reach the funeral courtyard.'

To a eunuch: 'Hasten to your master Brilla. Learn if he requires further materials or assistance building the funeral pyre. Help will be furnished him at once and without stint.'

To a captain of slingers: 'Double the guard on the walls. Yourself make the rounds. Quarmall must be entirely secure from outward assaults and escapes from within on this coming morn.'

To a richly-clad woman of middle years: 'To Quarmal's harem. See that his concubines are perfectly groomed and clad, as if their Lord himself meant to visit them at dawn. Quiet their apprehensions. Send to me the Ilthmarix Kewissa.'

In Hasjarl's Hall of Sorcery, that Lord let his slaves robe him for the obsequies, while not neglecting to direct the search for his traitorous champion Fafhrd, to instruct the shaft-watchers in the precautions they must take against Gwaay's attempts to return the poppy dust, perchance with interest, and to tutor his sorcerers in the exact spells they must use against Gwaay once Quarmal's body was devoured by the flames.

In the Ghost Hall, Fafhrd munched and drank with Friska a small feast he'd brought. He told her how he'd fallen into disfavor with Hasjarl and he mulled plans for his escape with her from the realm of Quarmall.

In Gwaay's Hall of Sorcery, the Gray Mouser conferred in turn with the eleven skinny wizards in their white loincloths, telling them nothing of Sheelba's spell, but securing from each the firm assurance that he was a magus of the First Rank.

In the steam room of Gwaay's bath, that Lord recuperated his flesh and faculties shaken by disease spells and drugs. His girls, supervised by Ivivis, brought him fragrant oils and elixirs, and scrubbed and laved him as he directed languidly yet precisely. The slender forms, blurred and silvered by the clouds of steam, moved and posed as in a languorous ballet.

The huge pyre was finally completed, and Brilla heaved a sigh of relief and contentment with the knowledge of work well done. He relaxed his fat, massive frame onto a bench against the wall and spoke to one of his companions in a high-pitched feminine voice:

'Such short notice, and at such a time, but the gods are not to be denied and no man can cheat his stars. It is shameful, though, to think that Quarmal will go so poorly attended: only a half dozen Lankhmarts, an Ilthmarix, and three Mingols – and one of those blemished. I always told him he should keep a better harem. However the male slaves are in fine fettle and will perhaps make up for the rest. Ah! but it's a fine flame the Lord will have to light his way!' Brilla wagged his hand dolefully and, snuffling, blinked a tear from his piggy eye; he was one of the few who really regretted the passing of Quarmal.

As High Eunuch to the Lord, Brilla's position was a sinecure and, besides, he had always been fond of Quarmal since he could remember. Once when a small chubby boy Brilla had been rescued from the torments of a group of larger, more virile slaves who had freed him at the mere passing-by of Quarmal. It was this small incident, unwotted or long forgotten by Quarmal, which had provoked a life-long devotion in Brilla.

Now only the gods knew what the future held. Today the body of Quarmal would be burned and what would happen after that was better left unpondered, even in the innermost thoughts of a man. Brilla looked once more at his handiwork, the funeral pyre. Achieving it in six short hours, even with hosts of slaves at his command, had taxed his powers. It towered in the center of the courtyard, even higher than the arch of the great gate thrice the stature of a tall man. It was built in the form of a square pyramid, truncated midway; and the inflammable woods that composed it were completely hidden by somber-hued drapes.

A runway was built from the ground across the vast courtyard to the topmost tier on each of the four sides; and at the top was a sizable square platform. It was here that the litter containing the body of Quarmal would be placed, and here the sacrificial victims be immolated. Only those slaves of proper age and talents were permitted to accompany their Lord on his long journey beyond the stars.

Brilla approved of what he saw and rubbing his hands, looked about curiously. It was only on such occasions as this that one realized the immensity of Quarmall, and these occasions were rare; perhaps once in his life a man would see such an event. As far as Brilla could see small bands of slaves were lined, rank on rank, against the walls of the courtyard, even as was his own band of eunuchs and carpenters. There were the craftsmen from the Upper Levels, skilled workmen all in metal and in wood; there were the workers from the fields and vineyards all brown and gnarled from their labors; there were the slaves from the Lower Levels, blinking in the unaccustomed daylight, pallid and curiously deformed; and all the rest who served in the bowels of Quarmall, a representative group from each level.

The size of the turnout seemed to contradict the dawn's frightening rumors of secret war last night between the Levels, and Brilla felt reassured.

Most important and best placed were the two bands of henchmen of Hasjarl and Gwaay, one group on each side of the pyre. Only the sorcerers of the twain were absent, Brilla noted with a pang of unease, though refusing to speculate why.

High above all this mass of mixed humanity, atop the towering walls, were the ever silent, ever alert guards; standing quietly at their posts, slings dangling ready to hand. Never yet had the walls of Quarmall been stormed and never had a slave once within those close-watched walls passed into the outer world alive.

Brilla was admirably placed to observe all that occurred. To his right, projecting from the wall of the courtyard, was the balcony from which Hasjarl and Gwaay would watch the consuming of their father's body; to his left, likewise projecting, was the platform from which Flindach would direct the rituals. Brilla sat almost next to the door whence the prepared and purified body of Quarmal would be borne for its final fiery cleansing. He wiped the sweat fom his flabby jowls with the hem of his under tunic and wondered how much longer it would be before things started. The sun could not be far from the top of the wall now, and with its first beams the rites began.

Even as he wondered there came the tremendous, muffled vibration of the huge gong. There was a craning of necks and a rustling as many bodies shifted; then silence. On the left balcony the figure of Flindach appeared.

Flindach was cowled with the Cowl of Death and his garments were of heavy woven brocades, somber and dull. At his waist glittered the circular fan-bladed Golden Symbol of Power, which while the Chair of Quarmall was vacant, Flindach as High Steward must keep inviolate.

He lifted his arms toward the place where the sun would in a moment appear and intoned the Hymn of Greeting; even as he chanted, the first tawny rays struck into the eyes of those across the courtyard. Again that muffled vibration, which shook the very bones of those closest it, and opposite Flindach, on the other balcony, appeared Gwaay and Hasjarl. Both were garbed alike but for their diadems and scepters. Hasjarl wore a sapphire-jeweled silver band on his forehead and in his hand was the scepter of the Upper Levels, crested with a clenched fist; Gwaay wore a diadem inlaid with rubies and in his hand was his scepter surmounted by a worm, dagger-transfixed. Otherwise the twain were dressed identically in ceremonial robes of darkest red, belted with broad leather girdles of black; they wore no weapons nor were any other ornaments permissible.

As they seated themselves upon the high stools provided, Flindach turned toward the gate nearest Brilla and began to chant. His sonorous voice was answered by a hidden chorus and reechoed by certain of the bands in the courtyard. For the third time the monstrous gong was sounded and as the last echoes faded the body of Quarmal, litter-borne, appeared. It was carried by the six Lankhmar slavegirls and followed by the Mingols; this small band was all that remained of the many who had slept in the bed of Quarmal.

But where, Brilla asked himself with a heart-bounding start, was Kewissa the Ilthmarix, the old Lord's favorite? Brilla had ordered the marshaling of the girls himself. She could not—

Slowly through a lane of prostrate bodies the litter progressed toward the pyre. The carcass of Quarmal was propped in a sitting posture, and it swayed in a manner horribly suggestive of life as the slavewomen staggered under their unaccustomed load. He was garbed in robes of purple silk and his brow bore the golden bands of Quarmall's Lord. Those lean hands, once so active in the practice of necromancy and incantations, were folded stiffly over the Grammarie which had been his bible during life. On his wrist, hooded and chained was a great gyrfalcon, and at the feet of its dead master lay his favorite coursing leopard, quiet in the quietness of death. Even as was the falcon hooded, so with wax-like lids were the once awesome eyes of Quarmal covered; those eyes which had seen so much of death were now forever dead.

Although Brilla's mind was still agitated about Kewissa, he spoke a word of encouragement to the other girls as they passed, and one of them flung him a wistful smile; they all knew it was an honor to accompany their master into the future, but none of them desired it particularly; however there was little they could do about it except follow directions. Brilla felt sorry for them all; they were so young, had such luscious bodies and were capable of giving so much pleasure to a man, for he had trained them well. But custom must be fulfilled. Yet how then had Kewissa—? Brilla shut off that speculation.

The litter moved on up the ramp. The chanting grew in volume and tempo as the top of the pyre was reached, and the rays of the sun, now shining full onto the dead countenance of Quarmal, as the litter turned toward it, reflected from the bright hair and white skin of the Lankhmar slavegirls, who had with their companions thrown themselves at the feet of Quarmal.

Suddenly Flindach dropped his arms and there was silence,

a complete and total silence startling in its contrast to the measured chant and clashing gongs.

Gwaay and Hasjarl sat motionless, staring intently at the figure that had once been the Lord of Quarmall.

Flindach again raised his arms and from the gate opposite to that from whence had come the body of Quarmal, there leaped eight men. Each bore a flambeau and was naked but for a purple cowl which obscured his face. To the accompaniment of harsh gong notes they ran swiftly to the pyre, two on each side and, thrusting their torches into the prepared wood, cast themselves over the flames they created and clambering up the pyramid embraced the slavegirls wantonly.

Almost at once the flames ate into the resinous and oil-impregnated wood. For a moment through the thick smoke the interlocking writhing forms of the slaves could be perceived, and the lean figure of dead Quarmal staring through closed lids directly into the face of the sun. Then, incensed by the heat and acrid fumes, the great falcon screamed in vicious anger and wing-flapping rose from the wrist of its master. The chains held fast; but all could see the arm of Quarmal lifted high in a gesture of sublime dismissal before the smoke obscured. The chanting reached crescendo and abruptly ended as Flindach gave the sign that the rites were finished.

As the eager flames swiftly consumed the pyre and the burden it bore, Hasjarl broke the silence which custom had enjoined. He turned toward Gwaay and fingering the knuckly knob of his scepter and with an evil grin he spoke.

'Ha! Gwaay, it would have been a merry thing to have seen you leching in the flames. Almost as merry as to see our sire gesticulating after death. Go quickly, Brother! There's yet a chance to immolate yourself and so win fame and immortality.' And he giggled, slobbering.

Gwaay had just made an unapparent sign to a page nearby and the lad was hurrying away. The young Lord of the Lower Levels was in no manner amused by his brother's ill-timed jesting, but with a smile and shrug he replied sarcastically, 'I choose to seek death in less painful paths. Yet the idea is a good one; I'll treasure it.' Then suddenly in a deeper voice: 'It had been better that we were both stillborn than to fritter our lives away in futile hatreds. I'll overlook your dream-dust and your poppy hurricanes, and e'en your noisome sorceries, and make a pact with you, O Hasjarl! By the somber gods who rule under Quarmall's Hill and by the Worm which is my sign I swear that from my hand your life is sacrosanct; with neither spells nor steel nor venoms will I slay thee!' Gwaay rose to his feet as he finished and looked directly at Hasjarl.

Taken unaware, Hasjarl for a second sat in silence; a puzzled expression crossed his face; then a sneer distorted his thin lips and he spat at Gwaay:

'So! You fear me more even than I thought. Aye! And rightly so! Yet the blood of yon old cinder runs in both our bodies, and there is a tender spot within me for my brother. Yes, I'll pact with thee, Gwaay! By the Elder Ones who swim in lightless deeps and by the Fist that is my token, I'll swear your life is sacrosanct – until I crush it out!' And with a final evil titter Hasjarl, like a malformed stoat, slid from stool and out of sight.

Gwaay stood quietly listening, gazing at the space where Hasjarl had sat; then, sure his brother was well gone, he slapped his thighs mightily and, convulsed with silent laughter, gasped to no one in particular, 'Even the wiliest hares are caught in simple snares,' and still smiling he turned to watch the dancing flames.

Slowly the variegated groups were herded into the passageways whence they had come and the courtyard was cleared once again, except for those slaves and priests whose duties kept them there.

Gwaay remained watching for a time, then he too slipped off the balcony into the inner rooms. And a faint smile yet clung to his mouth corners as if some jest were lingering in his mind pleasantly.

'... And by the blood of that one whom it is death to look upon...'

So sonorously invoked the Mouser, as with eyes closed and arms outstretched he cast the rune given him by Sheelba of the Eyeless Face which would destroy all sorcerers of less than First

Rank of an undetermined distance around the casting point – surely for a few miles, one might hope, so smiting Hasjarl's warlocks to dust.

Whether his Great Spell worked or not – and in his inmost heart he strongly mistrusted that it would – the Mouser was very pleased with the performance he was giving. He doubted Sheelba himself could have done better. What magnificent deep chest tones! – even Fafhrd had never heard him declaim so.

He wished he could open his eyes for just a moment to note the effect his performance was having on Gwaay's magicians – they'd be staring open-mouthed for all their supercilious boasting, he was sure – but on this point Sheelba's instructions had been adamant: eyes tightly shut while the last sentences of the rune were being recited and the great forbidden words spoken; even the tiniest blink would nullify the Great Spell. Evidently magicians were supposed to be without vanity or curiosity – what a bore!

Of a sudden in the dark of his head, he felt contact with another and a larger darkness, a malefic and puissant darkness, of which light itself is only the absence. He shivered. His hair stirred. Cold sweat prickled his face. He almost stuttered midway through the word 'slewerisophnak.' But concentrating his will, he finished without flaw.

When the last echoing notes of his voice had ceased to rebound between the domed ceiling and floor, the Mouser slit open one eye and glanced surreptitiously around him.

One glance and the other eye flew open to fullness. He was too surprised to speak.

And whom he would have spoken to, had he not been too surprised, was also a question.

The long table at the foot of which he stood was empty of occupants. Where but moments before had sat eleven of the very greatest magicians of Quarmall – sorcerers of the First Rank, each had sworn on his black Grammarie – was only space.

The Mouser called softly. It was possible that these provincial fellows had been frightened at the majesty of his dark

Lankhmarian delivery and had crawled under the table. But there was no answer.

He spoke louder. Only the ceaseless groan of the fans could be sensed, though hardly more noticeable after four days hearing them than the coursing of his blood. With a shrug the Mouser relaxed into his chair. He murmured to himself, 'If those slick-faced old fools run off, what next? Suppose all Gwaay's henchmen flee?'

As he began to plan out in his mind what strategy of airy nothing to adopt if that should come to pass, he glanced somberly at the wide high-backed chair nearest his place, where had sat the boldest-seeming of Gwaay's arch-magi. There was only a loosely crumpled white loincloth – but in it was what gave the Mouser pause. A small pile of flocculent gray dust was all.

The Mouser whistled softly between his teeth and raised himself the better to see the rest of the seats. On each of them was the same: a clean loincloth, somewhat crumpled as if it had been worn for a little while, and within the cloth that small heap of grayish powder.

At the other end of the long table, one of the black counters, which had been standing on its edge, slowly rolled off the board of the thought-game and struck the floor with a tiny *tick*. It sounded to the Mouser rather like the last noise in the world.

Very quietly he stood up and silently walked in his ratskin moccasins to the nearest archway, across which he had drawn thick curtains for the Great Spell. He was wondering just what the range of the spell had been, *where* it had stopped, if it had stopped at all. Suppose, for instance, that Sheelba had underestimated its power and it disintegrated not only sorcerers, but . . .

He paused in front of the curtains and gave one last over-the-shoulder glance. Then he shrugged, adjusted his swordbelt, and, grinning far more bravely than he felt, said to no one in particular, 'But they assured me that they were the *very* greatest sorcerers.'

As he reached toward the curtain, heavy with embroidery, it wavered and shook. He froze, his heart leaping wildly. Then the curtains parted a little and there was thrust in the saucy face of Ivivis, wide-eyed with excited curiosity.

'Did your Great Spell work, Mouser?' she asked him breathlessly.

He let out his own breath in a sigh of relief. 'You survived it, at all events,' he said and reaching out pulled her against him. Her slim body pressing his felt very good. True, the presence of almost any living being would have been welcome to the Mouser at this moment, but that it should be Ivivis was a bonus he could not help but appreciate.

'Dearest,' he said sincerely, 'I was feeling that I was perchance the last man on Earth. But now—'

'And acting as if I were the last girl, lost a year,' she retorted tartly. 'This is neither the place nor the time for amorous consolations and intimate pleasantries,' she continued, half mistaking his motives and pushing back from him.

'Did you slay Hasjarl's wizards?' she demanded, gazing up with some awe into his eyes.

'I slew *some* sorcerers,' the Mouser admitted judiciously. 'Just how many is a moot question.'

'Where are Gwaay's?' she asked, looking past the Mouser at the empty chairs. 'Did he take them all with him?'

'Isn't Gwaay back from his father's funeral yet?' the Mouser countered, evading her question, but as she continued to look into his eyes, he added lightly, 'His sorcerers are in some congenial spot – I hope.'

Ivivis looked at him queerly, pushed past, hurried to the long table, and gazed up and down the chair seats.

'Oh, *Mouser*!' she said reprovingly, but there was real awe in the gaze she shot him.

He shrugged. 'They swore to me they were of First Rank,' he defended himself.

'Not even a fingerbone or skullshard left,' Ivivis said solemnly, peering closely at the nearest tiny gray dust pile and shaking her head.

'Not even a gallstone,' the Mouser echoed harshly. 'My rune was dire.'

'Not even a tooth,' Ivivis reechoed, rubbing curiously if somewhat callously through the pile. 'Nothing to send their mothers.'

'Their mothers can have their diapers to fold away with

their baby ones,' the Mouser said irascibly though somewhat uncomfortably. 'Oh, Ivivis, sorcerers don't have mothers!'

'But what happens to our Lord Gwaay now his protectors are gone?' Ivivis demanded more practically. 'You saw how Hasjarl's sendings struck him last night when they but dozed. And if anything happens to Gwaay, then what happens to us?'

Again the Mouser shrugged. 'If my rune reached Hasjarl's twenty-four wizards and blasted them too, then no harm's been done – except to sorcerers, and they all take their chances, sign their death warrants when they speak their first spells – 'tis a dangerous trade.

'In fact,' he went on with argumentative enthusiasm, 'we've gained. Twenty-four enemies slain at cost of but a dozen – no, eleven total casualties on our side – why, that's a bargain any warlord would jump at! Then with the sorcerers all out of the way – except for the Brothers themselves, and Flindach – that warty blotchy one is someone to be reckoned with! – I'll meet and slay this champion of Hasjarl's and we'll carry all before us. And if ...'

His voice trailed off. It had occurred to him to wonder why he himself hadn't been blasted by his own spell. He had never suspected, until now, that he might be a sorcerer of the First Rank – having despite a youthful training in country-sorceries only dabbled in magic since. Perhaps some metaphysical trick or logical fallacy was involved ... If a sorcerer casts a rune that midway of the casting blasts *all* sorcerers, *provided the casting be finished,* then does he blast himself, or ... ? Or perhaps indeed, the Mouser began to think boastfully, he was unknown to himself a magus of the First Rank, or even higher, or—

In the silence of his thinking, he and Ivivis became aware of approaching footsteps, first a multitudinous patter but swiftly a tumult. The gray-clad man and the slavegirl had hardly time to exchange a questioning apprehensive look when there burst through the draperies, tearing them down, eight or nine of Gwaay's chiefest henchmen, their faces deathpale, their eyes staring like madmen's. They raced across the chamber and out the opposite archway almost before the Mouser could recover from where he'd dodged out of their way.

But that was not the end of the footsteps. There was a last pair coming down the black corridor and at a strange unequal gallop, like a cripple sprinting, and with a squushy slap at each tread. The Mouser crossed quickly to Ivivis and put an arm around her. He did not want to be standing alone at this moment, either.

Ivivis said, 'If your Great Spell missed Hasjarl's sorcerers, and their disease-spells struck through to Gwaay, now undefended . . .'

Her whisper trailed off fearfully as a monstrous figure clad in dark scarlet robes lurched by swift convulsive stages into view. At first the Mouser thought it must be Hasjarl of the Mismated Arms, from what he'd heard of that one. Then he saw that its neck was collared by gray fungus, its right cheek crimson, its left black, its eyes dripping green ichor and its nose spattering clear drops. As the loathy creature took a last great stride into the chamber, its left leg went boneless like a pillar of jelly and its right leg, striking down stiffly though with a heel splash, broke in midshin and the jagged bones thrust through the flesh. Its yellow-crusted, red-cracked scurfy hands snatched futilely at the air for support and its right arm brushing its head carried away half the hair on that side.

Ivivis began to mewl and yelp faintly with horror and she clung to the Mouser, who himself felt as if a nightmare were lifting its hooves to trample him.

In such manner did Prince Gwaay, Lord of the Lower Levels of Quarmall, come home from his father's funeral, falling in a stenchful, scabrous, ichorous heap upon the torn-down richly embroidered curtains immediately beneath the pristine-handsome silver bust of himself in the niche above the arch.

The funeral pyre smoldered for a long time, but of all the inhabitants in that huge and ramified castle-kingdom Brilla the High Eunuch was the only one who watched it out. Then he collected a few representative pinches of ashes to preserve; he kept them with some dim idea that they might perhaps act as some protection, now that the living protector was forever gone.

Yet the fluffy-gritty gray tokens did not much cheer Brilla

as he wandered desolately into the inner rooms. He was troubled and eunuch-like be-twittered by thoughts of the war between brothers that must now ensue before Quarmall had again a single master. Oh, what a tragedy that Lord Quarmal should have been snatched so suddenly by the Fates with no chance to make arrangement for the succession! – though what that arrangement might have been, considering custom's strictures in Quarmall, Brilla could not say. Still, Quarmal had always seemed able to achieve the impossible.

Brilla was troubled too, and rather more acutely, by his guilty knowledge that Quarmal's concubine Kewissa had evaded the flames. He might be blamed for that, though he could not see where he had omitted any customary precaution. And burning would have been small pain indeed to what the poor girl must suffer now for her transgression. He rather hoped she had slain herself by knife or poison, though that would doom her spirit to eternal wandering in the winds between the stars that make them twinkle.

Brilla realized his steps were taking him to the harem and he halted a-quake. He might well find Kewissa there and he did not want to be the one to turn her in.

Yet if he stayed in this central section of the Keep, he would momentarily run into Flindach and he knew he would hold back nothing when gimleted by that arch-sorcerer's stern witchy gaze. He would have to remind him of Kewissa's defection.

So Brilla bethought him of an errand that would take him to the nethermost sections of the Keep, just above Hasjarl's realm. There was a storeroom there, his responsibility, which he had not inventoried for a month. Brilla did not like the Dark Levels of Quarmall – it was his pride that he was one of the elite who worked in or at least near sunlight – but now, by reason of his anxieties, the Dark Levels began to seem attractive.

This decision made, Brilla felt slightly cheered. He set off at once, moving quite swiftly, with a eunuch's peculiar energy, despite his elephantine bulk.

He reached the storeroom without incident. When he had kindled a torch there, the first thing he saw was a small girl-like woman cowering among the bales of drapery. She wore a lustrous loose yellow robe and had the winsome triangular face, moss-green hair, and bright blue eyes of an Ilthmarix.

'Kewissa,' he whispered shudderingly yet with motherly warmth. 'Sweet chick . . .'

She ran to him. 'Oh Brilla, I'm so frightened,' she cried softly as she pressed against his paunch and hid herself in his great-sleeved arms.

'I know, I know,' he murmured, making little clucking noises as he smoothed her hair and petted her. 'You were always frightened of flames, I remember now. Never mind, Quarmal will forgive when you meet beyond the stars. Look you, little duck, it's a great risk I run, but because you were the old Lord's favorite I cherish you dearly. I carry a painless poison . . . only a few drops on the tongue, then darkness and the windy gulfs . . . A long leap, true, but better far than what Flindach must order when he discovers—'

She pushed back from him. 'It was Flindach who commanded me not to follow My Lord to his last hearth!' she revealed wide-eyed and reproachful. 'He told me the stars directed otherwise and also that this was Quarmal's dying wish. I doubted and feared Flindach – he with face so hideous and eyes so horridly like My Dear Lord's – yet could not but obey . . . with some small thankfulness, I must confess, dear Brilla.'

'But what reason earthly or unearthly . . . ?' Brilla stammered, his mind a-whirl.

Kewissa looked to either side. Then, 'I bear Quarmal's quickening seed,' she whispered.

For a bit this only increased Brilla's confusion. How could Quarmal have hoped to get a concubine's child accepted as Lord of All when there were two grown legitimate heirs? Or cared so little for the land's security as to leave alive even an unborn bastard? Then it occurred to him – and his heart shook at the thought – that Flindach might be seeking to seize supreme power, using Kewissa's babe and an invented death wish of Quarmal as his pretext along with those Quarmal-eyes of his. Palace revolutions were not entirely unknown in Quarmall. Indeed, there was a legend that the present line had generations ago clambered dagger-fisted to power by that route, though it was death to repeat the legend.

Kewissa continued, 'I stayed hidden in the harem. Flindach said I'd be safe. But then Hasjarl's henchmen came searching in Flindach's absence and in defiance of all customs and decencies. I fled here.'

This continued to make a dreadful sort of sense, Brilla thought. If Hasjarl suspected Flindach's impious snatch at power, he would instinctively strike at him, turning the fraternal strife into a three-sided one involving even – woe of woes! – the sunlit apex of Quarmall, which until this moment had seemed so safe from war's alarums . . .

At that very instant, as if Brilla's fears had conjured up their fruition, the door of the storeroom opened wide and there loomed in it an uncouth man who seemed the very embodiment of battle's barbarous horrors. He was so tall his head brushed the lintel; his face was handsome yet stern and searching-eyed; his red-gold hair hung tangledly to his shoulders; his garment was a bronze-studded wolfskin tunic; longsword and massy short-handled ax, swung from his belt, and on the longest finger of his right hand Brilla's gaze – trained to miss no detail of decor and now fear-sharpened – noted a ring with Hasjarl's clenched-fist sigil.

The eunuch and the girl huddled against each other, quivering.

Having assured himself that these two were all he faced, the newcomer's countenance broke into a smile that might have been reassuring on a smaller man or one less fiercely accoutered. Then Fafhrd said, 'Greetings, Grandfather. I require only that you and your chick help me find the sunlight and the stables of this benighted realm. Come, we'll plot it out so you may satisfy me with least danger to yourselves.' And he swiftly stepped toward them, silently for all his size, his gaze returning with interest to Kewissa as he noted she was not child but woman.

Kewissa felt that and although her heart was a-flutter, piped up bravely, 'You dare not rape me! I'm with child by a dead man!'

Fafhrd's smile soured somewhat. Perhaps, he told himself,

he should feel complimented that girls started thinking about rape the instant they saw him, still he was a little irked. Did they deem him incapable of civilized seduction because he wore furs and was no dwarf? Oh well, they quickly learned. But what a horrid way to try to daunt him!

Meanwhile tubby-fat Grandfather, who Fafhrd now realized was hardly equipped to be that or father either, said fearful-mincing, 'She speaks only the truth, oh Captain. But I will be o'erjoyed to aid you in any—'

There were rapid steps in the passage and the harsh slither of steel against stone. Fafhrd turned like a tiger. Two guards in the dark-linked hauberks of Hasjarl's guards were pressing into the room. The fresh-drawn sword of one had scraped the door-side, while a third behind them cried sharply now. 'Take the Northern turncoat! Slay him if he shows fight. I'll secure old Quarmal's concubine.'

The two guards started to run at Fafhrd, but he, counter-feiting even more the tiger, sprang at them twice as suddenly. Graywand coming out of his scabbard swept sideways up, fending off the sword of the foremost even as Fafhrd's foot came crushing down on that one's instep. Then Graywand's hilt crashed backhand into his jaw, so that he lurched against his fellow. Meanwhile Fafhrd's ax had come into his left hand and at close quarters he stroked it into their brains, then shouldering them off as they fell, he drew back the ax and cast it at the third, so that it lodged in his forehead between the eyes as he turned to see what was amiss, and he dropped down dead.

But the footsteps of a fourth and perhaps a fifth could be heard racing away. Fafhrd sprang toward the door with a growl, stopped with a foot-stamp and returned as swiftly, stabbing a bloody finger at Kewissa cowering into the great bulk of blanching Brilla.

'Old Quarmal's girl? With child by him?' he rapped out and when she nodded rapidly, swallowing hard, he continued, 'Then you come with me. Now! The castrado too.'

He sheathed Graywand, wrenched his ax from the sergeant's skull, grabbed Kewissa by the upper arm and strode toward the door with a devilish snarling head-wave to Brilla to follow.

Kewissa cried, 'Oh mercy, sir! You'll make me lose the child.'

Brilla obeyed, yet twittered as he did, 'Kind Captain, we'll be no use to you, only encumber you in your—'

Fafhrd, turning suddenly again, spared him one rapid speech, shaking the bloody ax for emphasis: 'If you think I don't understand the bargaining value or hostage-worth of even an unborn claimant to a throne, then your skull is as empty of brains as your loins are of seed – and I doubt that's the case. As for you, girl,' he added harshly to Kewissa, 'if there's anything but bleat under your green ringlets, you know you're safer with a stranger than with Hasjarl's hellions and that better your child miscarry than fall into their hands. Come, I'll carry you.' He swept her up. 'Follow, eunuch; work those great thighs of yours if you love living.'

And he made off down the corridor, Brilla trotting ponderously after and wisely taking great gasping breaths in anticipation of exertions to come. Kewissa laid her arms around Fafhrd's neck and glanced up at him with qualified admiration. He himself now gave vent to two remarks which he'd evidently been saving for an unoccupied moment.

The first, bitterly sarcastic: '... if he shows fight!'

The second, self-angry: 'Those cursed fans must be deafening me, that I didn't hear 'em coming!'

Forty loping paces down the corridor he passed a ramp leading upward and turned toward a narrower darker corridor.

From just behind, Brilla called softly yet rapidly, penurious of breath. 'That ramp led to the stables. Where are you taking us, My Captain?'

'Down!' Fafhrd retorted without pausing in his lope. 'Don't panic, I've a hidey-hole for the two of you – and even a girl-mate for little Prince-mother Greenilocks here.' Then to Kewissa, gruffly, 'You're not the only girl in Quarmall who wants rescuing, nor yet the dearest.'

The Mouser, steeling himself for it, knelt and surveyed the noisome heap that was Prince Gwaay. The stench was abominably strong despite the perfumes the Mouser had sprinkled and the incense he had burned but an hour ago. The Mouser had covered with silken sheets and fur robes all the loathsomeness of Gwaay except for his plagues-stricken pillowed-up face. The sole feature of his face that had escaped obvious extreme contagion was the narrow handsome nose, from the end of which there dripped clear fluid, drop by slow drop, like the ticking of a water clock, while from below the nose proceeded a continual small nasty retching which was the only reasonably sure sign that Gwaay was not wholly moribund. For a while Gwaay had made faint straining moanings like the whispers of a mute, but now even those had ceased.

The Mouser reflected that it was very difficult indeed to serve a master who could neither speak, write, nor gesticulate – particularly when fighting enemies who now began to seem neither dull nor contemptible. By all counts Gwaay should have died hours since. Presumably only his steely sorcerous will and consuming hatred of Hasjarl kept his spirit from fleeing the horrid torment that housed it.

The Mouser rose and turned with a questioning shrug toward Ivivis, who sat now at the long table hemming up two hooded black voluminous sorcerer's robes, which she had cut down at the Mouser's direction to fit him and herself. The Mouser had thought that since he now seemed to be Gwaay's sole remaining sorcerer as well as champion, he should be prepared to appear dressed as the former and to boast at least one acolyte.

In answer to the shrug, Ivivis merely wrinkled her nostrils, pinched them with two dainty fingertips, and shrugged back. True, the Mouser thought, the stench was growing stronger despite all his attempts to mask it. He stepped to the table and poured himself a half cup of the thick blood-red wine, which he'd begun unwillingly to relish a little, although he'd learned it was indeed fermented from scarlet toadstools. He took a small swallow and summed up:

'Here's a pretty witch's kettle of problems. Gwaay's sorcerers blasted – all right, yes, by me, I admit it. His henchmen and soldier fled – to the lowest loathy dank dim tunnels, I think, or else gone over to Hasjarl. His girls vanished save for you. Even his doctors fearful to come nigh him – the one I dragged here fainting dead away. His slaves useless with dread – only the tread-beasts at the fans keep their heads, and they because they haven't any! No answer to our message to Flindach suggesting that we league against Hasjarl. No page to send another message by – and not even a single picket to warn us if Hasjarl assaults.'

'You could go over to Hasjarl yourself,' Ivivis pointed out.

The Mouser considered that. 'No,' he decided, 'there's something too fascinating about a forlorn hope like this. I've always wanted to command one. And it's only fun to betray the wealthy and victorious. Yet what strategy can I employ without even a skeleton army?'

Ivivis frowned. 'Gwaay used to say that just as sword-war is but another means of carrying out diplomacy, so sorcery is but another means of carrying out sword-war. Spell-war. So you could try your Great Spell again,' she concluded without vast conviction.

'Not I!' the Mouser repudiated. 'It never touched Hasjarl's twenty-four or it would have stopped their disease-spells against Gwaay. Either they are of First Rank or else I'm doing the spell backwards – in which case the tunnels would probably collapse on me if I tried it again.'

'Then use a different spell,' Ivivis suggested brightly. 'Raise an army of veritable skeletons. Drive Hasjarl mad, or put a hex on him so he stubs his toe at every step. Or turn his soldiers' swords to cheese. Or vanish their bones. Or transmew all his maids to cats and set their tails afire. Or—'

'I'm sorry, Ivivis,' the Mouser interposed hurriedly to her mounting enthusiasm. 'I would not confess this to another, but . . . that was my only spell. We must depend on wit and weapons alone. Again I ask you, Ivivis, what strategy does a general employ when his left is o'erwhelmed, his right takes flight, and his center is ten times decimated?'

A slight sweet sound like a silver bell chinked once, or a silver string plucked high in the harp, interrupted him. Although so faint, it seemed for a moment to fill the chamber with auditory light. The Mouser and Ivivis gazed around wonderingly and then at the same moment looked up at the silver mask of Gwaay in the niche above the arch before which Gwaay's mortal remains festered silken-wrapped.

The shimmering metal lips of the statua smiled and parted

– so far as one might tell in the gloom – and faintly there came Gwaay's brightest voice, saying: 'Your answer: he attacks!'

The Mouser blinked. Ivivis dropped her needle. The statua continued, its eyes seeming to twinkle, 'Greetings, hostless captain mine! Greetings, dear girl. I'm sorry my stink offends you – yes, yes, Ivivis, I've observed you pinching your nose at my poor carcass this last hour through – but then the world teems with loathiness. Is that not a black death-adder gliding now through the black robe you stitch?'

With a gasp of horror Ivivis sprang cat-swift up and aside from the material and brushed frantically at her legs. The statua gave a naturally silver laugh, then quickly said, 'Your pardon, gentle girl, I did but jest. My spirits are too high, too high – perchance because my body is so low. Plotting will curb my feyness. Hist now, hist!'

In Hasjarl's Hall of Sorcery his four-and-twenty wizards stared desperately at a huge magic screen set up parallel to their long table, trying with all their might to make the picture on it come clear. Hasjarl himself, dire in his dark red funeral robes, gazing alternately with open eyes and through the grommeted holes in his upper lids, as if that perchance might make the picture sharper, stutteringly berated them for their clumsiness and at intervals conferred staccato with his military.

The screen was dark gray, the picture appearing on it in pale green witch-light. It stood twelve feet high and eighteen feet long. Each wizard was responsible for a particular square yard of it, projecting on it his share of the clairvoyant picture.

This picture was of Gwaay's Hall of Sorcery, but the best effect achieved so far was a generally blurred image showing the table, the empty chairs, a low mound on the floor, a high point of silver light, and two figures moving about – these last mere salamander-like blobs with arms and legs attached, so that not even the sex could be determined, if indeed they were human at all or even male or female.

Sometimes a yard of the picture would come clear as a flowerbed on a bright day, but it would always be a yard with neither of the figures in it or anything of more interest than an empty chair. Then Hasjarl would bark sudden for the other wizards to do likewise, or for the successful wizard to trade squares with someone whose square had a figure in it, and the picture would invariably get worse and Hasjarl would screech and spray spittle, and then the picture would go completely bad, swimming everywhere or with squares all jumbled and overlapping like an unsolved puzzle, and the twenty-four sorcerers would have to count off squares and start over again while Hasjarl disciplined them with fearful threats.

Interpretations of the picture by Hasjarl and his aides differed considerably. The absence of Gwaay's sorcerers seemed to be a good thing, until someone suggested they might have been sent to infiltrate Hasjarl's Upper Levels for a close-range thaumaturgic attack. One lieutenant got fearfully tongue-lashed for suggesting the two blob-figures might be demons seen unblurred in their true guise – though even after Hasjarl had discharged his anger, he seemed a little frightened by the idea. The hopeful notion that all Gwaay's sorcerers had been wiped out was rejected when it was ascertained that no sorcerous spells had been directed at them recently by Hasjarl or any of his wizards.

One of the blob-figures now left the picture entirely and the point of silvery light faded. This touched off further speculation, which was interrupted by the entry of several of Hasjarl's torturers looking rather battered and a dozen of his guards. The guards were surrounding – with naked swords aimed at his chest and back – the figure of an unarmed man in a wolfskin tunic with arms bound tight behind him. He was masked with a red silk eye-holed sack pulled down over his head and hair, and a black robe trailed behind him.

'We've taken the Northerner, Lord Hasjarl!' the leader of the dozen guards reported joyously. 'We cornered him in your torture room. He disguised himself as one of those and tried to lie his way through our lines, humped and going on his knees, but his height still betrayed him.'

'Good, Yissim – I'll reward you,' Hasjarl approved. 'But what of my father's treacherous concubine and the great castrado who were with him when he slew three of your fellows?'

'They were still with him when we glimpsed him near

Gwaay's realm and gave chase. We lost 'em when he doubled back to the torture room, but the hunt goes on.'

'Find 'em, you were best,' Hasjarl ordered grimly, 'or the sweets of my reward will be soured entire by the pains of my displeasure.' Then to Fafhrd, 'So, traitor! Now I will play with you the wrist game – aye, and a hundred others too, until you are wearied of sport.'

Fafhrd answered loudly and clearly through his red mask, 'I'm no traitor, Hasjarl. I was only tired of your twitching and of your torturing of girls.'

There came a sibilant cry from the sorcerers. Turning, Hasjarl saw that one of them had made the low mound on the floor come clear, so that it was clearly seen as a stricken man covered to his pillowed head.

'Closer!' Hasjarl cried – all eagerness, no threat – and perhaps because they were neither startled nor threatened, each wizard did his work perfectly, so that there came greenpale onto the screen Gwaay's face, wide as an oxcart and team, the plagues visible by the huge pustules and crustings and fungoid growths if not by their colors, the eyes like great vats stewing with ichor, the mouth a quaking boghole, while each drop that fell from the nose-tip looked a gallon.

Hasjarl cried thickly, like a man choking with strong drink, 'Joy, oh joy! My heart will break!'

The screen went black, the room dead silent, and into it from the further archway there came gliding noiselessly through the air a tiny bone-gray shape. It soared on unflapping wings like a hawk searching its prey, high above the swords that struck at it. Then turning in a smooth silent curve, it swooped straight at Hasjarl and, evading his hands that snatched at it too late, tapped him on the breast and fell to the floor at his feet.

It was a dart folded from parchment on which lines of characters showed at angles. Nothing more deadly than that.

Hasjarl snatched it up, pulled it crackingly open, and read aloud:

'Dear Brother. Let us meet on the instant in the Ghost Hall to settle the succession. Bring your four-and-twenty sorcerers. I'll bring one. Bring your champion. I'll bring mine. Bring your henchmen and guards. Bring yourself. I'll be brought. Or perhaps you'd prefer to spend the evening torturing girls. Signed (by direction) Gwaay.'

Hasjarl crumpled the parchment in his fist and peering over it thoughtful-evil, rapped out staccato: 'We'll go! He means to play on my brotherly pity – that would be sweet. Or else to trap us, but I'll out-trick him!'

Fafhrd called boldly, 'You may be able to best your death-rotten brother, oh Hasjarl, but what of his champion? – cunninger than Zobold, more battle-fierce than a rogue elephant! Such a one one can cut through your cheesy guards as easy as I bested 'em one-to-five in the Keep, and be at your noisy throat! You'll need me!'

Hasjarl thought for a heartbeat, then turning toward Fafhrd said, 'I'm not mind-proud. I'll take advice from a dead dog. Bring him with us. Keep him bound, but bring his weapons.'

Along a wide low tunnel that trended slowly upward and was lit by wall-set torches flaming no bluer-brighter than marsh gas and as distant-seeming each from the next as coastal beacons, the Mouser striding swiftly yet most warily led a strange short cortege.

He wore a black robe with peaked black hood that thrown forward would hide his face entirely. Under it he carried at his belt his sword and dagger and also a skin of the blood-red toadstool wine, but in his fingers he bore a thin black wand tipped with a silver star, to remind him that his primary current role was Sorcerer Extraordinary to Gwaay.

Behind him trotted two-abreast four of the great-legged tiny-headed tread-slaves, looking almost like dark walking cones, especially when silhouetted by a torch just passed. They bore between them, each clutching a pole-end in both dwarfish hands a litter of bloodwood and ebony ornately carved, whereon rested mattressed and covered by furs and silks and richly embriodered fabrics the stenchful, helpless flesh and dauntless spirit of the young Lord of the Lower Levels.

Close behind Gwaay's litter followed what seemed a slightly smaller version of the Mouser. It was Ivivis, masquerading as his acolyte. She held a fold of her hood as a sort of windbreak in front of her mouth and nose, and frequently she sniffed a handkerchief steeped in spirits of camphor and ammonia. Under her arm she carried a silver gong in a woolen sack and a strange thin wooden mask in another.

The splayed calloused feet of the tread-slaves struck the stony floor with a faint *hrush*, over which came at long regular intervals Gwaay's gargly retching. Other sound there was none.

The walls and low ceiling teemed with pictures, mostly in yellow ocher, of demons, strange beasts, bat-winged girls, and other infernal beauties. Their slow looming and fading was nightmarish, yet gently so. All in all, it was one of the pleasantest journeys the Mouser could recall, equal of a trip he had once made by moonlight across the roofs of Lankhmar to hang a wilting wreath on a forgotten tower-top statue of the God of Thieves, and light a small blue fire of brandy to him.

'Attack!' he murmured humorously and wholly to himself. 'Forward, my big-foot phalanx! Forward, my terror-striking war-cat! Forward, my dainty rearguard! Forward, my host!'

Brilla and Kewissa and Friska sat quiet as mice in the Ghost Hall beside the dried-up fountain pool yet near the open door of the chamber that was their appointed hiding place. The girls were whispering together, head leaned to head, yet that was no noisier than the squeaking of mice, nor was the occasional high sigh Brilla let slip.

Beyond the fountain was the great half open door through which the sole faint light came questing and through which Fafhrd had brought them before doubling back to draw off the pursuit. Some of the cobwebs stretching across it had been torn away by Brilla's ponderous passage.

Taking that door and the one to their hiding place as two opposite corners of the room, the two remaining opposite corners were occupied by a wide black archway and a narrow one, each opening on a large section of stony floor raised three steps above the still larger floor section around the dried-up pool. Elsewhere in the wall were many small doors, all shut, doubtless leading to onetime bed chambers. Over all hung the pale mortared great black slabs of the shallowly domed ceiling.

So much their eyes, long accustomed to the darkness, could readily distinguish.

Brilla, who recognized that this place had once housed a harem, was musing melancholically that now it had become a kind of tiniest harem again, with eunuch – himself – and pregnant girl – Kewissa – gossiping with restless high-spirited girl – Friska – who was fretting for the safety of her tall barbarian lover. Old times! He wanted to sweep up a bit and find some draperies, even if rotten ones, to hang and spread, but Friska had pointed out that they mustn't leave clues to their presence.

There came a faint sound through the great door. The girls quit their whispering and Brilla his sighs and musings, and they listened with all their beings. Then more noises came – footsteps and the knock of a sheathed sword against the wall of a tunnel – and they sprang silently up and scurried back into their hiding chamber and silently shut the door behind them, and the Ghost Hall was briefly alone with its ghosts once more.

A helmeted guard in the hauberk of Hasjarl's guards appeared in the great door and stood peering about with arrow nocked to the taut string of a short bow he held crosswise. Then he motioned with his shoulder and came sneaking in followed by three of his fellows and by four slaves holding aloft yellowly flaming torches, which cast the monstrous shadows of the guardsmen across the dusty floor and the shadows of their heads against the curving far wall, as they spied about for signs of trap or ambush.

Some bats swooped about and fled the torchlight through the archways.

The first guardsman whistled then down the corridor behind him and waved an arm and there came two parties of slaves, who applied themselves each to a side of the great door, so that it groaned and creaked loudly at its hinges, and they pushed it open wide, though one of them leaped convulsively as a spider fell on him from the disturbed cobwebs, or he thought it did.

Then more guards came, each with a torch-slave, and moved about calling softly back and forth, and tried all the shut doors and peered long and suspiciously into the black spaces beyond the narrow archway and the wide one, but all returned quite swiftly to form a protective semicircle around the great door and enclosing most of the floor space of the central section of the Ghost Hall.

Then into that shielded space Hasjarl came striding, surrounded by his henchmen and followed at heel by his two dozen sorcerers closely ranked. With Hasjarl too came Fafhrd, still arm-bound and wearing his red bag-mask and menaced by the drawn swords of his guards. More torchslaves came too, so that the Ghost Hall was flaringly lit around the great door, though elsewhere a mixture of glare and black shadow.

Since Hasjarl wasn't speaking, no one else was. Not that the Lord of the Upper Levels was altogether silent – he was coughing constantly, a hacking bark, and spitting gobbets of phlegm into a fiery embroidered kerchief. After each small convulsion he would glare suspiciously around him, drooping evilly one pierced eyelid to emphasize his wariness.

Then there was a tiny scurrying and one called, 'A rat!' Another loosed an arrow into the shadows around the pool where it rasped stone, and Hasjarl demanded loudly why his ferrets had been forgotten – and his great hounds too, for that matter, and his owls to protect him against poison-toothed bats Gwaay might launch at him – and swore to flay the right hands of the neglectful ones.

It came again, that swift-traveling rattle of tiny claws on smooth stone, and more arrows were loosed futilely to skitter across the floor, and guards shifted position nervously, and in the midst of all that Fafhrd cried, 'Up shields, some of you, and make walls to either side of Hasjarl! Have you not thought that a dart, and not a paper one this time, might silently wing from either archway and drive through your dear Lord's throat and stop his precious coughing forever?'

Several leaped guiltily to obey that order and Hasjarl did not wave them away and Fafhrd laughed and remarked, 'Masking a champion makes him more dreadsome, oh Hasjarl, but tying his hands behind him is not so apt to impress the enemy – and has other drawbacks. If there should now come suddenly a-rush that one wilier than Zobold, weightier than a mad elephant to tumble and hurl aside your panicky guards—'

'Cut his bonds!' Hasjarl barked and someone began to saw with a dagger behind Fafhrd's back. 'But don't give him his sword or ax! Yet hold them ready for him!'

Fafhrd writhed his shoulders and flexed his great forearms and began to massage them and laughed again through his mask.

Hasjarl fumed and then ordered all the shut doors tried once more. Fafhrd readied himself for action as they came to the one behind which Friska and the two other were hidden, for he knew it had no bolt or bar. But it held firm against all shoving. Fafhrd could imagine Brilla's great back braced against it, with the girls perhaps pushing at his stomach, and he smiled under the red silk.

Hasjarl fumed a while longer and cursed his brother for his delay and swore he had intended mercy to his brother's minions and girls, but now no longer. Then one of Hasjarl's henchmen suggested Gwaay's dart-message might have been a ruse to get them out of the way while an attack was launched from below through other tunnels or even by way of the air-shafts, and Hasjarl seized that henchman by the throat and shook him and demanded why, if he had suspected that, he hadn't spoken earlier.

At that moment a gong sounded, high and silver-sweet, and Hasjarl loosed his henchman and looked around wonderingly. Again the silvery gong-note, then through the wider black archway there slowly stepped two monstrous figures each bearing a forward pole of an ornately carved black and red litter.

All of those in the Ghost Hall were familiar with the tread-slaves, but to see them anywhere except on their belts was almost as great and grotesque a wonder as to see them for the first time. It seemed to portend unsettlements of custom and dire upheavals, and so there was much murmuring and some shrinking.

The tread-slaves continued to step ponderously forward and their mates came into view behind them. The four advanced almost to the edge of the raised section of floor and set the litter down and folded their dwarfed arms as well as they could, hooking fingers to fingers across their gigantic chests, and stood motionless.

Then through the same archway there swiftly paced the figure of a rather small sorcerer in black robe and hood that hid his features, and close behind him like his shadow a slightly smaller figure identically clad.

The Black Sorcerer took his stand to one side of the litter and a little ahead of it, his acolyte behind him to his right, and he lifted alongside his cowl a wand tipped with glittering silver and said loudly and impressively, 'I speak for Gwaay, Master of Demons and Lord of All Quarmall! – as we will prove!'

The Mouser was using his deepest thaumaturgic voice, which none but himself had ever heard, except for the occasion on which he had blasted Gwaay's sorcerers – and come to think of it, that had ended with no one else having heard either. He was enjoying himself hugely, marveling greatly at his own audacity.

He paused just long enough, then slowly pointed his wand at the low mound on the litter, threw up his other arm in an imperious gesture, palm forward, and commanded, 'On your knees, vermin, all of you, and do obeisance to your sole rightful ruler, Lord Gwaay, at whose name demons blench!'

A few of the foremost fools actually obeyed him – evidently Hasjarl had cowed them all too well – while most of the others in the front rank goggled apprehensively at the muffled figure in the litter – truly, it was an advantage having Gwaay motionless and supine, looking like Death's horridest self: it made him a more mysterious threat.

Searching over their heads from the cavern of his cowl, the Mouser spotted one he guessed to be Hasjarl's champion – gods, he was a whopper, big as Fafhrd! – and knowledgeable in psychology if that red silk bag-mask were his own idea. The Mouser didn't relish the idea of battling such a one, but with luck it wouldn't come to that.

Then there burst through the ranks of the awed guards, whipping them aside with a short lash, a hunch-shouldered figure in dark scarlet robes – Hasjarl at last! and coming to the fore just as the plot demanded.

Hasjarl's ugliness and frenzy surpassed the Mouser's expectations. The Lord of the Upper Levels drew himself up facing the litter and for a suspenseful moment did naught but twitch, stutter, and spray spittle like the veriest idiot. Then suddenly he got his voice and barked most impressively and surely louder than any of his great hounds:

'By right of death – suffered lately or soon – lately by my father, star-smitten and burned to ash – soon by my impious brother, stricken by my sorceries – and who dare not speak for himself, but must fee charlatans – I, Hasjarl, do proclaim myself sole Lord of Quarmall – and of all within it – demon or man!'

Then Hasjarl started to turn, most likely to order forward some of his guards to seize Gwaay's party, or perhaps to wave an order to his sorcerers to strike them down magically, but in that instant the Mouser clapped his hands together loudly. At that signal, Ivivis, who'd stepped between him and the litter, threw back her cowl and opened her robe and let them fall behind her almost in one continuous gesture – and the sight revealed held everyone spellbound, even Hasjarl, as the Mouser had known it would.

Ivivis was dressed in a transparent black silk tunic – the merest blackly opal gleaming over her pale flesh and slimly youthful figure – but on her face she wore the white mask of a hag, female yet with mouth a-grin showing fangs and with fiercely staring eyes red-balled and white-irised, as the Mouser had swiftly repainted them at the direction of Gwaay, speaking from his silver statua. Long green hair mixed with white fell from the mask behind Ivivis and some thin strands of it before her shoulders. Upright before her in her right hand she held ritualistically a large pruning knife.

The Mouser pointed straight at Hasjarl, on whom the eyes of the mask were already fixed, and he commanded in his deepest voice, 'Bring that one here to me, oh Witch-Mother!' and Ivivis stepped swiftly forward.

Hasjarl took a backward step and stared horror-enchanted at his approaching nemesis, all motherly-cannibalistic above, all elfin-maidenly below, with his father's eyes to daunt him and with the cruel knife to suggest judgment upon himself for the girls he had lustingly done to death or lifelong crippledness.

The Mouser knew he had success within his grasp and there remained only the closing of the fingers.

At that instant there sounded from the other end of the chamber a great muffled gong-note deep as Gwaay's had been silvery-high, shuddering the bones by its vibrancy. Then from either side of the narrow black archway at the opposite end of the hall from Gwaay's litter there rose to the ceiling with a hollow roar twin pillars of white fire, commanding all eyes and shattering the Mouser's spell.

The Mouser's most instant reaction was inwardly to curse such superior stage-management.

Smoke billowed out against the great black squares of the ceiling, the pillars sank to white jets, man-high, and there strode forward between them the figure of Flindach in his heavily embroidered robes and with the Golden Symbol of Power at his waist, but with the Cowl of Death thrown back to show his blotched warty face and his eyes like those of Ivivis' mask. The High Steward threw wide his arms in a proud imploring gesture and in his deep and resonant voice that filled the Ghost Hall recited thus:

'Oh Gwaay! Oh Hasjarl! In the name of your father burned and beyond the stars, and in the name of your grandmother whose eyes I too bear, think of Quarmall! Think of the security of this your kingdom and of how your wars ravage her. Forego your enmities, abjure your brotherly hates, and cast your lots now to settle the succession – the winner to be Lord Paramount here, the loser instantly to depart with great escort and coffers of treasure, and journey across the Mountains of Hunger and the desert and the Sea of the East and live out his life in the Eastern Lands in all comfort and high dignity. Or if not by customary lot, then let your champions battle to the death to decide it – all else to follow the same. Oh Hasjarl, oh Gwaay, I have spoken.' And he folded his arms and stood there between the two pale flame pillars still burning high as he.

Fafhrd had taken advantage of the shocks to seize his sword and ax from the ones holding them nervelessly, and to push forward by Hasjarl as if properly to ward him standing alone and unshielded in front of his men. Now Fafhrd lightly nudged Hasjarl and whispered through his bag-mask, 'Take him up on it, you were best. I'll win your stuffy loathy catacomb kingdom for you – aye, and once rewarded depart from it swifter ever than Gwaay!'

Hasjarl grimaced angrily at him and turning toward Flindach shouted, '*I* am Lord Paramount here, and no need of lots to determine it! Yes, and I have my arch-magi to strike down any who sorcerously challenge me! – and my great champion to smite to mincemeat any who challenge me with swords!'

Fafhrd threw out his chest and glared about through red-ringed eyeholes to back him up.

The silence that followed Hasjarl's boast was cut as if by keenest knife when a voice came piercingly dulcet from the unstirring low mound on the litter, cornered by its four impassive tread-slaves, or from a point just above it.

'I, Gwaay of the Lower Levels, am Lord Paramount of Quarmall, and not my poor brother there, for whose damned soul I grieve. And I have sorceries which have saved my life from the evilest of his sorceries and I have a champion who will smite his champion to chaff!'

All were somewhat daunted at that seemingly magical speaking except Hasjarl, who giggled sputteringly, twitching a-main, and then as if he and his brother were children alone in a playroom, cried out, 'Liar and squeaker of lies! Effeminate boaster! Puny charlatan! *Where* is this great champion of yours? Call him forth! Bid him appear! Oh confess it now, he's but a figment of your dying thoughts! Oh, ho, ho, ho!'

All began to look around wonderingly at that, some thoughtful, some apprehensive. But as no figure appeared, certainly not a warlike one, some of Hasjarl's men began to snigger with him. Others of them took it up.

The Gray Mouser had no wish to risk his skin – not with Hasjarl's champion looking a meaner foe every moment, side-armed with ax like Fafhrd and now apparently even acting as counselor to his lord – perhaps a sort of captain-general behind the curtain, as he was behind Gwaay's – yet the Mouser was almost irresistibly tempted by this opportunity to cap all surprises with a master surprise.

And in that instant there sounded forth again Gwaay's eerie bell-voice, coming not from his vocal cords, for they were rotted away, but created by the force of his deathless will marshaling the unseen atomies of the air:

'From the blackest depths, unseen by all, in very center of the Hall – Appear, my champion!'

That was too much for the Mouser. Ivivis had reassumed her hooded black robe while Flindach had been speaking, knowing that the terror of her hag-mask and maiden-form was a fleeting thing, and she again stood beside the Mouser as his acolyte. He handed her his wand in one stiff gesture, not looking at her, and lifting his hands to the throat of his robe, he threw it and his hood back and dropped them behind him, and drawing Scalpel whistling from her sheath leaped forward with a heel-stamp to the top of the three steps and crouched glaring with sword raised above head, looking in his gray silks and silver a figure of menace, albeit a rather small one and carrying at his belt a wineskin as well as a dagger.

Meanwhile Fafhrd, who had been facing Hasjarl to have a last word with him, now ripped off his red bag-mask, whipped Graywand screaming from his sheath, and leaped forward likewise with an intimidating stamp.

Then they saw and recognized each other.

The pause that ensued was to the spectators more testimony to the fearsomeness of each – the one so dreadful-tall, the other metamorphosed from sorcerer. Evidently they daunted each other greatly.

Fafhrd was the first to react, perhaps because there had been something hauntingly familiar to him all along about the manner and speech of the Black Sorcerer. He started a gargantuan laugh and managed to change it in the nick into a screaming snarl of, 'Trickster! Chatterer! Player at magic! Sniffer after spells. Wart! *Little Toad*!'

The Mouser, mayhap the more amazed because he had noted and discounted the resemblance of the masked champion to Fafhrd, now took his comrade's cue – and just in time, for he was about to laugh too – and boomed back, 'Boaster! Bumptious brawler! Bumbling fumbler after girls! Oaf! Lout! *Big Feet*!'

The taut spectators thought these taunts a shade mild, but the spiritedness of their delivery more than made up for that.

Fafhrd advanced another stamp, crying, 'Oh, I have dreamed of this moment. I will mince you from your thickening toenails to your cheesy brain!'

The Mouser bounced for his stamp, so as not to lose height going down the steps, and skirled out the while, 'All my rages find happy vent. I will gut you of each lie, especially those about your northern travels!'

Then Fafhrd cried, 'Remember Ool Hrusp!' and the Mouser responded. 'Remember Lithquil!' and they were at it.

Now for all most of the Quarmallians knew, Lithquil and Ool Hrusp might be and doubtless were places where the two heroes had earlier met in fight, or battlefields where they had warred on opposing sides, or even girls they had fought over. But in actuality Lithquil was the Mad Duke of the city of Ool Hrusp, to humor whom Fafhrd and the Mouser had once staged a most realistic and carefully rehearsed duel lasting a full half hour. So those Quarmallians who anticipated a long and spectacular battle were in no wise disappointed.

First Fafhrd aimed three mighty slashing blows, any one enough to cleave the Mouser in twain, but the Mouser deflected each at the last moment strongly and cunningly with Scalpel, so that they whished an inch above his head, singing the harsh chromatic song of steel on steel.

Next the Mouser thrust thrice at Fafhrd, leaping skimmingly like a flying fish and disengaging his sword each time from Graywand's parry. But Fafhrd always managed to slip his body aside, with nearly incredible swiftness for one so big, and the thin blade would go hurtlessly by him.

This interchange of slash and thrust was but the merest prologue to the duel, which now carried into the area of the dried-up fountain pool and became very wild-seeming indeed, forcing the spectators back more than once, while the Mouser improvised by gushing out some of his thick blood-red toadstool wine when they were momentarily pressed body-to-body in a fierce exchange, so that they both appeared sorely wounded.

There were three in the Ghost Hall who took no interest in this seeming masterpiece of duels and hardly watched it. Ivivis was not one of them – she soon threw back her hood, tore off her hag-mask, and came following the fight close, cheering on the Mouser. Nor were they Brilla, Kewissa and Friska – for at the sound of swords the two girls had insisted on opening their door a crack despite the eunuch's solicitous apprehensions and now they were all peering through, head above head, Friska in the midst agonizing at Fafhrd's perils.

Gwaay's eyes were clotted and the lids glued with ichor, and the tendons were dissolved whereby he might have lifted his head. Nor did he seek to explore with his sorcerous senses in the direction of the fight. He clung to existence solely by the thread of his great hatred for his brother, all else of life was to him less than a shadow-show; yet his hate held for him all of life's wonder and sweetness and high excitement – it was enough.

The mirror image of that hate in Hasjarl was at this moment strong enough too to dominate wholly his healthy body's instincts and hungers and all the plots and images in his crackling thoughts. He saw the first stroke of the fight, he saw Gwaay's litter unguarded, and then as if he had seen entire a winning combination of chess and been hypnotized by it, he made his move without another cogitation.

Widely circling the fight and moving swiftly in the shadows like a weasel he mounted the three steps by the wall and headed straight for the litter.

There were no ideas in his mind at all, but there were some shadowy images distortedly seen as from a great distance – one of himself as a tiny child toddling by night along a wall to Gwaay's crib, to scratch him with a pin.

He did not spare a glance for the tread-slaves and it is doubtful if they even saw, or at least took note of him, so rudimentary were their minds.

He leaned eagerly between two of them and curiously surveyed his brother. His nostrils drew in at the stench and his mouth contracted to its tightest sphincter yet still smiled.

He plucked a wide dagger of blued steel from a sheath at his belt and poised it above his brother's face, which by its plagues was almost unrecognizable as such. The honed edges of the dagger were tiny hooks directed back from the point.

The sword-clashing below reached one of its climaxes, but Hasjarl did not mark it.

He said softly, 'Open your eyes, Brother. I want you to speak once before I slay you.'

There was no reply from Gwaay – not a motion, not a whisper, not a bubble of retching.

'Very well,' Hasjarl said harshly, 'then die a prim shut-mouth,' and he drove down the dagger.

It stopped violently a hairbreadth above Gwaay's upper cheek and the muscles of Hasjarl's arm driving it were stabbingly numbed by the jolt they got.

Gwaay did open his eyes then, which was not very pleasant to behold since there was nothing in them but green ichor.

Hasjarl instantly closed his own eyes, but continued to peer down through the holes in his upper lids.

Then he heard Gwaay's voice like a silver mosquito by his ear saying, 'You have made a slight oversight, dear brother. You have chosen the wrong weapon. After our father's burning you swore to me my life was sacrosanct – until you killed me by crushing. "Until I crush it out," you said. The gods hear only our words, Brother, not our intentions. Had you come lugging a boulder, like the curious gnome you are, you might have accomplished your aim.'

'Then I'll have you crushed!' Hasjarl retorted angrily, leaning his face closer and almost shouting. 'Aye, and I'll sit by and listen to your bones crunch – what bones you have left! You're as great a fool as I, Gwaay, for you too after our father's funeral promised not to slay me. Aye, and you're a greater fool, for now you've spilled to me your little secret of how you may be slain.'

'I swore not to slay you with spells or steel or venom or with my hand,' the bright insect voice of Gwaay replied. 'Unlike you, I said nothing at all of crushing.'

Hasjarl felt a strange tingling in his flesh while in his nostrils there was an acrid odor like that of lightning mingling with the stink of corruption.

Suddenly Gwaay's hands thrust up to the palms out of his overly rich bedclothes. The flesh was shredding from the finger bones which pointed straight up, invokingly.

Hasjarl almost started back, but caught himself. He'd die,

he told himself, before he'd cringe from his brother. He was aware of strong forces all about him.

There was a muffled grating noise and then an odd faintly pattering snowfall on the coverlet and on Hasjarl's neck . . . a thin snowfall of pale gritty stuff . . . grains of mortar . . .

'Yes, you will crush me, dear brother,' Gwaay admitted tranquilly. 'But if you would know *how* you will crush me, recall my small special powers . . . or else *look up*!'

Hasjarl turned his head, and there was the great black basalt slab big as the litter rushing down, and the one moment of life left Hasjarl was consumed in hearing Gwaay say, 'You are wrong, again, my comrade.'

Fafhrd stopped a sword-slash in midcourse when he heard the crash and the Mouser almost nicked him with his rehearsed parry. They lowered their blades and looked, as did all others in the central section of the Ghost Hall.

Where the litter had been was now only the thick basalt slab mortar-streaked with the litter-poles sticking out from under, and above in the ceiling the rectangular white hole whence the slab had been dislodged. The Mouser thought, *That's a larger thing to move by thinking than a checker or jar, yet the same black substance.*

Fafhrd thought, *Why didn't the whole roof fall? – there's the strangeness.*

Perhaps the greatest wonder of the moment was the four tread-slaves still standing at the four corners, eyes forward, fingers locked across their chests, although the slab had missed them only by inches in its falling.

Then some of Hasjarl's henchmen and sorcerers who had seen their Lord sneak to the litter now hurried up to it, but fell back when they beheld how closely the slab approached the floor and marked the tiny rivulet of blood that ran from under it. Their minds quailed at the thought of those brothers who had hated each other so dearly, and now their bodies locked in an obscene interpenetrating and commingling embrace.

Meanwhile Ivivis came running to the Mouser and Friska to Fafhrd to bind up their wounds, and were astonished and mayhap a shade irked to be told there were none. Kewissa and

Brilla came too and Fafhrd with one arm around Friska reached out the wine-bloody hand of the other and softly closed it around Kewissa's wrist, smiling at her friendlily.

Then the great muffled gong-note sounded again and the twin pillars of white flame briefly roared to the ceiling to either side of Flindach. They showed by their glare that many men had entered by the narrow archway behind Flindach and now stood around him: stout guardsmen from the companies of the Keep with weapons at the ready, and several of his own sorcerers.

As the flame-pillars swiftly shrank, Flindach imperiously raised hand and resonantly spoke:

'The stars which may not be cheated foretold the doom of the Lord of Quarmall. All of you heard those two' – he pointed toward the shattered litter – 'proclaim themselves Lord of Quarmall. So the stars are twice satisfied. And the gods, who hear our words to each tiniest whisper, and order our fates by them, are content. It remains that I reveal to you the next Lord of Quarmall.'

He pointed at Kewissa and intoned, '*The next Lord of Quarmall but one* sleeps and waxes in the womb of her, wife of the Quarmal so lately honored with burnings and immolations and ceremonious rites.'

Kewissa shrank and her blue eyes went wide. Then she began to beam.

Flindach continued, 'It still remains that I reveal to you *the next Lord of Quarmall*, who shall tutor Queen Kewissa's babe until he arrives at manhood a perfect king and all-wise sorcerer, under whom our buried realm will enjoy perpetual inward peace and outward-raiding prosperity.'

Then Flindach reached behind his left shoulder. All thought he purposed to draw forward the Cowl of Death over his head and brows and hideous warty winy cheeks for some still more solemn speaking. But instead he grasped his neck by the short hairs of the nape and drew it upward and forward and his scalp and all his hair with it, and then the skin of his face came off with his scalp as he drew his hand down and to the side, and there was revealed, sweat-gleaming a little, the unblemished face and jutting nose and full mobile smiling lips of Quarmal, while his terrible blood-red white-irised eyes gazed at them all mildly.

'I was forced to visit Limbo for a space,' he explained with a solemn yet genial fatherly familiarity, 'while others were Lords of Quarmall in my stead and the stars sent down their spears. It was best so, though I lost two sons by it. Only so might our land be saved from ravenous self-war.'

He held up for all to see the limp mask with empty lash-fringed eyeholes and purple-blotched left cheek and wart-triangled right. He said, 'And now I bid you all honor great and puissant Flindach, the loyalest Master of Magicians a king ever had, who lent me his face for a necessary deception and his body to be burned for mine with waxen mask of mine to cover his poor head-front, which had sacrificed all. In solemnly supervising my own high flaming obsequies, I honored only Flindach. For him my women burned. This his face, well preserved by my own skills as flayer and swift tanner, will hang forever in place of honor in our halls, while the spirit of Flindach holds my chair for me in the Dark World beyond the stars, a Lord Paramount there until I come, and eternally a Hero of Quarmall.'

Before any cheering or hailing could be started – which would have taken a little while, since all were much bemused – Fafhrd cried out, 'Oh cunningest king, I honor you and your babe so highly and the Queen who carries him in her womb that I will guard her moment by moment, not moving a pace from her, until I and my small comrade here are well outside Quarmall – say a mile – together with horses for our conveyance and with the treasures promised us by those two late kings.' And he gestured as Quarmal had toward the crushed litter.

The Mouser had been about to launch at Quarmal some subtly intimidating remarks about his own skills as a sorcerer in blasting Gwaay's eleven. But now he decided that Fafhrd's words were sufficient and well-spoken, save for the slighting reference to himself, and he held his peace.

Kewissa started to withdraw her hand from Fafhrd's, but he tightened his grip just a little and she looked at him with understanding. In fact, she called brightly to Quarmal, 'Oh

Lord Husband, this man saved my life and your son's from Hasjarl's fiends in a storeroom of the Keep. I trust him,' while Brilla, dabbing tears of joy from his eyes with his undersleeve, seconded her with, 'My very dear Lord, she speaks only nakedest truth, bare as a newborn babe or new-wed wife.'

Quarmal raised his hand a little, reprovingly, as if such speaking were unnecessary and somewhat out of place, and smiling thinly at Fafhrd and the Mouser said, 'It shall be as you have spoken. I am neither ungenerous nor unperceptive. Know that it was not altogether by chance that my late sons unbeknown to each other hired you two friends – also mutually unknowing – to be their champions. Furthermore know that I am not altogether unaware of the curiosities of Ningauble of the Seven Eyes or of the spells of Sheelba of the Eyeless Face. We grandmaster sorcerers have a— But to speak more were only to kindle the curiosity of the gods and alert the trolls and attract the attention of the restless hungry Fates. Enough is enough.'

Looking at Quarmal's slitted eyes, the Mouser was glad he had not boasted and even Fafhrd shivered a little.

Fafhrd cracked whip above the four-horse team to set them pulling the high-piled wagon more briskly through this black sticky stretch of road deeply marked with cart tracks and the hoofprints of oxen, a mile from Quarmall. Friska and Ivivis were turned around on the seat beside him to wave as long a farewell as they might to Kewissa and the eunuch Brilla, standing at the roadside with four impassive guardsmen of Quarmall, to whom they had but now been released.

The Gray Mouser, sprawled on his stomach atop the load, waved too, but only with his left hand – in his right he held a cocked crossbow while his eyes searched the trees about for sign of ambush.

Yet the Mouser was not truly apprehensive. He thought that Quarmal would hardly be apt to try any tricks against such a proven warrior and sorcerer as himself – or Fafhrd too, of course. The old Lord had shown himself a most gracious host during the last few hours, plying them with rare wines and loading them with rich gifts beyond what they'd asked or what the Mouser had purloined in advance, and even offering them other girls in addition to Ivivis and Friska – benison which they'd rejected, with some inward regrets, after noting the glares in the eyes of those two. Twice or thrice Quarmal had smiled in too tiger-friendly a fashion, but at such times Fafhrd had stood a little closer to Kewissa and emphasized his light but inflexible grip on her, to remind the old Lord that she and the prince she carried were hostages for his and the Mouser's safety.

As the mucky road curved up a little, the towers of Quarmall came into view above the treetops. The Mouser's gaze drifted to them and he studied the lacy pinnacles thoughtfully, wondering whether he'd ever see them again. Suddenly the whim seized him to return to Quarmall straightway – yes, to slip off the back of the load and run there. What did the outer world hold half so fine as the wonders of that subterranean kingdom? – its mazy mural-pictured tunnelings a man might spend his life tracing ... its buried delights ... even its evils beautiful ... its delicious infinitely varied blacks ... its hidden fan-driven air ... Yes, suppose he dropped down soundlessly this very moment ...

There was a flash, a brilliant scintillation from the tallest keep. It pricked the Mouser like a goad and he loosed his hold and let himself slide backward off the load. But just at that instant the road turned and grew firm and the trees moved higher, masking the towers, and the Mouser came to himself and grabbed hold again before his feet touched the road and he hung there while the wheels creaked merrily and cold sweat drenched him.

Then the wagon stopped and the Mouser dropped down and took three deep breaths and then hastened forward to where Fafhrd had descended too and was busy with the harness of the horses and their traces.

'Up again, Fafhrd, and whip up!' he cried. 'This Quarmal is a cunninger witch than I guessed. If we waste time by the way, I fear for our freedom and our souls!'

'You're telling me?' Fafhrd retorted. 'This road winds and there'll be more sticky stretches. Trust a wagon's speed? – pah! We'll uncouple the four horses and taking only simplest victuals and the smallest and most precious of the treasure, gallop across the moor away from Quarmall straight as the crow flies. That way we *should* dodge ambush and outrun ranging pursuit. Friska, Ivivis! Spring to it, all!'

All these books are available at your local bookshop or newsagent, or can be ordered direct from the publisher.

To order direct from the publishers just tick the titles you want and fill in the form below.

Name ____________________

Address ____________________

____

Send to:
Grafton Cash Sales
PO Box 11, Falmouth, Cornwall TR10 9EN.

Please enclose remittance to the value of the cover price plus:

UK 60p for the first book, 25p for the second book plus 15p per copy for each additional book ordered to a maximum charge of £1.90.

BFPO 60p for the first book, 25p for the second book plus 15p per copy for the next 7 books, thereafter 9p per book.

Overseas including Eire £1.25 for the first book, 75p for second book and 28p for each additional book.

Grafton Books reserve the right to show new retail prices on covers, which may differ from those previously advertised in the text or elsewhere.